The 's Nest Mysteries

Book Four:

A FELONIOUS FINALE

By

C.S. McDonald

A FELONIOUS FINALE Book Information

The 's Nest Mysteries

A FELONIOUS FINALE

Book 4

by

C.S. McDonald

Contents

Cast of Characters

Recurring Characters:

Alexa Owl: Seamstress, who returns to her hometown of Pittsburgh with a generous divorce settlement to open a tailor shop, The Owl's Nest Couturier Shoppe. Reluctant time traveler.

Detective Bobby Starr: Angel. Why did he leave Heaven? Because he couldn't get into the Guardian Angel Squad until he resolved three murders, he left unresolved while he was living. Known as a bit of a scoundrel when alive, Bobby was married five times.

Bobby's wives:
    Catherine
    Cora Lee Baker-Starr
    Catherine Campbell-Starr
    Venetia Starr
    Katherine Fields-Starr

    Maisie: Bobby's daughter with Katherine Fields-Starr.

C.S. McDonald

Detective Cliff Slater: Alexa's love interest. Homicide detective in current times.

Detective Clifton Slater: Former homicide detective and Cliff's grandfather.

Wynona (Winnie) Mulaney: Feisty Irish woman whose parents used to own The Lazy Hound Pub in the mid 40's until '74, now The Owl's Nest Couturier Shoppe. She is the shop's manager.

Brian & Molly Mulaney: Winnie's parents and former owners of The Lazy Hound Pub.

Louie Santorini: Winnie's boyfriend.

Maggie: Winnie's older sister.

Holden Emery: Tailor for The Owl's Nest Couturier Shoppe. Good friend of Alexa and Winnie.

Guest Characters:
(In Order of Appearance)

Katherine Starr-Hathaway: Detective Bobby Starr's fifth wife, and diva of the On Stage Operetta Company.

Royce Hathaway: Tenor for the On Stage Operetta Company and Katherine's husband.

Piers Linney: (From Britain) Director of the On Stage Operetta Company.

Pooky Mateer: Seamstress for the On Stage Operetta Company.

Bert Mateer: Singer for the On Stage Operetta Company. Deceased husband of Pooky Mateer.

Olivia Shipman: Louie Santorini's daughter. Josh: Olivia's husband

Sergeant Joe Randolph: Pittsburgh police officer who works with Detective Clifton Slater.

Detective Vince Wheeler: Homicide detective for the Pittsburgh police department.

Louis Santorini: Louie's grandson.

Dean and Claire Santorini: Louie's son and his wife.

Brett and Stacy Santorini: Louie's son and his wife.

Tallis Chamberlain: Soprano for the On Stage Operetta Company.

Dorian Matias: Tallis's vocal coach.

Hazel: Pooky's sister.

Jeanette: Singer for the On Stage Operetta Company.

Adam Gless: Singer for the On stage Operetta Company.

Sister Viviana/Teresa: Novitiate nun.

Mother Viviana Reverent: The abbess at St. Elizabeth's and Sister Viviana's aunt.

C.S. McDonald

Prologue

Felonious Finale

The Carnegie Library and Music Hall, Carnegie, Pennsylvania 1965...

Joy filled Katherine Starr's heart when her small troop, Onstage Operetta Company, decided to produce *The Merry Widow*. She'd spent a lifetime dreaming of playing the role of Hanna Glawari, a beautiful, wealthy, young widow from the small and impoverished Balkan province of Pontevedro. Ambassador Baron Zeta is eager for Hanna to re-marry. Except, to keep her fortune in the country and save them all from ruin, he insists she marry a Pontevedrian and not a Frenchman. The clear choice is Count Danilo. However, there is a snag, Hanna and Danilo are old flames, and the Count is far too vain to marry her for her money.

Mix-ups and humorous intrigue abound when it comes to light that the Baron's wife, Valencienne, is having an affair with Frenchman Camille, Count de Rosillon! Hanna steps in to rescue the married woman's reputation. Much to the Pontevedrains' despair, Hanna declares it is *she* who plans to marry Camille, and that is when Danilo is forced to acknowledge his true feelings for Hanna.

Ah, Katherine never grew weary of the audience's anticipation at the finale…will they, or won't they?

Now, Katherine sat in her dressing room at the music hall, before her lighted mirror, smoothing on red lipstick, while her dear, bright yellow canary, Zippy, swung two and fro on its perch in the gilded cage nearby, twittering and singing her sweet song. Katherine had no sooner set the lipstick aside when there was a knock at the door.

"Katherine, may I come in?" Royce Hathaway, a talented baritone who played the role of Danilo, called from the hallway. His deep voice was on the edge of frantic.

"Yes, come in." Her expectant gaze clung to the mirror as Royce rushed through the door to stand behind her. Even through makeup, Katherine could see his handsome face was flushed. "What's wrong?"

"Bert Mateer won't be coming. He's very ill. Piers didn't feel the need to cover him with an understudy. He has no solo or lines, but he serves all the drinks for the party scenes and for the toasts. He's still quite important, and we've got no one to cover him. Everyone is on stage when he is, for the big scenes. Except…" Royce raised his eyebrows and cocked his chin to one side.

"Except, who?"

"Your husband."

"*Bobby*? But he just sets up the props. Makes sure the correct things are on stage at the correct time, fills the trays with drinks for Bert to serve. I'm not sure he knows what Bert actually does while he's on stage."

"I think Bobby knows. He's been to enough rehearsals. Sure, Bert hams it up as the waiter. It's his way to make up for being such a weak tenor and to be included in the show." Royce shrugged. "He does a good job. He gets laughs from the audience, but Bobby doesn't have to do that. I've seen the two of them talking backstage. I'm sure Bert has told him all about it. All Bobby has to do is serve the drinks. He doesn't even have to pretend to sing."

"Have you talked this over with Piers? He *is* the director," Katherine put in.

Royce's face pinched with guilt. "No, I haven't. He's very busy with last minute sound and light checks. I don't want to bother him with this." He gently laid his hands on her shoulders. "*Please*, Katherine, come with me to convince Bobby to do it and get him into costume. He looks to be about Bert's size. Don't you think?"

Katherine studied Royce's reflection in the mirror. He was right. The part of the waiter was small, yet significant, and this was something they could solve without bothering Piers. Lifting her lips into a demure curl, she patted his right hand. "Okay, I'll go with you, but no guarantees." Considering the blue, wide-brimmed hat festooned with mounds of white ostrich feathers on the brushed gold hat stand, but deciding to leave it behind, Katherine pushed up from her bench. She swept the long, ivory, and blue, brocade gown away from her legs. Her rhinestone choker and dangling earrings glinted in the lights outlining the mirror, as she stepped toward the bird cage to check the door. The last thing she wanted was for her darling Zippy to escape and fly through the auditorium during the performance.

"Hurry Katherine, we haven't much time," Royce agonized.

While sipping a cup of tea, Katherine peeked out from behind the curtain, stage right, marveling at her husband, Bobby Starr. Other than general performances in grade school, the man had never stepped on a stage, much less performed in an operetta. God bless him. He was doing a bang-up job after being basically forced to take Bert's place as the waiter mere moments before the opening night performance of *The Merry Widow*.

"He's doing a *top job*, Katherine. Bobby's a natural," Piers Linney's British whisper tickled Katherine's ear. The lanky, sandy-haired director had come to the Onstage Operetta Company by way of England four years ago. He'd been an asset to the company, offering amazing insights as a tenor, and his impressive performance and directing experiences. Piers's keen eye for talent and his charming demeanor had afforded the small company new, up-and-coming singers, not to mention one of Pittsburgh's best choreographers for this production.

Around a hushed chuckle, Katherine replied, "Obviously, you haven't heard him sing in the shower."

"Thankfully, no, but just *look at him*, Katherine. The audience is having a smashing good time. They're enjoying the music, the dancers, and Bobby is really putting on a show, taking a nip of the drinks before he offers them to the party goers. Look how he pauses to pump his eyebrows for the audience at the pretty dancers. He's out doing Bert by miles. *By God*, he's *got* to be part of our next show. The audience is eating out of his hand."

"You'll have to do some creative convincing, Piers. We practically had to get him dressed and on stage at gun point." She smiled at Bobby's fun antics. Presently, he was floundering toward stage left, struggling to balance the trayful of glasses, as if he'd had too much to drink, and he was quite realistic about it all. Although, bumping into the last dancer in the front row was a bit over the top for Katherine's liking. Piers and the audience gasped in unison at the move. The dancer stumbled but managed not to fall and even took a moment to help Bobby steady the tray. The young woman might very well ream Bobby out when she caught up with him later. In his defense, the debacle raised a laugh from the audience.

Still staggering about, he was a few steps away from stage left. Katherine took another quick sip of the tea, then handed the cup and saucer off to Piers. "He's making his exit. I'm on."

Arms open wide and a bright smile on her red lips, Katherine strolled onto the stage. She was about to sing when there was a loud *crash* from stage left. The noise took her by surprise, but she recaptured her poise and the audience's attention by singing the first line of her song, and that's when a horrific scream tore through the hall!

The singers and dancers' attention snapped toward stage left. Pooky Mateer shrieked, "He's dead! Oh, my God! He's dead!"

Chapter One

Rude Awakening

The bedroom door eased open. Moonlight sifting through the curtains lent a dim glow over the bed, revealing two sleeping figures tucked beneath blankets. Detective Bobby Starr slipped through the slight gap. With measured steps, he made his way to the foot of the bed. He couldn't be sure if it was a glint from the streetlamps or a glimmer from the moon sweeping over Alexa Owl's lovely face. Her long cinnamon brunette hair splayed over the pillow. The man next to her stirred, rolling over, tossing an arm across Alexa's body, then squirming against his pillow until he settled deeper into his sleep.

Bobby's face bunched in uncertainty. Six months had passed since last he saw Alexa. Would she be happy to see him or annoyed by his unexpected appearance? She looked so relaxed, content. He really hated to mess that up, but... "Alexa..." Bobby whispered. He wasn't sure why he was whispering. The man, Detective Cliff Slater, couldn't hear him. Wait…he leaned over the bed…yeah…it was Cliff. Maybe they were married by now. He tried again. "Alexa…" This time, she roused. Her brows furrowed and her head rolled toward the window. Hm. He was having second thoughts. If he woke her, she'd probably sit up quickly, waking Cliff. Not good. Too…annoying. He was really trying not to be so bothersome this time around. After all, he had six months and four assignments of guardian angel experience under his belt. Bobby wanted to impress Alexa, not upset her.

"What's goin' on, Starr? Is she willing to help or not?" Detective Clifton Slater asked. He was the latest angel to request admission into Saint Pete's Guardian Angel Squad. As Bobby and the rest of the squad, Slater had to resolve something he left unsettled before he died. Neither Bobby nor Slater knew what that something was just yet. Maybe it was learning to follow instructions. Slater was *supposed* to wait in the hallway, but instead, he was now standing at Bobby's shoulder.

"*Shhh!*" Bobby scolded.

Slater craned his neck to peer over Bobby's shoulder at the bed. "She's sleeping. Who's that with her?"

"Your grandson, Cliff."

Slater grinned. "Aww, did they get married?"

"I dunno. This isn't working. We're gonna have to move her."

"*Move her? Why?*"

"Because I don't want Cliff to wake up and I don't want her…" Bobby shook his head. "Never mind. We just gotta move her."

"*Where? How?*"

"Could ya stop with the questions and let me think?" Pushing his fedora back, Bobby scrubbed his fingers along his thick hairline as he walked in a small circle. He stopped and turned back to Slater. "Okay, I know where we'll take her."

"Again, *how*?" Slater pressed.

The right side of Bobby's lip arched. "Like this…" He clicked his fingers and in the next nanosecond, they were standing in a small, dimly lit living room. Pink floral drapes framed dusty rose vertical blinds drawn across a picture window. Slivers of light from the streetlamps seeped between the slats. Pillar candles stationed all around the room sent shimmering shadows across the hardwood floor and over the light cream walls. A bottle of wine and two glasses sat next to a flickering three-wick candle on the coffee table. A brown leather jacket lay over the floral stuffed chair next to the mauve couch.

Slater turned in a circle, taking in the unfamiliar surroundings. "Where are we?"

"Winnie Mulaney's place. I thought it would be better…somehow."

"If ya haven't noticed, we're here, but Alexa isn't. So, where is she?" Slater demanded.

Bobby raised his hands in a calming gesture. "Hold on, hold on, I'm sure she'll show up any minute. She's just a little…delayed."

"And what if she doesn't? What if ya sent her to…I dunno…Zimbabwe, then what?"

"Why would I send her to *Zimbabwe*?"

"Well, she's not *here, Starr*."

"What's going on?" Alexa asked in a woozy voice. Bobby and Slater swung around just in time to see her tumble off the sofa. *Thud.* Alexa raked her fingers through her mussed hair. "My head's spinning. It feels the same way when I'm in the port…" Her eyes met Bobby's. Alexa's jaw dropped. "Ooh…"

"I told ya she'd show up. I *know what I'm doin',*" Bobby snapped.

"Okay, fine, but if Cliff wakes up, won't he wonder where Alexa is?" Slater asked.

Bobby shrugged. "I've been told by Winnie that when she time travels, another Alexa takes her place. Lives her life and runs the shop while she's gone. Winnie says she's got no personality. They call her Zombie Alexa. I suppose she's in the bed with Cliff as we speak." Suddenly, he didn't feel so confident. He mumbled, "At least, I hope so."

"A little help here, please," Alexa croaked, struggling to climb from the floor onto the sofa while trying to keep her satin nightgown in place. Bobby and Slater rushed around the coffee table to help her onto the couch. Bobby sat down on her right and Slater to her left. Clearly attempting to get her bearings, Alexa studied Slater with narrowed eyes. "Slater…is that you?"

Slater's voice was soft and filled with pride. "Sure is. So, ya *did* marry my grandson, then?"

"What? Not yet." Alexa glanced around the room. "What are we doing at Winnie's house?"

Bobby began, "I thought…"

Closing her eyes, Alexa dropped her head against the couch. "Oh, God, it's Bobby. That explains *everything.*"

"C'mon, Owl, you know you're happy to see me," Bobby teased, that bad boy grin of his making a grand appearance.

"Us," Slater put in. "She's happy to see *us*."

"Of course, I am. But we need to be quick and quiet. Winnie's in bed." Brows furrowed; Alexa scanned the room. "Although, I'm surprised she left candles burning. Maybe she's not in bed. Maybe she's in the tub. What time is it?"

Bobby checked his watch. "Two a.m."

Alexa's face filled with concern until Bobby nodded at the bottle of wine and the empty glasses. Unease fled her expression as she leaned forward to give the angels a once over. "You both still look the same. Handsome as ever in a double-breasted suit, a striped tie, and, of course, that classic detective touch: a fedora."

"Of course, we're professionals," Bobby said.

"*One of us* was a professional," Slater stated concisely.

Bobby's face contorted beyond annoyance into irritation. Alexa was quick to change the subject. "Something's up. Angels don't appear on my doorstep, or in this case, Winnie's living room, for a cup of coffee. What gives, gentlemen?"

"That's exactly what I want to know," Winnie's whisper was filled with reprimand. The pure white mound that usually sat atop her head lay in silky tresses, caressing her shoulders. Winnie sported a long, blue satin robe trimmed with white piping on the cuffs and hem. One couldn't be absolutely certain, but it appeared the old Irish gal wasn't wearing anything under the robe.

"Why are you whispering?" Bobby asked.

"Look around ya, *Detective* Bobby Starr. Can't ya see I've been entertainin'?" Bobby's gaze flicked to the wine bottle and glasses, and then to his fellow intruders. Alexa's eyes were wide, and her right hand cupped over her mouth. Slater's chin was buried in his chest. Clearly, he was stifling a chuckle. Winnie added, "Ah, now you're catchin' on. I'll bet you've come along to visit Alexa…" Her gaze found Slater. She studied him for a moment, and then continued, "Hm, and if I was a wagerin' woman, I'd bet Slater wants help gettin' into that Guardian Angel Squad. Well, isn't that nice, then? But I haven't got a *baldy notion* what you're doin' *here*, in me livin' room at *two in the morning*, Bobby Starr."

Still reeling from the seventy-five-year-old woman's extracurricular activities, Bobby stammered, "Well… um…you're right. I'm acting as a mentor for Slater, and you're always there when we read the scroll and travel to another time. I…um…er…didn't want to leave you out, my wild Irish—"

"Ah, stuff the wild Irish rose nonsense and let's get on with it then," Winnie insisted. She turned to Slater. "Where's your scroll?"

"My *what*?"

Bobby leaned over Alexa to open the front of Slater's suit jacket and pull a scroll tied up with a gold ribbon from the inside pocket. Holding it up for Slater to see, he said, "Your scroll. St. Pete always provides a scroll with your assignment written on it. Usually, we find the scroll in ol' Charlie, but we're not at Alexa's place. And we have Winnie read the instructions, but it's your assignment, so do as you like." He dropped the scroll into Slater's hand.

Slater stared at the scroll, then lifted his baffled gaze to Bobby. "Who's Charlie?"

Alexa chuckled. "He was the dumb waiter behind the bar at The Lazy Hound Pub. It's still there, we still use it, and it leads up to the kitchen in my apartment. Winnie's mom, Molly, used to call it Charlie, the handiest man in the pub. For some reason, St. Pete always placed Bobby's scroll inside the old dumb waiter. Trust me, we never question what Pete does."

"Winnie…" a man's voice called from another room. "Winnie…are you coming back?"

Winnie's eyes popped wide. Her entire body stiffened. She scurried to the archway that evidently led to her bedroom. "I'll be right in, Louie. I found a message on me phone that needs me attention. It'll be a minute." She turned back to her not-so-welcome visitors. "Let's do this, then. Am I readin' it or are you, Slater?"

"*Louie's* in your bedroom?" Alexa questioned.

Bobby confirmed. "As in, Louie Santorini?" He jammed a thumb over his shoulder. "The guy who owns Louie's Little Mardi Gras Bar on Liberty Avenue?"

Winnie waved a dismissive hand. "Yes, yes, that's the one. And ya can quit whisperin'. From all those years of loud music in his pub, Louie's hearin' isn't too sharp. Now, let's get on with it."

Alexa giggled.

Slater extended the scroll toward Winnie. "Guess I shouldn't mess with tradition."

"Ya always were a wise man, Detective Slater." Winnie took the scroll from his hand, slipped off the ribbon, and unrolled it. "Well, St. Peter comes straight to the point

23

on this one, doesn't he? It reads, who killed Bobby Starr? Ya can't get more direct than that, can ya now?"

"That's it?" Alexa questioned.

"That's it. And you've got the standard three days to sort it, Detective Slater." Immediately, the scroll rolled up with a snap and disappeared. "Ha! I was ready for it this time," Winnie boasted.

Alexa turned to Slater. "So, Winnie was right. You're trying to get into the squad, and you want *my* help?"

Slater nodded. "I sure would. If you're willing."

"Of course, I will. I'm *honored* you want me to help. I'm...speechless."

"That won't last very long." Bobby said. Then his brows furrowed. That's right, he was the one suddenly annoyed. "Wait a minute...you're not gonna *think about it* for a day or two? No...I've got the Owl's Nest to run. I've got a serious relationship to tend to. Come back tomorrow. What happened to all *those excuses* you used to throw at me every time *I* showed up?"

Alexa tossed him an indifferent look. "In the end, I did help each and *every time*, didn't I?"

"Well...yeah."

"And Slater is asking for help in solving *your murder,* isn't he?"

"And that's another thing. I didn't know I was murdered." He turned to Slater. "Why didn't you get it solved in 1964?"

Slater lifted a flippant shoulder. "Lost interest, I suppose."

"You *lost interest*!"

"How could you *not know* you were murdered, Starr?" Slater bit out.

"It's like I told Alexa, one minute I was on the stage at one of Katherine's operas, and the next, I was…just dead."

"As usual, you had no idea what was going on," Slater said.

"Boys…*boys*…" Winnie interrupted. "That Viagra isn't gonna last forever, if ya don't mind me sayin'."

Bobby and Slater's stymied gaze snapped toward Winnie.

Alexa stabbed her fingers through her hair. "Oh, my God. Let's not go there, pleeeze."

"Now, if it's all the same to the lot of ya, I'd like ya to be on your way. Let me know the plans tomorrow, lass." With that, Winnie scooped up the bottle of wine and the two glasses from the coffee table, then marched down the hallway. They heard her announce as she stepped into her bedroom. "I'm *b-a-a-ack*!"

"Let's get outta here," Slater said.

"What's Viagra?" Bobby asked.

Alexa threw her right hand up. "No…no and *no!*"

Chapter Two

First Trip

Alexa woke with a start. The sun shone through the sheers, making her squint. Feeling a bit dazed, she glanced around the room. Yep, she was in her bedroom and her century. Wait…had she been in Winnie's condo, and did Slater want her to assist him in solving a murder? Bobby's murder? A dream. It was just a dream. Rolling over to duck the blinding rays, she found Cliff's side of the bed abandoned and the sheets cool to the touch. Scraping bed tousled tresses aside, she sat up, and in a sleepy voice called out, "Cliff…"

Cliff stepped out of the bathroom wearing a pair of dark green boxer briefs, black dress socks, and shaving cream slathered on his face. He looked like a really hot Santa Claus. Well, minus the socks. Smiling, he said, "Good morning, sleeping beauty. Wow! You were down for the count. You didn't even flinch when your cell phone rang. I hope you don't mind, but I answered it. Winnie was calling and I thought it might be important. She said she'd be late today. Maybe around nine. Something about her sleep being interrupted by noisy neighbors." He stepped back into the bathroom.

Nope. Not a dream. She really was with Bobby and Slater in Winnie's living room during the wee hours of the morning. Alexa had to chuckle at the memory of Winnie's noticeable frustration last night. Meh, she couldn't blame her. Stifling her amusement, Alexa replied, "She's never complained about her neighbors before."

"Maybe they just moved in. There's nothin' worse than a rowdy neighbor. I asked her if she wanted me to have an officer stop by and tell them to keep the noise to a minimum, especially after ten o'clock," Cliff said from the confines of the bathroom. He sounded like he was in a fishbowl.

"Oh? What did she say to *that* offer?"

Wiping his cheeks and neck with a hand towel, Cliff stepped out of the bathroom and toward the closet. "She said not to worry about it. They probably wouldn't be around, anyway." Cliff snatched a shirt from the closet, eddied into it, then buttoned it up.

"Mm. She's probably right." Alexa watched him hop around the room on one leg while stuffing the other into his slacks. Her ex-husband had never been that entertaining in the morning. Dennis was never entertaining. Ever. One of the *many* reasons he was no longer her husband.

"I won't be back until late." He zipped up, then as he tucked the shirt into his slacks, he added, "I've got an errand to run. Don't forget we're going to my parents' for dinner Friday night."

"Gawd, we sound like an old married couple," Alexa said.

Shoving his feet into his shoes, Cliff grinned. "I know, right?" He trotted to the bed and kissed her lips. "Gotta go."

"Be careful out there."

"Yes, dear," Cliff called over his shoulder, then leaned back into the room, grabbed his tie off the dresser, and hurried toward the door.

Alexa listened to the apartment door open, slam closed, and the sound of Cliff's rushed footfalls descending the stairs into the couturier shop, then the shop's door open and slam closed. Around a sigh, she muttered, "Coffee." She tossed the blankets away and swung her legs over the side of the bed. Just then, a bright yellow bird soared across the room. Alexa ducked then dared a look to see a little canary land on the headboard. Another beleaguered sigh. "And so, it begins."

While padding down the hallway toward the kitchen, Alexa wiggled into a robe. The comforting aroma of coffee wafted through the apartment. Evidently, Cliff had made coffee. Whatta guy. She plucked a mug from the cabinet, poured a cup of Joe, then slipped onto a stool at the island to enjoy a quiet moment before showering and starting her day in the shop. If she remembered correctly, there were no appointments today, just lots of alterations were on the agenda.

Without warning, Slater appeared on the other side of the island. "Are you ready?"

Now, most people would be terrified to suddenly find an apparition in their kitchen. For Alexa, it had become part of her normal. She casually peered over the rim of her coffee cup. "Do I *look* ready? I'm in my jammies. We're not going to *Walmart,* are we?"

"I hadn't planned on it. Do you need to pick something up before we go?"

Bright eyed, Alexa straightened in her seat, and plopped the mug onto the island. "That's right. You've lived in the twenty-first century. I'm not talking to 1960s Clifton Slater; I'm talking to the *present* Clifton Slater." Her brows furrowed at his double-breasted suit, red tie, and grey fedora. "I mean, you're dressed like 1960 Slater, and you look like him too—just as handsome as your grandson. You don't look like the man I met in the nursing home just six months ago."

"Thank God for that. He was one decrepit ruin of a man," Slater said.

Alexa's voice was soft and genuine. "No. He was *wonderful.* I loved the 1963 version of you, but I absolutely *adored* the twenty-first century version of you, and so did Cliff." She smiled at the memory, and then shook it away before it overwhelmed her. "That said, because you've only been dead for six months, you know what a computer is, a cellphone, DNA, Walmart…" she chuckled. "…and a *Roomba* too, right?"

Slater laughed at the mention of a Roomba. "Just because I know what a computer is, doesn't mean I know how to use one effectively. Never did catch on to that very well. Just a warning: I type with one finger, and I'm not very good at coming up with or remembering usernames or passwords."

"Is anybody?"

Slater chuckled. "I doubt it. The good news is I won't shoot your Roomba this time around." He glanced around. "Do you still have one?"

"Couldn't live without it."

Slater grinned at her comment, then looked down at his attire. "I guess I look like the 1960s version of me because that's where we're heading, 1965. So, are you gonna get dressed, or are you going in your *jammies*?"

"Where's Bobby?"

He lifted a shoulder. "I dunno. He's probably off doing stuff for the squad. Do you need him to be here?"

"Nooo. I was just wondering. Thinking back, when Bobby showed up here the first time, he didn't have anyone with him. I suppose it makes sense that you wouldn't either. Like you said, he's probably got a customer or a client or whatever you call them."

"MITs."

Alexa's brows furrowed. "What?"

"MITs. 'Mortals In Trouble', that's what they're called."

"Ah…MITs…cute." Alexa grabbed the mug from the granite countertop and made her way toward the living room. "I'm not ready to go just yet." She plopped down in the closest chair, tucked her legs under her, then took a sip of coffee. "First, I need some information…" Just then, the canary flew into the room to perch on the mantle above the electric fireplace. Alexa hitched her chin toward the bird. "Like, who does *that* belong to?"

Clearly stymied by the canary, Slater rubbed the back of his neck as he wandered toward a chair and sat down. "I dunno. How did it get in here?"

"It's not really here. It's a ghost bird. Just like Walter was a ghost dog. You could see him. Winnie, Bobby, and I could see him, but no one else could. Each time I've time traveled; I've been host, here in the twenty-first century, to someone's pet. Cora Lee Starr's cat, Garbo. A poodle named Trixie, Walter, and evidently this little canary." The canary flicked its head about, checking out the items on the mantle, then hopped up onto the round mantle clock. "I hope it doesn't poop everywhere."

"Even if it did, the poop wouldn't be there because it would be ghost poop, right?" Slater pointed out.

Alexa half smiled. "I guess. Anyway, I've got some questions."

"Uh, oh, Bobby warned me about your questions." Slater slipped the fedora from his head, crossed his right leg over his left, then hung the hat on his knee.

"Good, then you're prepared."

"I wouldn't be so sure."

"Let's start with what we know. Even though I don't know very much, I'll go first. Bobby told me Katherine was a singer in a local operetta company…"

"Onstage Operetta, Janey used to drag me to their shows every once in a while," Slater put in.

"Did you ever see Katherine perform?"

"Probably, but I couldn't say for sure. I wasn't exactly an enthusiastic member of the audience. I finally got smart and started buying tickets for Janey, my mother-in-law, and her sister, Mary, to go to the shows."

"That was generous," Alexa noted.

"Self-preservation."

"You're such a man."

"Yes, I am." He shot her an ornery smirk that instantly reminded her of Bobby's bad boy grin—the one she never quite knew how to handle. Now, it seemed Slater owned one of those sexy yet somehow perplexing smiles, too. Funny, he was so much like his grandson, and yet she'd never seen such an expression on Cliff's lips.

"*Anyway*, these operettas were performed at the Carnegie Library and Music Hall. Bobby said he was on the stage, and then he was *just dead*. He didn't know how. He simply died. And that's all I know," Alexa explained.

"I don't have my notes from the crime scene or interviews, and this took place a long time ago. So, I'm shooting from the hip here, but I'll do my best. We were called to the music hall around eight o'clock that night. I remember because we never got called to the music hall, and certainly never to the *library*. When we got there, the audience was pretty much gone, only a few stragglers. Everyone from the operetta company was still there. The light and sound crew were closing up shop, and of course, Katherine Starr was backstage. Obviously, she was upset." Slater sagged deeper into the chair. His contemplative gaze focused on something past Alexa's shoulder, although she didn't believe he was seeing it. No. He was recreating the scene at the music hall.

"Are you sure he didn't have a heart attack or a stroke? It seems odd, to me anyway, that he didn't know he'd been murdered."

"It is odd, but he was definitely murdered. The coroner was new, but he was good, the first of his kind for Pittsburgh. He was actually a doctor and immediately recognized the signs of poisoning. Maybe that's why he didn't realize he'd been murdered because it was so unexpected. After talking with some of the stage crew who saw Bobby collapse, they described many of the symptoms of poisoning—confusion, dizziness, difficulty breathing—which backed up the coroner's diagnosis. The director, I think his name was Piers…Piers Lindley…no, that wasn't it. Lindy? I'll have to think about that. Anyway, the director told me Bobby was playing the part of the waiter, and he was taking drinks from all the wine glasses that were on the tray he was using. So, of course, we gathered them all up to be tested for poison. But they came out clean, unless someone was quick enough to remove the poisoned drink during the chaos. At least, that's what we originally thought. Obviously, that wasn't the case, since here we are."

"I'm assuming no cylinders of cyanide were found in the music hall."

"That's right."

"Why was Bobby on stage? He's not a singer," Alexa fished.

"Katherine and another cast member talked him into taking another singer's place who'd suddenly became sick. Can't remember his name at all…wait…Bert…his name was Bert. Turned out he wasn't sick. He'd been poisoned, cyanide. He died too."

"So, Bobby wasn't the intended victim?"

"Dunno for sure. Do you think St. Pete will provide my old notes?" Slater inquired.

"Doubt it. We're starting from scratch and that may very well be a good thing. It removes all preconceived notions about the case. With that in mind, it sounds like we solve Bobby's murder, we solve Bert's murder too." She glanced up at the canary, now sitting on the corner of the flat screen TV affixed to the wall above the mantle. "Two birds, one stone."

"We've only got one bird," Slater said.

"Let's hope it stays that way."

After showering and dressing, Alexa returned to the living room to find Slater standing at the window, drinking a cup of coffee while watching the traffic on Penn Avenue. She'd pulled her hair up in a messy bun, slipped on a pair of skinny jeans, and a floral peasant blouse. No real need to get too dressed up. St. Pete would make sure she arrived appropriately clad for the time period. The buzzer sounded, indicating the shop's door had opened from the outside. Slater spun around. "What was that?"

"Winnie must be here. Which is good. I can't go until I talk to her," Alexa said.

"Why not?"

"Winnie's the shop manager. She needs to know that I'm actually leaving, mainly because she'll soon be dealing with Zombie Alexa. Besides, she always gives an Irish blessing of sorts before we go for good luck. It's kind of a little ritual. Not to mention, we ruined her date last night, and I think we owe her an apology," Alexa said.

Slater lifted a hand in justification. "Going to Winnie's place was *Bobby's* idea. I didn't have anything to do with *that* decision. We were suddenly…there."

"Well, I don't think she appreciated it very much, and I don't blame her."

"Are ya up there, lass?" Winnie called from the bottom of the staircase.

Alexa hurried down the hallway to the apartment door and opened it. "I'll be right down." She turned to find Slater walking toward her. "This won't take long. Let's go."

They descended the stairs into the Owl's Nest Couturier Shoppe. The two majestic crystal chandeliers were the first thing to catch one's eye. They dangled over the open area where a free-standing, full-length triple mirror stood. The cream-colored French provincial sofa with a tufted ottoman, flanked by two over-stuffed chairs, was keenly positioned ten feet back from the mirror. The sunshine beaming through the storefront window provided a brilliant sheen over the hardwood floor.

"How much money could you possibly make as a *seamstress*?" Slater inquired.

Alexa found his continued amazement at how *fancy* the shop was for just a *sewing business* amusing. Pride in her voice, she replied, "I manage quite well."

"Sure, looks that way," Slater mumbled.

They made a right at the bottom of the staircase to find Winnie standing behind the long cherry bar counting the money from the register. Many a pint had been served across the bar when it was part of The Lazy Hound Pub. Winnie's parents, Brian and Molly Mulaney, owned and operated the pub from the 1940s until the early '70s. Nowadays, one end of the bar was the cash desk, and the other end provided a coffee bar for Alexa's clients. As per usual, Winnie's red tote bag lay atop the bar at the coffee end. The old Irish gal loved to bake something each day for everyone to enjoy, usually drenched in Jameson whiskey. Winnie was a gem.

"Well, well," Winnie's Irish lilt sounded a tad irked. "If it isn't one of the *scoundrels* who thought it a good idea to drop by me house *uninvited* and drag this poor lass along in her jim-jams."

Alexa shot Slater a raised eyebrow. He sighed. "Look, Winnie, I'm really sorry about that. But it wasn't my idea. This is my first time at this guardian angel thing. I'm gonna make mistakes…"

"And your *first mistake* was listenin' to *Bobby Starr*, if ya don't mind me sayin'. Me father used to say, you've got to do your *own growin'*, no matter how tall your grandfather was, or in your case, your mentor," Winnie said.

"I think we're being a bit too hard on Bobby. He was just trying to do the best he could under the circumstances. He didn't want to wake Cliff and make things difficult for me. I think that was quite…*angelic* of him."

"Now that you mention it, why aren't you and Cliff married? You're obviously living together," Slater asked.

"No, we're not. He hasn't asked me to marry him yet."

"Why not?"

"Don't know. You'll have to ask *him*."

"I intend to," Slater stated concisely. "Mm, don't know how St. Pete would feel about that."

"So, you'll be off then? We have a fairly quiet day today. I'm assuming Zombie Alexa will handle the alterations on the list. Holden won't be in until tomorrow," Winnie said as she dropped the bills into the cash drawer and pushed it closed with a *click*.

"There's someone I won't be bumping into this time, since I'm in spirit form," Slater pointed out.

"Ah, he's a dear lad for sure. Now, you'd best be on your way. You've only got three days to sort out Bobby's murder," Winnie said.

My, wasn't she being pushy? "Are you trying to get rid of us?" Alexa asked.

"I might be. Now, off with you." Winnie flicked her hands at them as she made her way around the bar.

Slater pumped his eyebrows at Alexa. Quashing a giggle, her lips quivered. Her gaze slid toward the red tote at the other end of the bar. "What did you bake?"

Winnie's head snapped toward the tote. "Oh, I figured I'd be alone today, so I just brought a small bit of leftover coffee cake. You know, for me lunch. Don't worry, I'll have something extra tasty when you come back."

Good thing liar's pants really didn't catch fire, but Alexa rolled with it. "Okay, we should go. But aren't you forgetting something, Winnie?" She asked, once again trying to keep a giggle from bubbling to the surface.

"I don't think so. Mrs. Welling will be in at ten-thirty to pick up her mother-of-the-bride dress. Shannon McGill will be dropping by around noon to pick up her weddin' gown, and then I think Cliff's brother, Sean, is comin' for that jacket that Holden put a new zipper in. He didn't make an appointment. I think he's stoppin' by after work hours. Other than that, I'll be in me office workin' on this quarter's taxes."

"Mm, don't do anything I wouldn't do, lass," Alexa teased.

"Well, that leaves me day wide open, doesn't it then?"

Alexa's eyes brightened. "Wait…isn't tonight the toga party you talked Louie into having at the bar? The one his daughter wasn't so keen about?"

"Tonight's the night, and Olivia isn't keen on too much when it comes to Louie having any fun, especially if that fun includes me," Winnie said.

Alexa turned to Slater. "Oh, you should see the beautiful toga Holden made for Winnie. Gorgeous red shoulder shawl with gold trim draped over an ankle-length satin tunic, and a gold and red Greek key design belt. He used the Greek key ribbon trim around the bottom of the toga too. Holden's eye for detail is amazing. Winnie ordered a gold leaf headdress to top it all off. She'll be the bell of the ball, or maybe I should say the *Aphrodite* of the party. And she and Louie have been practicing a special karaoke act to kick off the karaoke competition they're holding."

"That should be fun," Slater said.

Alexa turned back to Winnie. "I just don't get Olivia. *Everyone* loves you."

"Ah, lass, I'm not dating everyone's daddy." Winnie waved a flippant hand. "Awe, she's just a stick in the mud. I'm meeting Louie at Olivia's house. It's Louis's eighth birthday; that's Louie's grandson. Hopefully, we won't be there long. Now, if that's all…"

"Not exactly. I was waiting for the Irish blessing," Alexa said.

"Oh, yes, yes, yes. Now…which do I use for this *special* occasion: Detective Clifton Slater's first day on the job as a guardian angel trainee?" Lifting her finger in the air, she announced, "Ah, I've got just the one. Here's to a long life and a merry one. A quick death and an easy one. A *frothy* pint, and another one." She flicked her hands at them again. "Off with you now. I've got that daft zombie to deal with and taxes to prepare."

"And a toga party to attend," Alexa added.

"Wouldn't want to get in the way of that," Slater said. He let out a wary breath, then reached for Alexa's hand.

Placing her hand in his, she inquired, "Ready?"

Slater let out another breath. "I sure hope so."

Closing his eyes, he squeezed Alexa's hand. Immediately, she felt the familiar downward suction toward another time, another place, another adventure, only this time, with a new and promising guardian angel.

They were gone. As always, Winnie felt a terrible sensation of trepidation wash over her when Alexa traveled to the past with Bobby, and now Slater. She would wait for Zombie Alexa to show up, and it wouldn't be too long—it never was. Alexa was right. Olivia simply didn't like her relationship with Louie, and she couldn't figure a way to win the woman over.

Out of nowhere, something small and bright yellow swooped over her head. Winnie flinched and ducked. "Good Lord in the mornin'! What was that?"

Chapter Three

Different Angel, Different Place

"Whoa, whatta trip," Slater's voice sounded close, yet Alexa couldn't be sure from which direction it was coming from nor how close he was standing because there was so much… noise. As with every journey through the portal she'd made with Bobby, she felt lightheaded when landing in the past. Except this time, there were so many voices, and sounds…footsteps, a chair sliding over the floor, phones ringing, and…were those typewriters? She felt a hand squeeze her shoulder. "Alexa…are you alright?" Slater asked.

"Hey, Slater, I thought you weren't comin' in today. What've ya got there? A drunk?" a man's voice said.

"Naw, this is a friend of mine. She's not feeling well. Get her some water, would ya?" Slater said.

"Sure, sure," the man replied. His blurry form hurried away.

Massaging her forehead with the pads of her fingers, Alexa whispered, "I'll be okay. I just need a moment." Slowly, her eyes came into focus. When she traveled through the portal with Bobby, they usually landed in or around The Lazy Hound Pub. That's not where she and Slater had arrived. Alexa was fairly sure they were in a police station, a squad room. Hokay, different angel— different location…it made sense.

Just then, the man returned. He handed Slater a pointy paper cup. "Here ya go. Is she okay? Who is she?"

Slater gave Alexa the cup. She took a sip. "I'm fine now, thank you. I was just a little lightheaded, but it's passed now."

"Good. This is a colleague of mine, Sergeant Joe Randolph. Joe, this is Alexa Owl she's…um…er…"

Smiling, Alexa reached her hand out to Joe. "I'm a friend of the family. It's nice to meet you, Joe."

"Are you from out of town?" Joe inquired.

"No. I live in Mount Lebanon on Hoodridge Drive."

"Nice area," Joe replied. He had that *I'm very interested and getting ready to flirt* sound to his voice.

"Don't you have something to do, Joe?" Evidently, Slater heard the tone too and didn't appreciate the way Joe was looking at his grandson's girlfriend. Suddenly, it occurred to Alexa she hadn't checked out what attire St. Pete had chosen for this 1960s visit. She hoped it wasn't something ghastly, like the last time. Fact was, 1960's fashion could be amazing or perfectly…ghastly. She dared a peek. Nice! Very…classic. Alexa wore a mustard yellow, short-sleeved, scoop neck, thigh-length tunic, with matching, flair-legged slacks. A silver chain belt hung low on her hips. Alexa fingered her cinnamon brunette hair swept back with a psychedelic scarf knotted at the back of her neck. Her hair was teased at the top of her head behind the scarf and flipped at her shoulders. Delightful 1960's fashion—good job, Pete!

Flinching back into the moment, Joe cleared his throat. "Oh, yeah, we're following some leads on the Commuter Bandit. Ya know, I think you might be right."

Forcing her attention from her fabulous duds, Alexa could see Slater searching his mind for his former statement. She had no doubt he remembered the case, which certainly had her intrigued, yet it was clear Slater simply couldn't recall what he'd told Joe. Giving up, he fished, "Right about what?"

"You said he's probably a suburbanite, hitting the banks in town, like the North Side Bank last week, then he heads back home where he leads a perfectly respectable life. Possibly with a wife and kids," Joe said.

"Yeah, that's exactly what I think. You'd better get on it. Bank tellers all over the city are jumpy. And why shouldn't they be? He's eluded us since '63. He's making us look like idiots," Slater griped.

Joe nodded his agreement, shot a parting grin at Alexa, then headed for the door.

Slater turned to Alexa. "How did you come up with all that so fast?"

"With what?"

"Where you live. You even gave him an address," Slater said.

"I didn't *come up* with anything. That's where I *did* live…with my parents…since the early 2000s. We were

Cliff's next-door neighbors, the La Pearles." By the looks of him, Slater wasn't making the connection. "My maiden name was La Pearle, *Alexa La Pearle*." He still wasn't getting it. "Sam and Jennifer La Pearle were my parents."

Finally, she'd hit the right relationship. Slater's face brightened with recognition. "Yes, yes, Sam and Jen, I remember them now. Very nice people. How are they?"

"My parents are gone, I'm afraid."

"I'm sorry."

"I am too. I miss them terribly." Alexa glanced around the squad room. All men, and most of them quickly averted their gaze when hers swept in their direction. "In any case, here we are in the very mega center of your expertise. I would think your files or notes would be somewhere in your desk."

"That all depends. You heard what Joe said. I'm not here today." He looked down at the white planner on his desk advertising Mellon Bank, and the month of May 1965 in bold black print across the top of the calendar. Random notes, phone numbers, thoughtless circular doodles, and dried dribbles of coffee blotted the page. Slater tapped the week of May fourth with his fingertips. "If I remember correctly, this was about the time the baby…"

"Cliff's dad, Thom?" Alexa confirmed.

Slater's lips lifted. "Yeah, Tommie. Man, he suffered horribly with ear infections. Poor little guy would cry for hours. Janey was beside herself. Never got any sleep. So, I'd take some time off now and then to help her out. Speaking of babies, did you know Bobby's daughter, Maisie, was born the same day as our Tommie?"

"I did not know that."

"Yeah, September ninth. The nurse no sooner came to the fathers' waiting room to tell me that Thom had arrived, when another nurse came in to tell Bobby that Maisie was here." Slater turned from the desk to lean his behind against it. Crossing his arms, he dropped his chin to his chest. Alexa considered the detective's thoughtful demeanor. He appeared reflective, just this side of regretful. Slowly, he lifted his gaze to meet hers. "Ya know, we spent hours in that fathers' waiting room together, Bobby and me. Never spoke a word until our kids were born, and then the joy of becoming fathers seemed to just…I dunno…take over. We shook hands and congratulated each other. He slapped me on the shoulder like we were old buddies. Except, I got to raise my son. Bobby only enjoyed his daughter for about a year." Slater shook his head. "Funny, I'd forgotten all about that moment until just now."

Alexa's heart swelled. Slater was in the midst of realizing something intimate had passed between him and Bobby all those years ago—parenthood. Detective Clifton Slater was a tough detective with a soft heart, maybe even for that pain in the neck, Detective Bobby Starr.

Slater emerged from his funk with a different cast to his expression. "In any case, I always took my notebook home with me. Detectives keep their notebook with them at all times. It's almost like a Bible." He dug into his jacket pocket to pull out and hold up a small, black notepad. "All I've got is this brand new one." A careworn sigh. "But you're right, the case file should be around here…somewhere." Stuffing the pad back into the pocket, he pushed off the desk to reach down and yank the left side file drawer open, then walked his fingers through the tightly packed folders. Shaking his head, he straightened, then slammed the drawer closed with his knee. "Not in that one." A renewed sense of determination to find Bobby's killer was clearly in control now. Slater tugged the matching drawer to the right. He rifled through another collection of jammed folders. "Gotcha," he declared, slipping a folder from the lot, slamming the drawer, then laying it open atop the calendar.

Alexa moved closer to examine the information from the crime scene. "What've we got?"

Slater slid several 8x10 photos from under the typed pages. "Crime scene photos." Evidently, he saw Alexa wince. "You gonna be okay with this?"

She looked away. "I don't know if I've got what it takes to look at such awful pictures of Bobby."

Slater held the photographs up, turning them this way and that. "Oh, I dunno. I think the photographer got his good side."

Alexa's head snapped up. "*Clifton Slater*!"

Slater blinked back. "You sounded just like Janey."

"*Good.*"

"I'm sorry. I was teasing. It was in bad taste."

"It certainly was, *Detective*." Alexa met his gaze. Slater was holding the pictures against his chest. Knots twisted in her stomach. Investigating Bobby's death was one thing, but coming face to face with his corpse was quite another. Okay, it wasn't really his dead body, it was merely photographs of his body. Still... She swallowed back the urge to wretch.

Slater tucked the photos under the report. "We don't have to look at them first thing. Let's look at my report, help jar my memory a little, then if you're up to it, we'll look at the pictures." His voice softened. "It's not necessary for you to look at them at all, if you don't want to."

Alexa let out a careworn breath. "You're right. Let's ease into the photos, shall we? What's in the report?"

Slater picked up the file and studied it. "This file has quite a few pages. My interviews with the cast and some of some of the crew. There were a lot of people to talk to." He spent time with the information on the top sheet, then remarked, "This is my interview with Piers Linney."

"I believe you said he was the director of the opera," Alexa put in.

"Yeah, he was British. Moved to the U.S. about four years prior to this incident. He told me Bobby had done a terrific job replacing Bert Mateer as the waiter. Luckily, no singing required, he said." Slater looked up at Alexa. "It's not in the report, but I remember him saying how Bobby was hamming it up and had the audience eating out of his hand. Mr. Linney was thrilled about it because he'd arranged for a scout from Pittsburgh Opera to be in the audience to watch Katherine. Of course, he hadn't told Katherine about it. He didn't want to make her more nervous than necessary, but then everything went wrong."

"So, Katherine lost her husband and her shot at becoming an opera star with a big company," Alexa said.

"Guess so. I haven't kept in close touch. I don't really know if she went back to performing after Bobby's death or not. Anyway…" He ruffled through the pages and slipped out another sheet. "Here's an interview that we may want to revisit, Pooky Mateer. She was Bert Mateer's wife and the company's seamstress."

"*Pooky*? Surely, that can't be her real name."

Chuckling, Slater flipped through the paperwork until he found what he was looking for. "Naw, her real name is Patrice. I don't know why they called her Pooky. Just a silly nickname. Mrs. Mateer was standing just off stage left when Bobby staggered toward her and collapsed. I remember she was pretty rattled when I spoke with her. Who wouldn't be, right?"

"Didn't you say Bert Mateer didn't show up to perform because he was sick, and he died too?" Alexa inquired.

"Yep."

"And he was poisoned also?"

"Yep."

"So, why was the seamstress standing in the wings if her husband wasn't on stage?"

Slater lifted the page to read deeper into the interview. "I must've asked her something similar to that because it says here a dancer had lost a button and her top was sagging forward. Pooky was waiting for her to come off stage so she could replace the button."

"So, her husband is poisoned the same way as Bobby, she leaves him at home alone even though he's very sick, *and* she's standing right there when Bobby comes off stage. Pretty big coincidence, don't you think?"

"I do. The coroner said according to blood samples he took from Mr. Mateer, he was poisoned over a period of time. Small, consistent doses. Like I said, this guy was good."

"Wait, in small doses? I thought cyanide was lethal in any amount, and if ingested would kill you within twenty minutes," Alexa said.

"Usually, yes. But the doc said the amount Bert must've received, on a daily basis, may have been as little as a drop from an eyedropper. We're talkin' 0.05 milliliter here and may have been diluted in something, like a beverage of some sort, coffee maybe. When Wheeler searched the Mateer's house, he didn't find cyanide anywhere. Honestly, Mrs. Mateer didn't seem strong enough to murder her husband, or anyone else, for that matter."

"How's that?" Alexa asked.

"Eh, she was a mousey woman. As I remember, she was quite tall but very mousey. Not that those kinds of women can't do something out of character, but Pooky was well-liked and respected for her sewing skills. I remember, everyone in the cast and crew said Bert idolized her, and she loved Bert. No kids. That said, the conversation I had with Pooky Mateer at the music hall was the only one I had."

"Why?"

"She was way too rattled to discuss Bobby's death, and then Joe and I didn't handle Bert Mateer's death at all. Pooky found him when she went home that night. We were still working the scene at the music hall. Wheeler was called out to the Mateer residence." He replaced the papers in the folder, closed it, then glanced at his watch.

"It's almost lunchtime. I'm starvin'. How about we drive over to the Hound, grab a burger, and we'll go over the interviews while we eat?" Slater tidied up the papers, then slid them back into the folder.

"Sounds good, but first I want to look at those photographs," Alexa said.

Slater's gaze slid to meet hers. "You sure?"

Alexa took a deep breath. No, she wasn't sure. She had grown to love Bobby. That ornery, scatter-brained, inconvenient, hard to deal with, big-hearted, handsome, charming, bad boy angel. Regardless of the fact that he was, indeed, dead, Alexa simply never thought she'd have to actually see him that way. This was a murder investigation—*Bobby's* murder investigation. Crime scene photos were part and parcel to that inquiry. Calling out every bit of courage, Alexa replied, "I'm sure."

Slater slipped the photos from under the paperwork and handed them to Alexa. Another stabilizing breath was required before she dared a look. She gulped back when she laid eyes on the first photo: Bobby lay on his back on the wooden floor surrounded by broken glasses. His right arm was laid out and his head turned in the same direction. He was sporting a typical, period waiter's uniform: a black suit, white shirt, and black bowtie. The shirt was soiled. His face was bloody.

Slater pointed to the blotches over the white fabric. "Of course, the cider splashed all over his shirt when he fell."

"Cider?"

"Yeah, they don't put wine in the glasses for the performance, it's cider. I know this is a black-and-white photo, but the stains on his shirt aren't red, like wine would be, it's brown in color, more like blood would be after it dried. He broke his nose when he fell, that's why his face is bloody and some of the stains on his shirt are blood."

Alexa set the photo aside. The second was the dreaded head shot. Bobby's was cringeworthy. Pushing against tears, she lay the photo in the folder atop the first. The third was a different angle from the first, a better view of the broken glasses, shards of glass, and spillage. The tray he was using lay halfway under a side curtain. "Was this tray moved or did it bounce when Bobby fell?"

"I dunno. It may have been kicked aside when people were trying to help him. Many of the back-stage crew were treated for cuts from the broken glass, including Pooky. I think she required a few stitches," Slater supplied.

Tossing the last picture on the folder, Alexa sank into Slater's chair. She covered her eyes. "I didn't sign on for this. I know he's dead, but I didn't want to actually…" Her voice melted away.

Slater squeezed her shoulder. "That was hard. I know. From the moment I met you, Alexa Owl, I knew you were a strong woman. What you just did took a lot of strength."

Dropping her hands from her face into her lap, Alexa managed a slender smile. "Thank you for that."

"C'mon, let's get something to eat," Slater said. He gathered the folder together.

Alexa touched his wrist. "Wait…there's a note paper-clipped to one of the last pages."

Slater fingered through the pages until he came to the paperclip. "What's this?" He tugged the folded paper from under the clip.

"What does it say?" Alexa pushed up from the chair.

"Says here, I saved Bobby's shirt for future reference. Glad I was smart enough to write a note. I would've, or should I say, *I did* forget all about that."

"Oh my God, Slater, you were *way ahead* of your time. Where is it?"

Obviously thwarted, Slater searched the desktop as if the shirt would suddenly materialize. "I'm not sure."

"What does that mean?"

"I put it in one of *those* places."

"What place? The evidence room? A lockup of some kind?"

"No. Not a place of official capacity. You know, a place where it would be safe…" Letting out a disgusted sigh, Slater dropped a fist onto the file. "…and now I can't remember where that place is."

Chapter Four

Sister Mary Alexa

Alexa leaned a hip against Slater's desk. "Hm. Would you have taken the shirt home to put it in a closet or under a bed?"

"No. The shirt was police business. I don't mix police investigations with home life. Besides, Janey would've been upset if she found a blood-stained shirt under the bed," Slater reasoned.

"Point taken. Well, it's gotta be around here somewhere, and we've got to find it."

"And then what? We've just got an old, stained shirt. This isn't the twenty-first century, ya know," Slater put in.

"True, but your gut told you to hold on to that shirt and you did. When we find it, you'll turn it into the pathologist. If he's as good as you said he was, I'll bet he'll be interested in running some tests on the shirt. Ya never know, he may find something that was missed in the original investigation. Now, let's rip this desk apart and see if it's in there." Alexa pointed to the right side of the desk. "I'll take this side, and you take that side."

"Okay, but we gotta be careful with the files. I don't want me to come back and have trouble finding information on a case," Slater said.

Just as Slater bent down to grab the handle on the left drawer, a short, stalky man wearing a crumpled suit with a badge on the right lapel approached Slater's desk. His hair was thinning, and a rosy red tinged his cheeks. Alexa sensed his probing gaze sweep over her. Yeah, he was doing more than just undressing her with his eyes. He reached his hand out toward her and asked, "Hey, Slater, who's this tall drink of water?"

Following the man's gaze, Slater stepped in front of Alexa, blocking the man's view and his handshake. Slater's timbre was concise. "She's my *sister-in-law*. She's staying with Janey and me for a day or two. On her way to the *convent*." Slater followed up his statement with a hefty glare.

Smiling, the man replied, "*Whoa*. She doesn't look like no nun."

"I'm a flying one," Alexa mumbled under her breath.

Slater scowled all the more. The man threw his hands up. "Okay, okay, take it easy, Slater. I didn't know you were Catholic."

"I'm *not*." Slater stabbed his thumb over his shoulder at Alexa. "*She is*." The man turned to make his way back to his desk. Slater leaned in close to whisper, "That's Detective Vince Wheeler. He's one of those perverts."

Alexa's eyes snapped up to meet Wheeler's. Grinning, he winked at her. "Imagine my surprise," she whispered, rolling the file drawer open.

"Let's just say he arrests a lot of hookers, then let's them off with a *warning*. Although, I gotta say, there haven't been any hookers in the holding cells for a while now," Slater said. He yanked the drawer open, started pulling out files, and piling them on the desk. He glanced up. Alexa followed his gaze. It seemed Slater was checking Wheeler's location. Evidently satisfied, he quietly added, "Like I said, Wheeler handled the call to the Mateer residence because Joe and I were still working the music hall scene."

"Does that mean Bert Mateer's death is his case?" Alexa asked.

"Yep. They're definitely connected. Problem is, we can't figure how either man ingested the cyanide," Slater began. "Wheeler isn't exactly forthcoming with his information."

"Mm, that doesn't mean we can't question Pooky about Bobby, then just slip in questions about Bert."

"No, it doesn't." Only half the files were out of the drawer when Alexa heard Slater let out a frustrated breath, then the sound of files sliding from the desktop and dropping back into the drawer.

Then another man said, "Thought you were stayin' home today, Slater."

Feeling it was best, Alexa kept her nose in the file drawer. Slater replied, "I was supposed to. Turned out, I needed a file."

"Is this a new…assistant?" the man queried.

Another sigh. "Not really, um…Sister Mary *Alexa* of the Holy Virginity…" Alexa's gaze flashed toward Slater's laughing eyes. "I'd like to introduce you to Detective Sawyer. His wife, Colleen, is very active in the choir at Saint Mary's. She'll probably be in the choir this Sunday when you direct." He swung back toward his fellow detective. "Sister Alexa is Janey's younger sister. She's very talented with music. She's in town for a short time as part of her training before she goes on to the convent. Janey was feeding the baby, so Sister Alexa came along to help me locate the file." He returned his attention to a shell-shocked Alexa. "Have you found it, Sister?"

Okay, to her limited knowledge, his explanation didn't quite add up to how becoming a nun worked, but she saw no reason not to play along. Quickly regaining her composure, Alexa folded her hands together at chest level. "I'm sorry, I haven't. I will certainly keep the family of the victim close to my heart and in my nightly prayers, Clifton." She fought to keep a straight face while looking into Detective Sawyer's stupefied expression.

"But she's not dressed like…" Most likely thinking better of calling the nun a liar, the detective backpedaled and stammered, "It was nice to meet you, Sister Virgin…I mean, Sister Virginit…er…Sister Alexa…" Obviously giving up the fight, he crossed himself.

"Oh! Yes, of course," Alexa said softly, bowing her head and crossing herself. The detective hurried toward the door, tossing Detective Wheeler a dirty look as he passed. He hesitated just long enough for Joe Randolph to step through the door before making his desperate exit. From the corner of her eye, Alexa saw Joe saunter to his desk, open the right top drawer, take out a crinkled paper bag, and pull out a sandwich. Alexa gathered the files she'd placed on the desk. "Well, there's nothing in my drawer either. Think…where could you have put it other than here? Are you sure you didn't put it in the lockup?"

Slater flinched when Joe asked, "What're you lookin' for, Slater?"

"A white shirt from the Bobby Starr investigation."

"Bobby Starr? You mean that guy who dropped dead at the opera last year?"

"Yeah," Slater growled. Nodding his understanding, Joe took a bite of his sandwich, then plunked down in his chair. Scrubbing a hand over the nape of his neck, Slater watched Alexa slide the last two files into the drawer and close it. Self-reprimand filled his tone. "I just can't imagine where I could've put that stupid shirt. It's not like me to misplace something. Especially something important."

Alexa let out a beleaguered sigh. "In your defense, you probably didn't necessarily consider the shirt important, but for some strange reason, you kept it."

"And now it's driving me nuts."

"Is this what you're lookin' for?" Joe asked.

Alexa and Slater swung around to see Joe holding up a crinkly, stained white shirt. "Where did you find that?" Slater demanded more than asked.

"In my desk. Right where you asked me to put it a year ago. It was right after we'd left the music hall. We were sitting at The Hound. You were havin' a Rueben sandwich, and I had the corned beef on rye. Mrs.

Mulaney was upset over that Starr guy dyin'. She was sobbin' all over her husband's shoulder…"

Slater impatiently blurted, "*Anyway*…"

"Anyway, *you said* you wanted to save the shirt; in case we would ever need it for evidence. I couldn't figure out why we would, but you didn't have room in your desk. So, you told me to stuff it in mine." He took a bite of his sandwich. Around a mouthful and a shrug, he added, "So, I did."

Slater's face looked like it was about to burst into flames. Alexa held her hand up for him to take a breath. Using her right pointer and thumb, she gingerly took the shirt from Joe's hand. "And it looks like that's *exactly* what you did—*stuffed it* into your desk." During her earlier visits to the past, the police were completely ignorant about how to handle evidence, and it looked like they hadn't gained much more respect for it in the 60s either. Alexa wasn't sure what kind of forensic knowledge was available in 1965, but whatever the shirt had to offer may have been critically compromised. She slid her gaze to meet Slater's. "Would you happen to have a bag?"

"I've got my lunch bag," Joe said. He rushed to his desk to dump an apple and a plastic baggie filled with cookies from the brown paper bag onto his desk, then scurried back to offer it to Alexa.

Dismayed, Alexa looked at the bag and then into Joe's beaming eyes. She grumbled, "At this point… what the heck?" While he held the back open, she carefully wiggled the dilapidated shirt into the unsterile sack.

Slater clapped his hands together in victory. "Good. We'll drop it off at the lab on our way to The Hound and see what the doc can find."

"And then it's off to the convent," Alexa said under her breath.

Alexa and Slater settled at a table tucked in the farthest corner of The Lazy Hound Pub. The first time Alexa's time travel excursions took her to The Lazy Hound was 1953. Other than the tablecloths, not much had changed. The wood floor was scuffed and stained, and the long cherry bar still provided twelve well-worn bar stools. As before, two older gentlemen sat on the stools with a pint in front of them. Her gaze glided to the big storefront window that looked out onto Penn Avenue. The old sleeping hound dog curled up around a mug of beer painted on the glass looked weathered, as did the green lettering that announced The Lazy Hound Pub, corralling the slumbering, floppy-eared, mongrel. Petula Clark's unmistakable crisp English-accent wafted through the pub. Alexa's wandering gaze found a jukebox stationed near the staircase. The jukebox was a new addition since her last visit in 1963. She paused to listen to Petula's words about going downtown.

Slater sliced through her musing by slapping the case file onto the table. "Okay, here's the file. We've got a lot of interviews to go over." He looked up. "Oh, good. Here comes Maggie."

Alexa glanced up to find Winnie's older sister approaching the table while sliding a notepad and a nubby pencil from her green-and-white striped apron. Maggie had a different look about her since the last time Alexa had been to the pub, which, according to the time travel table, would have been two years prior. It was hard to keep track of the ages of those from the past. Actually, she was never quite sure how old Maggie or Winnie was when she visited. In 1953, Maggie appeared to be in the early stages of her teen years and Winnie approximately eight. Now, in 1965, Maggie was probably in her late twenties. Her tired, haggard, and rail-thin appearance gave the impression she'd been run ragged. The dark circles beneath her eyes signaled the young woman wasn't getting much sleep. Her long, curly auburn hair was in disarray. Over the years, Maggie's hair was always so lovely. The young woman's undone appearance had Alexa wondering if she'd gotten married and was now chasing after a toddler or two—that would surely drive anyone to exhaustion.

Around a careworn sigh, Maggie asked, "Whatta ya be havin' then, Detective Slater?"

"I'll have the roast beef sandwich, coleslaw, and a beer."

Maggie's weary gaze slid from her notes toward the brunette sitting with Slater. "And what'll your friend be havin'?"

It was business as usual in the good ol' time travel zone. No matter how many times Alexa returned to the past, no one remembered her from the time before. In fact, even Winnie, who was part and parcel to the whole time travel and seeing apparitions in the twenty-first century, did not remember her encounters with Alexa in the twentieth century. As she'd been reminded, on several occasions, Alexa had never actually existed there. "I'll have a burger with cheese and ketchup, please. Oh, and a root beer float, too." The Hound offered the best root beer floats Alexa had ever tasted. She was always sure to savor at least one when visiting the past.

"Comin' right up," Maggie said before spinning on her heels and scurrying away. As the young Irish girl departed, Alexa noticed her shoes were scuffed and worn. The hem of her plaid skirt was coming loose. Yep, something had changed for Maggie. While the Mulaney's weren't wealthy people, their children's shoes and clothes were always in good condition. On the other hand, Molly's daughters were no longer children; they were young adults. Alexa figured Winnie would be about… wow…twenty by now. She made a mental note to keep an eye on Maggie.

Again, Slater pulled her from her funk. Laying several files before her, he said, "I'd like to review the cast members first. It's nice we have the case files, but I wish we had my handwritten notes. I tended to write little details down that I didn't include in the case files." He handed her a slip of paper. "Luckily, I kept a list of the cast with the files."

Alexa studied Slater's typed catalog:

The Merry Widow

Director: Piers Linney

Singers:

Katherine Starr: Hanna Glawari – a wealthy widow (soprano)

Royce Hathaway: Count

Danilo – First Secretary of the Pontevedrian embassy (baritone)

Ben Landis: Baron Zeta – the Ambassador (baritone)

Tallis Chamberlain: Valencienne – Baron Zeta's wife (soprano)

Nick Ferroni: Camille, Count de Rosillon – French attaché to the embassy (tenor)

Bert Mateer (deceased): Waiter, older actor who Bobby replaced.

Alexa's eyebrows rose. "I disagree. This is *very* detailed, Slater. You've even listed what role and what kind of singer each individual was. Impressive." Her gaze met his. "Before we move forward, did the production happen?"

"You know what they say, the show must go on, but in this case, it didn't. The stage, the dressing rooms, even the library itself became a crime scene. We shut the whole thing down. I think the cast was so overwhelmed by the incident that they simply didn't want to do the show. As far as I know, there hasn't been another show at the music hall since."

"That's a shame."

"It was. *But* my understanding of the current situation is they've decided to put the show on within the week. They're in rehearsal now. Same cast. It's a great opportunity to revisit the cast members and re-familiarize myself with the case." He tapped his pointer finger on a file. "I want to talk with *her* first."

The file in question drew Alexa's attention. A black-and-white photograph of a beautiful young woman was stapled to the corner of the page. Long, dark tresses spilled about her shoulders. Her dark, seductive eyes were as captivating as her plump lips. Alexa was taken aback by the size of her mouth, very large, yet mesmerizing, and in perfect symmetry with her features. She flipped the picture up to read the name on the file. "Tallis Chamberlain. Tallis, what an interesting name. Is it a stage name or is that her real name? She's…more than just beautiful, she's…quite…*spellbinding*."

"Yes, she is, and yes, Tallis is her real name."

"Any special reason you want to talk with her first?"

"She was, or should I say still is, a *spellbinding* woman. She was about ten years younger than me, and as far as I know, she is still alive in your time. Did you know Katherine was twelve years younger than Bobby?"

"I did not. Seems I'm learning a lot about Mr. Starr on this trip. Is Katherine still living? I mean, in the *twenty-first* century?"

"I believe so. Into her eighties by now."

"Did Katherine ever remarry?"

"I think she married a fellow opera singer soon after Bobby's death. So, that means they're newlyweds right about now. In fact…" He flipped through the files, slipped another sheet out, and placed it in front of Alexa. "I believe she married this guy…Royce Hathaway. Get this, she kept the name Starr as a stage name."

"Can't say that I blame her. Katherine Starr is more...*stagey* than Katherine Hathaway," Alexa said, as she studied the photo of Royce stapled to the sheet. "Mm, he's quite handsome. Very...oh, what was his name? Tony Curtis. Yeah, he looks a lot like Tony Curtis—even that *sexy,* errant curly lock of dark hair on his forehead."

Eyes narrowed in curiosity; Slater leaned in close to look at the photo. "Yeah, he does kinda look like Curtis. They're entertainers. Of course, they're good-looking."

"Jimmy Durante wasn't good-looking."

"I stand corrected."

"Do you have pictures of all the cast members?"

"Sure do. Again, they're entertainers. They were all more than willing to provide me a *headshot*." Slater's tone dripped with cynicism.

Holding the photo aside with her finger, she perused the notes on Royce Hathaway. "Says here, Royce talked Bobby into taking Bert's place on stage. Wait...he *and* Katherine convinced Bobby?" Alexa's brows drew downward. Her lips pressed together.

"What's *that* look?" Slater asked.

"Nothing. There was no *look*."

"There was a look. I used to get a similar look when I'd miss dinner or a special occasion, which was more often than not."

Chuckling, Alexa returned her attention to the Hathaway file. Askance, she noticed Maggie approaching the table with their lunch order on a tray. She set the file aside. "I agree. We need to revisit the cast. Now, according to Royce's file, he has a day job, as I'm sure most amateur opera singers do. You have him down as an agent for Lifetime Investments."

"That's on Carson Street," Slater supplied.

"Hm." Alexa glanced at her watch. "It's about one o'clock. Royce is probably at work, as well as most of the singers. Let's stop by the library and find out what time rehearsals usually start."

Slater snorted. "It's obvious you're not a cop. We have no qualms about visiting suspects at their workplace. When we show up at their office, or wherever, it tends to throw them off and we get a better feel for what they might be hiding."

"You think Royce Hathaway is hiding something?"

"I intend to find out." Slater replied. Maggie set a beer and a plate with a roast beef sandwich and a generous dollop of coleslaw down in front of Slater. Then carefully placed the root beer float and cheeseburger down for Alexa. Slater grinned. "But first…*lunch*."

Chapter Five

Toga Trouble

"Your destination is on the right. You have arrived," the GPS system announced. Winnie rolled her orange metallic Volkswagen Beetle to a stop in front of the charming Cape Cod house on Elizabeth Lane in the West Mifflin neighborhood of Pittsburgh. She was dressed in the elegant toga costume Holden had made for her. Winnie's gold leaf headdress lay on the passenger seat next to her purse. The usually confident Irish gal wasn't accustomed to these recent feelings of insecurity. Tiny tight knots tangled in her stomach every time she came in contact with Olivia Shipman were definitely a new twist. Clearly, Louie's daughter was doing a job on her. Winnie didn't understand the young woman's attitude, and she didn't much like it either. Louie had three children; Dean, Brett, and Olivia, who was a late-in-life birth, which probably accounted for her possessiveness toward daddy.

From the moment she and Louie started dating, Olivia was up-in-arms. Seems she didn't appreciate her father seeing another woman after her mom, Barbara's death, and she wasn't shy about expressing her displeasure. "I'm surprised Dad would be interested in a woman such as yourself. Mom was *so* different." Such as the likes of you, Winnie translated. "Mom was a…*sophisticated* woman." *Yep, that's exactly what Olivia meant.* And yet the comments got worse. Winnie wondered if she were tripping over her words, or she was purposely voicing her exact thoughts. "She took care of the books for the bar, but she didn't drink there. Mom wasn't much of a partier, she was more…*demure* than you," Olivia said when they first met. Winnie was most certain Olivia wasn't tripping over anything. She was being direct. *Very* direct.

Evidently, Louie hadn't informed his daughter they had dated years ago, before he met Barbara, and it was Winnie who had broken off the relationship. Actually, Winnie didn't consider what they had now a serious relationship. It was more companionship they shared. Regardless, Louie had insisted she wear her toga costume so Olivia and Louis could see them dressed up for the party.

Holden had outdone himself on her toga. It was lovely, but she wasn't so sure how Olivia would react. She tipped down the visor and picked up the headdress. Using the mirror affixed to the visor, she slipped the headdress into her white hair in front of her braided bun. "Here goes nothin', Wynona Mulaney," she said to her reflection before pushing the visor up, grabbing her purse, and shouldering the door open. When she reached the front door, she heard Olivia's voice from the other side. "You look ridiculous. What's going on with you, Dad? A *toga party. Really*? Are you going through a mid-life crisis?"

Louie chuckled. "I'm much too old for that, Liv. I'm just having fun. What's wrong with that?"

The poor man seemed to be in the need of rescuing. Winnie boldly rapped on the door. A dog's deep bark bellowed from somewhere inside. She could hear the dog's footfalls scampering toward the door, and when it swung open, Louie's ear-to-ear grin and a curly, black cocker spaniel greeted her. Winnie couldn't have prevented herself from smiling if she'd tried. Louie looked genuinely happy in his knee-length, short-sleeved, white tunic featuring a royal blue drape that looped over his right shoulder to cross over his left hip, and then back to his shoulder. He was sporting a gold headband and a pair of black sandals.

"Oh! Don't you look handsome," Winnie said. The dog danced around her legs, sniffing her tunic. She patted his head. "And who's this darlin' pup?"

"That's Allister," a young, blonde-haired boy with big blue eyes said.

Winnie smiled at the boy. "You must be Louis. Happy birthday."

"Your costume looks beautiful, Winnie. Come in," Louie said. He took her by the hand to lead her into a small foyer. Louis tossed a small red ball down the hallway and Allister took off after it.

"Louis, stop throwing that ball around. You're gonna break something, and I'm not going to be happy." Olivia cried out, then swung around to manage a forced smile. "You look very nice, Winnie. That's a lovely costume, not at all what I expected."

"What were you expectin', lass?"

"Oh…I'm not sure. Something one-shouldered, perhaps?"

"I think this is more age-appropriate," Winnie replied.

Louie held out his cell phone toward his daughter. "Could you take a picture of us?"

Another faux grin. "Sure."

Smiling brightly, Louie wrapped an arm around Winnie to pull her close, and with that, Olivia grudgingly lifted the phone to take aim and press the button. She gave the phone back to her father. Louie inspected the picture, showed it to Winnie, and said, "I'll text you the picture. We'd better get going."

"Um…could I talk to you for a moment before you go?" Olivia asked. Her gaze flicked to Winnie and then back to her father. "Privately." Reluctantly, Louie followed Olivia into another room.

While Winnie couldn't make out the conversation, she could hear Olivia's whispers and Louie's low responses. The whispers had a tense tone. Only a moment had passed when Allister came bounding into the foyer with the red ball clenched in his teeth and Louis on his heels. Winnie stepped back as the boy wrestled the ball from the spaniel's grip and then tossed it into the living room. The ball hit the corner of the coffee table, bounced upward to smack an angel figurine on a nearby bookcase, and then rolled off the shelf onto the floor, where the dog scooped it up and scurried out of the room. Winnie gasped. Louis's eyes were wide with trepidation. Winnie quickened to the bookcase. The delicate porcelain angel lay on her side. Her head was broken off, as were both of her wings. Bits and pieces and shards of porcelain lay scattered over the shelf.

"Mom's gonna *kill* me," Louis muttered.

Winnie carefully gathered up the pieces. "I don't think there's much that can be done to fix this poor little fallen angel." The boy's lips bunched. There was scant purpose in pointing out the child's error in judgment. What was done was done. Winnie felt bad for him. After all, it was his birthday. Her gaze slid to the foyer and then back to Louis. Quietly, she said, "Don't worry, lad. This will be our secret."

Louis's brows furrowed. "*How*? Mom's gonna notice the angel's broken. She's gonna be *really* mad. I didn't think I threw the ball hard. I meant for it to roll across the room, but it bounced. And…"

Just then, Olivia and Louie stepped into the room. It wasn't more than a nanosecond when Olivia noticed the broken pieces in Winnie's hand. First her eyes widened, and her shoulders braced. Olivia rushed toward Winnie, gasping when she realized what she was holding. She spun to face her son. "*Louis*! I told you not to throw that ball around!" Tears welled in her eyes. "That was grandma's favorite figurine!" Turning back, she cupped her hands for Winnie to gingerly spill the fragments into them. "This was her mother's and she treasured it. This figurine was at least eighty years old. It's unreplaceable!" Her flushed face pinched in anger, and again she whirled toward Louis. "Go to your room, immediately!" Louis hung his head and started across the room.

"Now, hold on a minute, Olivia. The boy didn't break the little angel…I did."

Olivia and Louie's eyes snapped toward Winnie. Louis came to an instant halt to turn and stare at Winnie, slack jawed. Olivia muttered, "*You* did?"

"I'm so sorry, but yes, I did." Much to her own surprise, Winnie was stammering. "The dog wanted someone to play with him…so, I gave the ball a little toss, but it bounced against the coffee table and hit the angel. I'm…I'm…I…"

Louie came to her aid. "We should be going. It's *just* a figurine, Liv."

"It was *Nana's*! Mom *loved* this little angel. She entrusted me with it."

"If your mother were here, she would tell you to leave it alone, Liv. It was an *accident.* Now, we're going to the bar to finish setting up the party. Your brothers are coming with their wives. I would be happy if you and Josh came too. No pun intended but, the ball's in your court. See ya later." With that, Louie palmed Winnie's elbow to usher her out of the house. He paused at the door. "Oh, and thanks for the *talk*."

"Daddy!"

Louie let the screen door slam closed behind him. Invisible to all, Bobby Starr leaned against the wall with his arms crossed over his chest. Lips curled; Louis walked past him.

71

Louie's Little Mardi Gras Bar had been a staple on Liberty Avenue in Downtown Pittsburgh since the late 60s. The bar was known for its Mardi Gras theme the year through. Just a few steps inside the door, a long bar ran the length of the wall. Mardi Gras masks of all shapes, sizes, colors, and characters filled every available spot on every wall. Large urns overflowing with vibrant Mardi Gras beads stood prominent places throughout the saloon. Twenty tables had a good view of the small stage at the farthest reach of the vast space. A small disco ball dangled above the stage, designated for Thursday night karaoke.

Even though Louie's bar entertained a Mardi Gras theme and atmosphere, the patrons were enthusiastically participating in this evening's toga party. Bar-goers were sporting togas of all kinds: short, *too short*, long, mid-length, conservative tunics, sexy one-shouldered togas, gold-leafed crowns, headbands, wrist cuffs, and more. In keeping with the traditional theme, some of the patrons were sporting masks featuring Greek characters, Zeus, Athena, Aphrodite, and even the Roman emperor, Caesar. Louie and his staff were pouring drinks at a fever pitch, and the crowd was having a great time.

Winnie, Louie's sons, and their wives sat at a table near the bar. Dean's wife, Claire, said over the din of partiers, "I feel bad that Liv is giving you such a rough time, Winne. You're the best thing to happen to Lou since Barbara's death. He's busy with the bar and getting the new wine cellar ready, but he was lonely before you came along. There's a difference between busy and lonely, ya know." She chuckled. "You've really livened up his life."

"I think she's jealous," Stacy, Louie's other daughter-in-law, stated. "She's always had daddy's undivided attention until you showed up. Now, she doesn't know how to handle the competition."

"There's more to it than that," Brett said, before taking a swig of his beer.

Winnie suspected jealousy fueled Olivia's disdain for her, but Brett's statement had her wondering. "What then?"

"She's worried you'll marry dad and take a chunk of our inheritance when he dies," Brett explained.

"She thinks I'm a *gold-digger,* does she?"

"You shouldn't have said anything, Brett," Dean scolded. "But yeah, she does. Don't worry about it, Winnie. Liv will come around and don't worry about breaking the little statue either. Something was bound to get broken sooner or later the way Louis carries on with that dog, and he gets away with it too."

"Louis gets away with *most* things," Claire added concisely.

"He's a good boy and Allister's a good dog, but they can be a little out-of-hand sometimes. It's just the way eight-year-olds are," Dean said.

Louie's announcement interrupted their conversation. "Okay, everybody it's time for our toga party karaoke competition!" Standing in front of the microphone, Louie studied a clipboard, then added, "Looks like we've got ten acts ready to perform, but if you want to get in on the action, the sign-up sheet is at the end of the bar. Here's our first act, Missy, Kayla, and Samantha performing Venus by Bananarama!" Louie swept his arms toward three young women dressed in one-shouldered, very short toga dresses, giggling, and stumbling toward the stage.

Stacy leaned close to Winnie. "I thought you and Louie were going to do a karaoke to kick things off."

Winnie sighed. "We were, but I don't think Louie's much in the mood now."

Chapter Six

Different Century, Same Job

Slater took Alexa aback when he pulled into the Greentree Manor Apartments on Greentree Road. "What are we doing here? I thought we were going to Mt. Lebanon."

"Thought we'd drop in on Pooky Mateer before we stop by Tallis Chamberlain's house. C'mon."

Alexa followed the detective along the sidewalk toward another building she was acquainted with. Only, the apartment complex looked newer than its twenty-first century counterpart. While the Greentree Manor Apartments were well kept, in her era, they still had a dated appearance. However, in 1965, they looked quite modern. Slater held the door open while she stepped into a small lobby. They took the elevator to the second floor and walked along the hallway until they came to apartment 226. Slater rapped on the door. No response.

He tapped again, and still no one acknowledged the summons.

A woman from across the hall opened her door to peek out. "She's not home." The woman's voice had an older timbre, yet the gap she peered through was so slight it was hard to get a feel for her age or what she looked like.

"Do you know when she'll be back?" Slater inquired.

"No. You just missed her. She left about fifteen minutes ago," the woman volunteered. "Can I tell her who stopped by?"

"Yes, tell her Detective Clifton Slater wants to talk with her."

Still, she didn't open the door any farther, but the lift of her eyebrow was visible through the crack. "Hm, you're the second policeman to visit today. I was having coffee with her right around one o'clock, or maybe it was noon, when another detective came to see her. I didn't catch his name. Pooky gave me the bum's rush. Hope everything's okay. I'll tell her you were here."

"Thank you, ma'am," Slater said. The woman closed her door. The lock clicked. He turned to Alexa to mumble, "Someone beat us to the punch."

"Wheeler?" Alexa questioned.

"That would be my guess."

Slater pulled the police department's unmarked, black Rambler into the driveway of a three-story Tudor-style home in the Mount Lebanon neighborhood. "This house isn't far from my parent's home. I used to drive past it all the time," Alexa said.

"This is where Tallis Chamberlain lives," Slater supplied.

"Whoa, the house sold for over a million about a year ago. Well, a year ago in the *twenty-first* century. What does Tallis do for a living?"

Before sliding out of the car, Slater tossed Alexa a wink. "She married well."

Alexa pushed the car door open to take in the huge sandstone blocks that climbed halfway up the home. Tall, pointed, Tudor-style gables flanked each end of the structure, and a curved archway provided a protected canopy for the beveled front door. Perfectly manicured, hip-level boxwood hedges led the way to the entrance. The triple-garage doors near the back of the house were closed. Parked just outside the first door was a sleek, dark green, 1965 Corvette Convertible. "Yeah, looks like she did okay." Alexa muttered as she slid out of the car and slammed the door.

Slater nodded toward an older red Ford sitting at the farthest reach of the driveway. "Wonder whose got the Ford. Tallis is married to Leland Chamberlain. He's old, feeble, and in a wheelchair. Tallis is wife number three. He likes them young, but as history shows, it never turns out well for him."

"How old is Mr. Chamberlain?"

"Well into his eighties. Old money—railroads."

They stepped through the archway into a small, dank entrance. Slater knocked on the door. Alexa said, "She'll be set for life when he kicks."

Slater snorted. "I think that was the plan for all three wives. Tallis just might be the lucky one."

The door opened and a slight, middle-aged, dark-haired woman wearing a pristine, white maid's uniform, and holding a small silver tray with a glass of red wine, stood before them. Slater shot Alexa a *guess-we-know-who-owns-the-Ford* look.

"Can I help you?" the woman asked. From somewhere in the house, a piano played while a strong soprano voice sang something in Italian.

Slater produced his badge. "I'm Detective Clifton Slater, homicide. I was hoping to speak with Mrs. Chamberlain, please."

The woman glanced over her shoulder, then turned back. "She's in the middle of her singing instruction. Mrs. Chamberlain doesn't like to be disturbed. Her vocal coach really hates it."

"I'm sorry. We'll try to be as brief as possible, but we do need to talk with her…now."

Her pursed lips clearly conveying her annoyance, the maid opened the door wider and stepped aside to give them entry into an elegant foyer. The crystal chandelier overhead cast prisms across red and gold damask wallpaper. A gorgeous mahogany table supported by a Greek lyre base stood against the wall beneath the curved staircase. Fresh white roses in a Waterford crystal vase sat atop the table. Now inside the house, Alexa could hear the piano music and Tallis's voice were coming from upstairs. Closing the door, the maid said, "I'll tell Mrs. Chamberlain you're here."

"Thank you," Slater replied. The woman made no attempt to hurry up the staircase; rather, she climbed with meticulous steps, unerringly balancing the tray, glancing down at them with ambiguous eyes. Alexa wondered if she were overprotective of her boss or concerned neither singer nor instructor would receive her in a pleasant manner.

Moments after she was out of sight, they heard the piano come to an abrupt stop. Muffled, impatient words were exchanged, and then the maid returned to the apex of the staircase to call down, "Mrs. Chamberlain said to come up to her music suite. She doesn't wish to come down the stairs."

"Fair enough," Slater said. Alexa followed him up the stairs to meet the maid in a hallway as elegant as the foyer. No longer carrying the tray, she led them across the space into a lovely room. When they stepped through, she closed the door behind them. The music room's walls were painted a soft blue with wide, ornamental, white trim, and crown molding. The black baby grand piano was stationed in front of a bay window that looked out over a small but decorative courtyard. Next to the piano stood a mahogany music stand. Several sheets of music were spread over the shelf. Just beyond the window was a large portrait of a young woman dressed in a delicate white lace frock. Her dark, curly tresses held back by a small gold crown, she stood before a music stand, posed as if she were about to burst into song. Two wide, tufted, linen barrel chairs were positioned beneath the portrait. Between the chairs was a small, round table with a rotary phone and a photograph of Tallis, garbed in a velvet gown, singing on a stage stationed on top. The far wall was lined with four mahogany sheet-music cabinets.

A reed-thin man with a rather large nose was seated at the piano. He picked up the glass of wine that had been placed on the piano and held it out toward the maid. "Take this away. Tallis doesn't need to drink alcohol so early in the day," he said with a note of haughty disgust in his voice.

Tallis whined, "Dorian, it's not *that* early, and it's not very much wine…"

Pitching her a raised eyebrow and turned down lips, he extended his long arm out farther toward the maid. "I said, take it away. You don't want to turn out like my worthless drunk of a mother, do you, Tallis? Besides, I'm not sure red wine is good for the voice. We must always consider our voice, mustn't we?"

Tallis rolled her eyes as the maid took the glass and sauntered from the room, closing the door behind her. Tallis must have noticed Alexa admiring the artwork and used the moment to escape Dorian's reprimand. "That is a portrait of the great Angelica Catalani. She was a famous Italian opera diva. It was said her soprano voice was of the *purest* quality. In fact, Napoleon was so besotted with her, he would not grant her passage to England. She disguised herself as a nun to escape to London, where she was an instant success. Angelica was wined and dined by all the socialites of the time, including the king." Alexa couldn't take her eyes off Tallis's mouth as she spoke—it was so large and mesmerizing. Her full lips were splashed with a ruby red lipstick which only accentuated the movement of her mouth. She imagined a boisterous sound would come out when Tallis sang.

Quickly, Alexa snapped her gaze away from Tallis's mouth. That's when she noticed Tallis was wearing a soft, pink, lace frock, much like the one Angelica was sporting in the portrait. Alexa replied, "It's a beautiful portrait."

With his hands folded, not-so-patiently, on his lap, Dorian said, "I hope you'll be quick about this. We've got much work to do this afternoon before Tallis's rehearsal this evening." He flicked his hand toward the portrait. "She doesn't have time to stand around talking about paintings on the wall." The black, lightweight, fitted turtleneck sweater, and dark slacks he sported accentuated his thin frame. Alexa had his age figured to be forty, maybe forty-five. He had bushy eyebrows, long sideburns, and dark, shoulder-length hair pulled back with a red satin ribbon tied in a tidy bow. He made no attempt to hide his impatience or his quirks.

Retrieving the notepad and a pen from his pocket, Slater inquired, "And you are…"

Snatching a tissue from the box atop the piano then dabbing his forehead, the man replied, "I'm Tallis's vocal coach, of course, Dorian Matias."

Alexa considered the sum of his attire, Saks, Hudson's, at the very least, Macy's.

"I'll be as brief as possible, Mr. Matias." Slater turned his attention to Tallis. "Mrs. Chamberlain, you were among the cast of The Merry Widow last year when Mr. Starr collapsed backstage."

"Yes. I sang the role of Valencienne, the Baron Zeta's wife. I do remember you, Detective Slater and recall giving you a full statement back then. So, what are you doing here today? As Dorian said, I'm very busy. I'm sure you're not aware, but we're performing The Merry Widow very soon."

"Will you be singing the same role?" Alexa asked.

"Valencienne, yes," Tallis replied.

"Katherine Starr will *try* to sing the lead. Frankly, Tallis should have sung the role of Hanna…" Dorian spoke purposefully as if addressing idiots. "That's Hanna Glawari, who is the actual merry widow, in the first place. Tallis's soprano is more suited to the role. Personally, I think *that director* favors Katherine, in more ways than one." He patted his cheeks with the tissue.

"If that's true," Tallis began. "He's missed his opportunity. She's married to Royce Hathaway now."

"Maybe he doesn't like girls," Dorian put in.

"Like you?" Tallis remarked. Dorian rolled his eyes. She turned to Slater. "That's a suspicious union."

"What is?" Slater questioned.

"Katherine and Royce. You know they talked Bobby into taking Bert's place, don't you? Then the poor man is poisoned…shifty, in my book. I thought so from the start."

Just then, the door opened, and the maid peeked in. "There's a call for you, Mrs. Chamberlain." The maid dipped out of the room, gently closing the door.

"*More interruptions*," Dorian griped, throwing his hands in the air. "This entire session is a *complete waste*. I should just go." Fervently, he began gathering the music from the piano.

"Patience, Dorian, patience," Tallis said over her shoulder as she made her way to the phone on the small table beneath the portrait. She lifted the receiver to her ear. "Hello…" letting out a disgusted sigh, she demanded, "That won't do at all. What are we going to do?" She listened again, then rolled her eyes. "Well, find someone quickly, and let me know."

"What's wrong?" Dorian queried.

Tallis plunked the phone onto the cradle. "Seems our dear, *inept* Pooky has decided she simply cannot continue as the seamstress for the show. The gown I'm supposed to wear for the big party scene…" she turned toward Alexa and Slater. "That's the scene where Bobby was serving the drinks, and then collapsed after he made his exit, stage left. Ugh! My gown is lying in pieces on Pooky's table in the costume room. She was taking it in. They'd better find someone soon."

Alexa glanced at Slater, then announced, "I could help. I'm a professional seamstress."

Tallis's eyes widened. "That's wonderful! Are you looking for a job?"

"Not really, but I'd work the show to help out," Alexa replied.

Tallis's gaze slid to Slater, then back to the brunette. Her brows dropped into a V. "If you're a seamstress, what are you doing here with a police detective?"

The singer was quick. Alexa had to be as well. "Oh… ah…I'm writing a book. A mystery…and I'm following Detective Slater today to see how he…you know, his process for investigating a murder."

Seemingly accepting of the answer, Tallis's expression softened. "How interesting, a seamstress who writes. You'll fit in with our merry band of artists just fine."

"Maybe this interruption wasn't a total loss," Dorian put in.

"Indeed. They say there is a purpose for everyone you meet. Show up at the Carnegie Library and Music Hall, the one in Carnegie, tonight at six o'clock. I'll let them know we've got a new seamstress." Tallis's gaze moved to Slater. "Back to you, Detective. I was on stage when Bobby collapsed. Before that, I was in my dressing room. Dorian was there, weren't you, dear?" Dorian nodded his confirmation. "I believe that's as good an alibi as any. I have nothing to hide."

"There were rumors you were upset that Mr. Linney provided tickets for a scout from Pittsburgh Opera to watch Mrs. Starr," Slater said.

"I was…at first. Then I realized he would see my performance as well. You're barking up the wrong tree, Detective. I have no reason to be jealous of Katherine Hathaway. I have an eighteenth-century vibrato that is very rare these days. Katherine, on the other hand, is *just* a soprano."

"Will that be all?" Dorian exacted more than inquired.

"For now. Thank you for your time," Slater said, and with that, Alexa followed him toward the door.

Tallis called out, "Wait…what's your name, dear? I'll need to say who our new seamstress is."

"Alexa…Alexa Owl."

"See you at six, Alexa, and *please*, be prompt."

The moment they were out of the room, and the door was closed, the piano began to play. Tallis's big voice boomed throughout the upstairs. As they made their way down the staircase, Slater said, "Evidently, the scout wasn't all that impressed with her eighteenth-century… um…whatever it was. She's still singing in the operetta company."

Alexa chuckled. "I know, right?"

"Pretty fast thinking on your part, taking the seamstress position." Slater chuckled. "Maybe I won't take you to the convent."

"Gee thanks. Now we have a mole on the inside of the production."

"A what?"

Alexa sighed. "A spy."

Slater stepped from the stairs into the foyer. "Why didn't ya say so?"

"I did *say so*."

Out of nowhere, the maid said, "Have a nice afternoon."

Alexa and Slater's attention flicked toward the sound of her voice. The maid was holding the front door open, and there was that look again. Alexa caught a sideways glimpse of the wine glass sitting on the decorative table. The glass was empty, and the maid closed the door immediately upon their exit.

They made their way back to the car, but before Alexa opened the door to slip inside, she paused to admire the Corvette. "I wonder how much money a vocal coach makes." She looked over the roof of the Rambler to find Slater considering the sports car too.

"I was wondering the same thing," he replied.

Far less uptight or unfriendly than the Chamberlain's maid, the middle-aged secretary at Lifetime Investments on Carson Street, in downtown Pittsburgh, cordially led Alexa and Slater to Royce Hathaway's office. It was an actual office, not a cubicle. It was a small room with a desk, a nameplate that read, *Royce Hathaway*, file cabinets, and a typewriter. Small but it was, in fact, an office. Old school—no computer. Work was done with pencil and paper.

Leaning into the room, the secretary said, "Mr. Hathaway, there is a Detective Slater and Alexa Owl here to see you."

Royce looked up from some paperwork. He was sporting a pair of round, black-rimmed glasses. The specs were just like those Tony Curtis had worn in the movie, *Some Like it Hot*. Wait, at this time, that movie was a mere six years old, and Monroe had died just three years ago. Alexa was impressed. Royce Hathaway was indeed a doppelganger for Tony Curtis. His blue tie dangled loosely from the collar of his white shirt. A black suit jacket was neatly slung over the back of the chair. His brows furrowed and his lips tightened into a straight line as if to quash the whisper, *what the heck do they want?* Pushing up from the chair, Royce pulled the glasses from his face and tossed them on top of the paperwork. "What can I do for you, Detective Slater?"

"I understand you and Mrs. Hathaway, the former Mrs. Starr, will be performing in The Merry Widow soon," Slater said.

Royce's gaze slid to the brunette with the detective and then back to Slater. Clearly, he was apprehensive of the unexpected visit, and it was even more evident he intended to measure his words. In an obvious attempt to convey a relaxed demeanor, Royce provided a hesitant smile. "Yes, the cast was shocked and saddened by the unfortunate events last year, and we simply couldn't find it in our hearts to continue with the production. Piers Linney, the director, called us all together about two months ago at the music hall to see if we, the cast…I mean, to see if we were ready to resume rehearsals and put on the show. We all agreed it was time to move forward, so…" A shrug. "We did."

"And your wife was okay with the decision?" Slater fished.

"Piers had called her a few weeks before the meeting to talk it over with her. Of course, Katherine was the most affected by what…what happened…oh, and of course, Pooky, our seamstress, too. Katherine and I talked it over and after much soul searching, she felt she could do it. She called Piers back and he notified everyone about the meeting." Shaking his head, Royce dropped his gaze to the desk, then lifted it to meet Slater's. Around a careworn sigh, he added, "I just received a call that Pooky has decided she can't continue. The woman's been quite emotional since we started back up. Understandable. As with all productions, there are complications, and now we don't have a seamstress."

"Who's taking Mr. Mateer's place in the show?" Slater asked.

"Piers found a new, young tenor, Jack Holland. He's pretty good. Not as good as Bert was at hamming it up, but he's young and can sing. Bert could carry a tune, that was about it. He was basically part of the chorus, but he wouldn't dress in their dressing room. He dressed in the costume room. The singers in the chorus used to make jokes about it." Again, his questioning gaze glided to the brunette.

"How is Mrs. Hathaway handling things? Has she been emotional?" Slater inquired.

Royce's gaze slid back to the detective. "Katherine has struggled. That's to be expected, but she's doing okay."

"If I recall correctly, it was you and Mrs. Hathaway, who at the time was Mrs. Starr, talked Bobby Starr into taking Mr. Mateer's place on stage."

Royce's eyes narrowed. He cocked his head to one side. "Yes…"

"What was your relationship with Katherine before Mr. Starr's death?"

Now, it was more than obvious Royce was calculating his response. He left Slater's question floating in the air for a long moment. Alexa was beginning to think he was going to ignore it all together. Finally, he said, "We were friends…fellow opera singers and cast members of four productions together."

"Nothing more? You married her soon after Mr. Starr's death. I mean, you do understand how that looks, right?"

"We were *friends*, Detective Slater. When someone loses a loved one, everyone says, if there's anything I can do, just call. But they don't mean it. I wanted to be there for my friend, and we grew closer as she mourned her husband. No, I did *not* take advantage of her situation. We fell in love, and now we're married. That's *all*." While well chosen, his words and tone were on the shady side of concise.

Slater nodded and then turned to go. Alexa followed.

Before they reached the door, Royce inquired, "I'm sorry." They turned. He lifted a hand in the brunette's direction. "I missed this young woman's name."

"She's your new seamstress, Alexa Owl," Slater replied.

"That's a relief," Royce said.

They turned to leave, then Alexa turned back. "By the way, has anyone told you…"

"That I look like Tony Curtis. All the time. In fact, I was in New York City several years ago. Someone yelled, 'Look! It's Tony Curtis!' Well, I was surrounded within seconds. Everyone was shoving paper at me for an autograph. I tried to explain, but they wouldn't listen." A shrug. "So, I just started signing autographs. They were probably disappointed when they moved away to find Royce Hathaway on their napkins, notepads, and whatever else I signed."

Alexa laughed. "That's a fantastic story."

Chapter Seven

Katherine with a K

A gentle rain started to fall. The lamps along the parking lot outside the Carnegie Music Hall cast glaring stalks over the pavement. Alexa and Slater sat in the Rambler, watching individuals huddled under umbrellas scurry through the stage door. "I don't think you should come inside with me," Alexa said. "I think the cast would be more comfortable if they don't relate me to the police. Especially, the detective who's investigating Bobby's murder."

"I don't think you should be in there alone. While we don't know for sure, there may be a murderer among the group," Slater countered.

"Maybe. But I need them to trust me, and that would include the murderer. We don't know if this is the *exact* same cast as the last production. While the leads may be the same, there might be different singers in the chorus or different dancers. I'll try to find out who has returned for this show, and who hasn't. Besides, the murderer could be a member of the stage crew or the orchestra or they may have skipped the show all together. If *I* had killed someone and gotten away with it, I think I'd steer clear of the next production. Most likely, I'd skip town as well."

"You're using common sense, Alexa. Murder is not a sensible act, and it certainly isn't one of common sense. Oftentimes, murderers return to the scene of a crime, especially if they've gotten away with it. That said, I don't believe we're dealing with a serial murderer here. I believe this person had a purpose in mind."

"I think so too. But I *don't* believe they're going to trust me if you're attached to my butt," Alexa insisted.

Slater held his hands up in surrender. "Okay. Like the last time, we need a compromise. You go in. I'll wait ten or fifteen minutes, and then I'll come in and sit in the back."

"I'm hearing a but…"

"*But*…the whole idea of coming here tonight was to re-interview the cast, wasn't it?"

Alexa blew out a breath. "Yes, it was. And you should do that. But try to make every attempt to stay away from me. That should be easy enough. I'll probably be in the costume room working on Tallis's gown and who knows what else."

"There ya go. Compromise achieved. Problem solved." He checked his watch. "It's almost six. You'd better get in there. Sorry, I don't have an umbrella to offer."

"That's okay, I won't melt." As Alexa stepped out of the car, she was suddenly wearing a tan raincoat, hood up. Smiling, she glanced upward. "Thanks, Pete." With that, she trotted up the sidewalk toward the stage door, pulled it open, and stepped into a long corridor that ran parallel to what appeared to be the backstage area. The music hall was bursting with sound, musical instruments warming up, conversations between members of the stage crew filled with instructions, and melodious voices ascending the scales. She wasn't sure what direction she should head. Follow the conversations or the scales? Tallis would certainly be where the singing was taking place, so that seemed like the best place to start.

Making her way down the corridor, Alexa stepped over wires and squeezed past crew members who were laying the wires and setting up lighting. As she drew closer to the room where the singers were warming up, she heard a woman instruct, "Good. Now, men, lip trills please…five-six-seven-eight…" instantly, low, wooly vibrations emerged from the nearby room. It sounded like a group of men blowing water in unison. "Do-Mi-Sol-Do-Mi-Sol…" Weird sound, but she could make out the scales they were using. The woman announced, "Good! Good! Now, ladies…five-six-seven-eight…" The women repeated the exercise, only on a higher octave than the men.

Feeling a bit insecure, yet having to make her presence known, Alexa stepped into the doorway to look around the small rehearsal room. The men, about ten in all, including Royce Hathaway, were standing to the left, and the women, of the same count, to the right. Metal music stands filled with sheet music stood before each person. From the headshots Alexa had seen in the case file, she immediately recognized Katherine Starr-Hathaway, and of course, Tallis Chamberlain, who immediately held a hand up for her to wait. The older, grey-haired woman conducting the singers turned at Tallis's gesture to the brunette standing on the threshold. With a wave of her hands, the woman cut the singers off. "May I help you?" she asked.

Tallis stepped forward. "This is the seamstress I was telling everyone about. Her name is Alexa." The group smiled and many nodded their hello. "We don't have time for intros at this time, my dear, but you'll find the costume room farther down the hall, take a right, then the last door on the left past the dressing rooms. It isn't far. At the end of the hall, it's the only room without a door. You'll see a table with a coffeemaker and carafes filled with hot water for tea, and a bowl of tea bags. Help yourself."

"Thank you," Alexa said, and with that, she followed Tallis's directions until she came to a narrow corridor. A payphone secured to the wall was the first thing she noticed, yet sure enough, there was a small table pressed against the wall at the very end of the hall that held the coffeemaker and tea bags, as Tallis described. The old music hall was drafty, and the rainy night added a chill to the air. A cup of warm coffee sounded good, so she stopped long enough to grab a Styrofoam cup from the tall pile to pour a cup, spoon in some creamer, and then head for the costume room. Almost to the doorway, the sound of singing drifting down the corridor reminded her the cast was still busy warming up. Alexa paused.

Most likely, no one would be in the dressing rooms. Why not have a look?

With measured steps, she made her way to the first door. Affixed to the old wooden door was a small chalkboard. Scribbled in white chalk was the name *Royce Hathaway*. Alexa glanced up the hallway. Empty. Quietly, she knocked on the door with her knuckles. No response. Another peek up the hall, then she turned the knob to open the door, stepped inside, and closed the door. The room was small. Cracked plaster walls were painted a dingy white. The floor was bare, cold cement.

The only illumination in the room came from the lighted mirror above a vanity positioned on the wall directly across from the door. Glancing over her shoulder, she found a clothes rack. A suit covered in a plastic bag hung on the rack. Royce's costume, she presumed. The black suit jacket that was in his office that afternoon was draped over the chair in front of the vanity. A damp, black umbrella leaned against the wall next to the vanity. Droplets tumbled down the folds of the umbrella, forming a tiny puddle under the pointed tip.

Royce's dressing room was void of any personal items. It appeared he was using it for a place to leave his suit jack and umbrella, for the time being anyway. Alexa opened the door, peered down the hall, and listened to the singing. Yep, they were still at it. She stepped out of the room. The next door's blackboard was marked *Katherine Hathaway*. It made perfect sense to have her room next to her husband's, but Alexa had to wonder if Royce's room was always next door, or had it only been since the marriage. She let herself into Katherine's accommodation. This room was much the same as the first: small, cracked plaster, drab paint, a cement floor, and a lighted vanity on the wall. Except Katherine had personalized her space with a green throw rug and framed photos on the wall of past performances. The pictures intrigued Alexa, and while she could still hear the cast singing, she took the opportunity to peruse a few.

The first photograph was marked *Pirates of Penzance*, *Mabel*. Katherine looked beautiful wearing a red wig and a white, frilly Regency style bonnet. Long, tightly curled locks fell across her shoulders. She was garbed in a long, white Victorian style dress with a lavender sash around her tiny waist. Behind her stood a pirate holding a fencing sword. It appeared the singer had grown a beard for the role, very cool. A closer look revealed Royce was the pirate. He smiled brightly, arms outstretched, full, flowing sleeves seemingly billowing in the ocean breeze.

Thinking back to her last trip with Bobby, Alexa remembered him mentioning Katherine was starring in *The Pirates of Penzance*; therefore, the photo must've been taken in '63. The second photograph was marked, Yum-Yum, *The Mikado*. Again, a stunning photo of Katherine dressed in a luxurious silk Kimono, her mouth open in song, while holding a bright blue floral fan over her head. Katherine's dark hair was swept up in a traditional Nihongami style.

Suddenly, a flutter of movement and a tiny *chirp* made Alexa jump and turn. In the far corner of the room, just beyond the vanity, stood a tall, gold birdcage stand. Dangling from the hook was a gilded birdcage. A tiny yellow canary sat on a swing, twittering. Alexa made her way across the room, past the costume rack where several long dresses and a formal gown hung in plastic garment bags. She peered into the cage. "Well, hello there. I believe we've met before in my apartment, only in a different century. You must belong to Katherine. I hope you're not giving Winnie too much trouble." The little canary cocked its head, studying her as it swung to and fro. She glanced around the damp space. "Seems like a strange place to keep a bird." Alexa paused to listen. The singers were silent. Time to go.

Quickly, Alexa crossed the small room to crack the door open and peek into the hallway. No one was about. She slipped through the gap, closed the door behind her, and hurried across the hall to the doorless costume room. Just as she was about to step over the threshold, she heard the click of a door. Trepidation washing over her, Alexa glanced down the hallway. A young man with rather shaggy, dark hair dashed down the hallway. Had he seen her come out of Katherine's room, or had he been in one of the others? Feeling uneasy, she entered the costume room where she found an emerald green velvet dress lying on a large cutting table. Setting her coffee aside, she scrutinized the small room while stripping out of the now dry raincoat and tossing it on a nearby wooden chair. She glanced over her shoulder at the doorway. Nothing.

The cutting table took up most of the space. A Singer sewing machine was nestled in a corner on the other side of the room. The machine was vintage in her twentieth-century world standards—most likely circa 1950s. Alexa had never used anything so…old, but she'd have to make the best of it. A clothing rack stood against the wall to her far left. Several costumes hung on the rack. Had the costumes been finished or were they waiting to be mended or altered? First things first. She picked up the cup, took a sip of the coffee, and considered the velvet dress spread out over the table. Straight pins lined up like tiny soldiers, armed with tiny sharp points, pinched the seams. The remainder of the jaggy little army was jammed into a bright red pin cushion shaped like a tomato sitting near the dress. Some of the pins had colorful balls on the top. Several safety pins were stuck to the cushion. Two ordinary white buttons were stuck to the cushion with straight pins. Her lips curled. She remembered seeing a cushion exactly like it on her grandmother's sewing machine. Come to think of it, Gran had a Singer sewing machine much like the one in the corner. A pair of dressmaker's shears and a rolled-up measuring tape lay near the dress. Evidently, Pooky wanted her replacement to find the necessary tools to work on the costumes easily. Thanks, Pooky.

The orchestra started to play. Two male voices wafted down the corridor. The rehearsal had begun. A twinge of anxiety coiled through her. Had the young man seen her? If so, who would he tell, or maybe he didn't belong in the rooms either? Another quick peek at the doorway. Again, nothing. No one. She would have to be extra careful next time. For now, she needed to get to work. She had no doubt Tallis would stop in to check on her progress when the rehearsals were through. Alexa was sure there had better be progress.

Shaking off the rain, Slater made his way along a narrow corridor toward the auditorium. He'd promised Alexa he'd keep his distance, so he'd parked the Rambler at the farthest reach of the lot where the lamp was out. Hopefully, no one would see who she was getting into the car with. He'd be sure to retreat to his vehicle well before rehearsals ended.

As he made his way down several steps, past a balcony, Slater noticed Piers Linney seated in the middle of the second row. The director wasn't lounging; rather, he was leaning on the theater seat in front of him, scrutinizing the two men standing center stage, singing. If his memory served him correctly, the taller man was Nick Ferroni, the second was Royce Hathaway. While he knew Mr. Linney would not be happy to see him, nor want to take time to answer questions, he appeared to be the most accessible at the moment.

Slater sidestepped his way down the row toward Piers and then eased down into the seat next to him. Over the orchestra and the men's voices, he heard the director let out a long-suffering sigh, and then he turned toward the detective.

His British lilt was that of congenial conciseness. "Royce told me you visited his office today and basically accused him and Katherine of setting Bobby up to be killed. That's rubbish, Detective Slater. Absolute rubbish."

"You don't find their marriage so soon after Mr. Starr's death a little too convenient?"

"I warned Royce people would look at it that way. But after Bobby's death, Royce stepped in and took care of Katherine, and they fell in love. That's not a crime in Britain. I certainly hope it's not in this country. Besides, both Royce and Katherine were on stage when Bobby was poisoned. I've never heard that the police found out where the poison came from or how he ingested it, have you?"

"No, we haven't."

"Look, do I believe someone inside the music hall killed Bobby and Bert? Probably, yes. I mean, it only makes sense, doesn't it? Do I think Royce or Katherine are that clever or devious? I'm sorry, I don't."

"Got anyone in mind who is?"

Piers sat back against the seat. "There's a loaded question if ever I heard one."

"Okay. Do think the murderer is among your cast?"

"Show business is a vindictive enterprise, Detective. It doesn't matter what level you're at, everyone's trying to get one up on the other."

"Like Tallis Chamberlain?"

Piers shot Slater a look, then stood and clapped his hands loudly. The orchestra reluctantly stopped playing. "Royce, could you sing that last bit for me again? Not sure you're getting your point across to the audience. I want them to know how *desperate* you are."

now only the fitting remained. Gathering the gown from the table, she carried it to the rack to hang it up, when a woman's voice caught her off guard.

"Hello…" she turned to find Katherine filling the doorway. When Alexa last saw Katherine, she wore her hair in short, loose pin curls. Now her dark hair flipped at her shoulders. She sported a basic black pencil skirt and white blouse. Katherine had been Bobby's fifth wife. Out of his five wives, three bore the name Catherine. Alexa remembered Bobby always referred to this particular one as '*Katherine with a K, the best Katherine.*' She looked tired, but her smile was sincere as she moved closer, extending her hand. "I saw the light was still on, so I thought I'd step in and introduce myself. I'm Katherine Hathaway."

Quickly, Alexa hung the gown on the rack and took Katherine's hand. How strange. She'd never really had any contact with Bobby's wives. He was divorced from Catherine number one when she met Bobby. Cora Lee was dead by then; however, she'd met Catherine number two during Cora Lee's murder investigation and before she became Bobby's third wife. Venetia, the exotic dancer, and wife number four had left him before Alexa's last trip to the past. Yet here she was, Katherine with a K, standing directly in front of her. "It's nice to meet you, Katherine. I hope I get a chance to see you perform."

"Oh, I don't know about that. The cast kept Pooky very busy right up to curtain time and even sometimes *during* the show. The costumes are rather old. You never know when a button will pop, or a zipper will give way." She paused for a moment, gazing down at her black, patent leather pumps, then cocking her head to one side, she added, "My husband mentioned he met you this afternoon at his office. He said you were with Detective Slater. While you can't believe everything Tallis says, she told everyone you're writing a book."

Alexa knew she had to maintain a level of complacency when it came to her association with Slater. Then again, the fact Tallis had been talking about her was working in her favor. "Yes, a mystery. I spent the day traveling with Detective Slater to learn his investigative procedures. I want to make sure that I'm correct in how police-work is done."

"Is the book about the opera or what happened here last year?"

Alexa smiled. "Goodness no, but when Mrs. Chamberlain mentioned the company needed a seamstress, I offered my services."

"But you *are aware* of what happened?"

"Yes. I read about it in the papers. I'm so sorry for your loss, Mrs. Hathaway. That said, I'm not part of the investigation. I'm just studying proper police procedure and repairing or altering costumes. Nothing more."

Just then, Royce stepped into the room. He was wearing his suit jacket, while holding the birdcage completely draped with a cloth in one hand, a raincoat, and umbrella in the other. "Hello again, Miss Owl." Alexa smiled and nodded her greeting. "Katherine, we'd better go. It's getting late. Winnie probably has Maisie in bed by now. I'm sure the girl is anxious to get home. It's pouring buckets outside." He set the cage and the umbrella on the floor, then held up the raincoat for Katherine to slip into.

Alexa went to the door to peek into the hallway. A tall, thin brunette wearing a pair of black crop pants and a multi-colored polka-dotted blouse was pouring a cup of coffee. Alexa stepped back into the costume room. "I thought Mrs. Chamberlain would stop by to try on her gown."

"Maybe tomorrow night," Katherine began, as she shimmied into the coat. "I saw her walk out the stage door right after rehearsal ended."

"I suppose I'm waiting for nothing. I should get going then. Before I do, where's the bathroom?" Alexa asked.

"All the way down the hallway, past stage right, and then turn right," Katherine replied.

Royce scooped up the birdcage and umbrella, then palming Katherine's elbow, he said, "Have a nice evening, Miss Owl." With that, they made their way out of the room. Alexa followed. The brunette was gone.

Alexa was certain Slater was waiting for her in the parking lot. Still, she didn't want the lights to go out and be stuck feeling her way through the darkness to the stage door. After a quick wave goodbye to Katherine and Royce, as they headed for the stage door, she hurried forward toward the bathroom.

On her way back from the bathroom to the costume room to gather her coat and shut out the lights, Alexa heard voices echoing from the music hall. Several people were still about. Good. She snatched the raincoat from the chair and as she pressed her arms into it, something on the cutting table caught her eye. She approached the table. Next to the sewing shears, the rolled-up tape measure, and tucked under her Styrofoam cup was a handwritten note that read…

Careful what you drink.

"What?" Alexa murmured. She glanced around the room furtively, hoping no one was lurking in a corner or behind the clothing rack. "Who…" Just then, that all too familiar vacuum began its unrelenting quaff, dragging her down, down, down—back to the twenty-first century.

Chapter Eight

Big and Small Potatoes

"Hey…don't ya think it's time to get up? Or do you have a light schedule today?" Cliff's voice stirred Alexa from a deep sleep. The bed felt cozy, warm, and soft. She rolled over to find him hovering over the bed. Clearly, St. Pete had sent her home. Cliff was holding a coffee mug. "Are you with me? I've got coffee."

Alexa ran her fingers through her bed tossed hair. Her voice was soft and woozy. "Not really. Coffee appreciated. What time is it?"

"Eight-fifteen. I heard the front door buzzer about twenty minutes ago, and then again, a few minutes ago. So, the gang's all here." He extended the mug toward her. "Feeling better today?"

"What do you mean?"

"You weren't really yourself yesterday. You were… um…"

"Zombie-like?"

"You weren't trying to eat my brains, but yeah, zombie is a good description."

Alexa chuckled. Yep, even Cliff had to deal with Zombie Alexa in her absence—even if he didn't know about it. "I was feeling kind of like a zombie. I'm better today, thank you." At least for the time being. Pushing up from the pillows to take the mug from him, she kissed his lips, and then took a sip. That's when she realized Cliff was dressed casually. He was wearing the dark plum polo shirt she'd bought him for his birthday and a pair of jeans. He looked yummy. A flit and a twit caught her attention. There it was, the little canary, perched on the windowsill. Katherine's canary. She asked, "So, what're you still doing here? Are you off today?"

"Not really. I'm not working cases today, like I *should* be. I've got that benefit golf outing for the Children's Hospital Free Care Fund today. Remember?"

No. Alexa didn't remember, but she had no intention of admitting it. "Oh, yeah, that's right. What time do you have to be there?"

Cliff looked at his watch. "In forty minutes. Better get a move on. Who knows what the parkway looks like." He bent down and kissed her lips. When he pulled away from the kiss, he started for the bedroom door. "See ya." That's when the little canary pushed off the windowsill to fly across the room and took a tiny, runny, white dump on Cliff's shoulder. Alexa gasped. Cliff swung around. "Are you okay?"

Quickly, Alexa conjured up a yawn and a stretch. "Oh, yes, I was just…yawning."

Shooting her a look, Cliff continued into the hallway and out the apartment door.

Alexa sat straight up. The poop wouldn't really be there. No. It wouldn't. Right? She set the coffee mug on the nightstand, ripped the blankets away, and swung out of the bed.

Standing at the coffee service end of the bar at the Owl's Nest Couturier Shoppe, Winnie thumbed a text message, then pressed *send*. This was the second text she'd sent to Louie this morning with no reply. She tucked the cell phone into the pocket of her sweater, then removed a square casserole dish from her red tote bag resting atop the bar. The alluring smell of freshly baked cinnamon rolls floated through the shop just as Holden Emery walked through the door. The tall, well-muscled, dark-haired, handsome man had been the tailor for the Owl's Nest for two years.

"Ah, you're just in time, lad." Winnie sliced a thick chunk, generously slathered with icing from the dish and set it on a small paper plate. "These rolls just came out of the oven not twenty minutes ago."

Holden crossed the shop toward the bar. "So, how'd the toga party go last night? Looks to me like you and Louie are getting serious."

"I'm not sure how serious I'm willin' to go." She handed him the plate. "Give a taste, then."

Holden took the plate from Winnie and bit into the roll. He pressed his eyes closed in pure pleasure. Around a mouthful, he said, "Mm, that has got to be the best cinnamon roll I've ever tasted." He licked some errant icing from his lips. "Seriously Winnie, why didn't you ever get married?"

Shrugging, Winnie cut a piece for herself. "Eh, I never had a mind to. After all, things went badly when me sisters tied the knot. Ellie fell out with me father because she married a Jew. They never did patch things up. Maggie and I kept in touch with Ellie. She was our *sister*. I was thankful me mum was willin' to come together with Ellie and meet her grandchildren before she passed." Carrying her plate, she traversed the room to have a seat on the sofa. Holden followed. "Now, poor Maggie's marriage was in trouble from the start. We had the reception right here at the pub. About a week after the weddin', she found out her husband had been *on the job* with one of the wedding guests back in the storage room." Winnie shook her head at the memory. "Oh, Cullen Duffy was a handsome lad and a charmer, too. Me father thought the world of him. Mainly because his parents had immigrated from Ireland about the same time as he and me mum did. Cully, as Maggie used to call him, was a useless sort. Never kept a job. He drank too much, and he suffered from a double dose of original sin. Ah, but Maggie found it in her heart to forgive him on many occasions, especially after the children were born. Well, me father was *furious* when she announced she'd thrown Cully out and was divorcin' him." She took a bite of her cinnamon roll.

"*Why?* Cully was cheating on his daughter. You'd think he'd be furious with *Cully*, not Maggie," Holden reasoned.

"Brian Mulaney was a staunch Catholic, ya know. Back then, ya stuck it out with your husband, no matter how much of a *blaggard* he was. Poor Maggie was back to working in the pub to make ends meet. She moved into one of the apartments upstairs with her two kids. Her life was hard for a long time. Back then, I was goin' to business school, and I decided I wasn't gonna let no man wreck me life. And I'll tell ya this; I've got no regrets, Holden. Not one." Furtively, she slipped the cell phone from her pocket. No new messages. She let the phone slip from her fingers to glide back into place.

"So, that's it? You're not willing to have a relationship with Louie?"

"I *do* have a relationship with Louie. I believe nowadays it's called friends with benefits."

Holden's brows furrowed. "I don't mean to be disrespectful, Winnie, but…aren't you a little old for that?"

"Ah lad, ya don't have to worry about *bein' old*. Ya have to worry about *thinkin' old*." Winnie checked her text messages again. Nothing. Teasingly, Holden craned his neck to see Winnie's texts. She pressed the phone to her chest while tossing him a playful smirk.

Winnie's cell phone rang. Around a quiet chuckle, Holden pushed up from the sofa and moved toward the cash desk. Winnie slid the phone from her pocket, glanced at the screen, and smiling, she set the paper plate aside, then pressed the *talk* button. "Well, hello there. How's me favorite barkeep this mornin'?"

Louie's voice was strained. "Winnie…I'm not sure how to say this, so I'm just gonna say it. I've thought about it and…well, things are too…complicated. I don't think we should see each other anymore."

Winnie's smile faded, and her uplifted tone fled. "I don't know what to say, Louie. Is it Olivia?"

There was a long pause. For a moment, she thought he may have hung up. Then she heard him sigh. "She's my daughter, Winnie. I don't want to have to choose between the two of you, but…she's my daughter. I've got to choose her."

Winnie's voice grew small. "I see. Well…if that's the way ya feel, there's nothin' more to say, is there?" Winnie's thumb found the end button to press it down, hard. Disheartened, she pushed up from the sofa and slowly made her way to the bar, passed Holden, and toward her office.

Holden's timbre held concern. "Is everything okay, Winnie?"

Winnie paused at the doorway but didn't turn to face him. "Louie just broke it off with me." She waved a dismissive hand. Around a faux chuckle, she turned. "What am I sayin'? There was nothin' to break. We had no commitments. No promises made. As they say, no rings, no strings, and I didn't want any parts of that, did I then?" With that, she went into her office and closed the door.

Holden had just finished booting up the computer atop the register, counted the petty cash, and checked the day's schedule when he heard footsteps on the staircase. He hurried around the corner of the bar to meet Cliff almost at the bottom of the stairs. "Is Alexa up?"

The right side of Cliff's lip hitched. "Almost, but not quite. Is there a problem?"

Holden leaned back to check Winnie's office door. Still closed. "I think Winnie needs a friend right about now. A *girlfriend*. Louie broke up with her."

"Uh, oh. I thought they were getting along good." He turned to go back up the stairs when Alexa came rushing out of the apartment door to clamber down the stairs. The red silk robe she wore hung open, flickering behind her, revealing the red silk nightgown trimmed in lace. Her right hand slid down the chunky cherry railing while she clutched a bright blue polo shirt in her left.

"Cliff! You need to change that shirt," she announced. Her tone was just this side of panicked.

Cliff looked down at his shirt, then glanced at Holden, who couldn't figure what was wrong with the polo shirt he was already wearing. He considered it a wonderful shade of purple. "What's wrong with his shirt?" Holden inquired.

Alexa stopped short. Her mouth opened but nothing came out. The bright white dollop of do-do on his shoulder was quite evident—to her anyway. "Um…it has a stain. I don't think you should show up at benefit with a stain on your shirt, Detective Slater."

Holden moved closer to Cliff, appraising his shirt. "I've never worn it before. I don't see a sta—"

110

Just then, Winnie stepped out of her office. "What's all this, then…" her eyes widened, and her brows arched. She looked up to meet Alexa's gaze. "Surely, it's not really there," Winnie quietly muttered.

"You see it?" Alexa asked her Irish cohort.

"See *what*?" Holden asked.

"Well…I do…yes. But I don't think it will be noticeable to anyone but you and I…I…I mean, it's so *tiny*…"

"I've brought a fresh shirt. He may as well change, and I'll work on that stain," Alexa insisted.

What is up with her? She was acting strange all day yesterday. Holden mused.

"I don't have time to argue about this," Cliff began. "I'll just change my shirt." Quickly, he pulled the purple shirt over his head, revealing his sculpted chest and abs.

Holden murmured, "Whoa."

Winnie elbowed him.

Alexa tossed the blue shirt to Cliff, and in return, he tossed the purple one to her, then pulled the blue shirt on. With open arms, he looked up at her. "Better?"

She smiled. "Have a good time." With that, Cliff hurried to the door.

Shaking her head, Winnie turned and walked toward her office. "That'll be the easiest stain in the world to fix. I've got taxes to work on."

Alexa started back up the stairs. When Holden heard the click of the office door closing, he called out, "Alexa, wait." She turned and he trotted up the four steps to meet her, then he explained about the phone call Winnie had received from Louie. He finished up with, "She's been in her office with the door closed ever since. I'm worried.

111

I've never seen her like this, Lex. She's pretending it's no big deal, but it is. I know it is."

"Ho-boy," Alexa sighed. "I'll talk with her, but I should get dressed before anyone arrives. I'll be down shortly." She trotted up the stairs.

Time was of the essence. Alexa never knew how long she would remain in her own century when St. Pete sent her back. Winnie was hurting and she wanted to be there for her, not Zombie Alexa, the real Alexa.

Not certain what the day's schedule held, Alexa rushed through getting ready, choosing a pair of black leggings and a black, high-low tunic. She finished the look with a long, silver chain and hoop earrings. Still in the process of pulling her hair into a low ponytail, she rushed out the door and down the stairs. Holden was on the phone. She pointed to the office. He nodded.

Alexa tapped on the door. Winnie called from the other side, "Come in."

When she pressed the door open, Alexa was most surprised. Winnie sat in her black leather swivel chair, and the little canary was perched on her shoulder. What was most surprising was Bobby Starr was sitting on a stool next to Winnie's desk. They each were sipping coffee. Quickly, Alexa closed the door. She kept her voice low. "Bobby…"

"I see you're home for your first break. How's the case going?" he inquired.

How should she handle that question? This was the first time she'd been involved in a case where the murder victim was able to provide pertinent information. There were questions in her mind she had no doubt Bobby could satisfy, yet she felt it was not a good idea to discuss the current condition of his murder investigation. A watered-down answer may be the best course of action. "Good. Slow but good." Alexa crossed the small room to touch Winnie's shoulder. The canary swiftly flew to perch on the filing cabinet. "I heard about Louie. What happened?"

"*Olivia* happened. Now, I don't want a bunch of fussin'. What's done is done. I haven't had the likes of Louie Santorini in me life for fifty years, and I doubt I'll be needin' him now. Me father used to say, Wynona, ya got to take the small potato with the big potato, and if you're lucky enough to be Irish, well then, you're lucky enough." She pushed to her feet. "Now, this shop isn't gonna run itself. I'd best get the fittin' room ready for the young bride-to-be that's expected in fifteen minutes." With that, Winnie walked out of the office. The canary was quick to fly out the door before she closed it.

Alexa and Bobby sat in silence for several moments. Finally, she said, "I'm surprised to see you here. I thought you'd be on a case."

Bobby lifted a shoulder and let it drop. "I am."

Chapter Nine

Pooky

It had been a long day in the Owl's Nest Couturier Shoppe, and Alexa had spent the entire day in the shop. St. Pete had not sent her reeling through the portal back to 1965. No doubt Slater was hard at work on Bobby's murder case. In truth, the well-seasoned detective didn't need her assistance. Perhaps she wouldn't be returning at all, and Alexa felt a little bummed-out about that possibility. Working the investigation on Bobby's death was important to her. She wanted to be a part of resolving his murder. Alas, her involvement may have been nothing more than an exercise in getting Slater settled. While she was thankful for the opportunity, she hoped not.

After a somber Winnie gathered her red tote and headed for home, and Holden finished up hemming a bridesmaid gown, Alexa locked up the shop and climbed the stairs to her apartment. As she stepped through the door, the Roomba swept past. A smile lifted her lips at the memory of Slater's unexpected visit to the twenty-first century last year, and his first and only encounter with the vacuuming device. Not knowing what it was and horrified because it was following him down the hallway, he pulled out his revolver and shot it. The defenseless Roomba shattered into smithereens. A chortle tumbling from her lips, she made her way to the kitchen, and that's when her gaze fell upon the built-in wine rack at the end of the island. Uh, oh, the rack was empty, not a bottle of wine to be had. How had she allowed that to happen? The Roomba glided over the living room floors while the canary watched from atop the TV. She wished she knew the little thing's name.

Alexa glanced out the window. The first kiss of dusk was settling over Penn Avenue. Still, the weather was pleasant, and while the vacuum was doing its thing, she decided to take a stroll to the Good Wine and Spirits store and grab a few bottles of wine, then settle in for the evening, watch a movie, and wait for something to happen—*if* it was going to happen.

It was still rush hour in the Burgh and the traffic along Penn Avenue was slow and tight. Weary drivers were sipping coffee from travel mugs, talking on cell phones, tapping the pads of their fingers on the steering wheel, and they all had one thing in common: frustration. Happy to be walking along the avenue to her destination, Alexa stepped through the glass, gliding doors of the Good

Wine and Spirits store. The vast shop was a wine drinker's paradise, tendering wines from everywhere and vintages to satisfy everyone's pallet, as well as other spiritous offerings. Grabbing a cart, Alexa set her purse in the child seat, then proceeded to peruse the aisles. She had just picked up a pinot noir when she heard a familiar voice near the Chairman's Select Wine section. She paused to listen. Yes, it was Louie Santorini's voice, along with the shop manager, Eric. Setting the wine back onto the shelf, Alexa left the cart but grabbed her purse, then made her way to the end of the aisle to peer around the shelves. Sure enough, Louie was examining a bottle of wine from the select section.

"I want to offer only the highest quality vintages for my tasting room. I'd also like to provide Pennsylvania wines for the cellar. I'm considering having a competition next month with local home winemakers," Louie said.

"That sounds fun. What a great idea," Eric said.

Louie's voice softened. "Yeah…a friend of mine came up with it." Alexa had a strong idea who that friend could be, and by the looks of him, Louie had one, Wynona Mulaney, on his mind.

"How soon would you need delivery?" Eric inquired.

"As soon as possible. I'd like to open this weekend. Can you handle it?"

"Certainly. Let's put together an order. I'll get a form and check our delivery schedule for this week, then meet you at the front counter in just a minute." He called to a young woman stocking the vodka section as he hurried away. "Tammy, I'll need you to cover the register for a little while, please."

"Sure thing," Tammy replied, then abandoned her chore to make her way toward the front of the store.

"Thanks, Eric. I knew I could count on you," Louie said. He slipped another bottle from the shelf to read the label.

This was a perfect opportunity to talk with Louie, except Alexa wasn't sure it was her place to do so. After all, Bobby said he was on a case. She didn't press the angel for details, aware it may not have been appropriate to do so. She had to wonder who Bobby had been assigned to help. Winnie or Louie or possibly Olivia? Louie slipped the wine bottle back into place and turned to head for the counter. On a braced breath, and not exactly sure how she was going to approach the subject, she made her way toward him.

Alexa made every attempt at a casual tone, hoping for success. "Louie…"

He turned. Clearly, he was making every attempt to match her casual manner. "Alexa…how nice to see you." She was certain his greeting wasn't sincere. Oh, no, he didn't think it was nice to see her at all. Alexa reached for his hand in another attempt to breach the awkward meeting. Smiling, Louie accepted her touch. Alexa's mind was racing. How could she begin a conversation? Louie took the reins. "Alexa…before you even speak, please know my heart is broken. I want to be with Winnie…"

"Then be with her, Louie."

"It's not that simple. I've got other relationships to consider."

Alexa squeezed his hand. "Does your daughter love you?"

"Of course she does."

Alexa kept her voice at a calm, easy level. "I have no doubt you're right. But can she provide you with all the companionship you need?" Louie appeared to struggle with an answer. "Louie…after my dad died, I know my mom struggled with loneliness. At the time, I lived in Columbus, Ohio. I had a business to run. My sister, Natalyn, was finishing up her last year of law school. We simply couldn't fill the void. If Mom would've started dating, I would've been thrilled. You need to talk with Olivia. Tell her how you need Winnie for companionship because I know her heart is broken, too." Alexa kissed his cheek. "You think about it." Giving his hand one more squeeze, she added, "I'll be dropping in on that new cellar of yours. Hope you'll have my favorite wine."

Louie smiled. "If I don't, I'll get it."

Alexa nodded her goodbye and a wink for good measure, then made her way back to the aisle she came from. Hoping she hadn't done more damage than good, Alexa reached for the bottle of pinot noir she'd had in her hand moments ago. Immediately, she felt the pull of the portal. Okay, could it be Pete wanted her to bump purposely into Louie before she left this century? Maybe Winnie is Bobby's case. Maybe not. Nevertheless, 1965 was calling…

"We've got to stop meeting like this, Miss Owl." Alexa heard Slater say, then felt his steadying hand on her shoulder. The world was swirling. He whispered, "C'mon, lean on me. Are you okay?"

She tried to bring him into focus. "Just give me a minute." Alexa blinked and blinked again, trying to grab her bearings. Finally, the blur gave way and her head stopped spinning. She looked around. They were standing outside the police station. If she were being honest, she preferred landing at The Lazy Hound. The Hound simply had a more welcoming feel. "I'm okay. So, what have we got?"

"Don't know. I've just arrived myself. Are you sure you're, okay?"

"That portal always beats me up. I'll be fine." Slater opened the door for her. Alexa paused to see what she was wearing this day. It appeared Pete was keeping it uber-casual this trip. She sported a pair of black, stretchy crop pants, black flats, and a sleeveless top with a houndstooth print. Once again, her hair was swept up in a wide scarf that tied beneath her hair and dangled halfway down her back. Alexa didn't mind the relaxed attire; it was very comfortable. She stepped through the door, then they made their way through the busy squad room and to Slater's desk.

Slater pulled out his chair. "Why don't you have a seat until you've got your bearings?" Alexa complied, noting Wheeler's heavy gaze upon them.

Joe Randolph seemed to be waiting for Slater's arrival. He was quick to approach the desk with a file in hand. "The doc sent over the tests he made on that shirt."

His gaze slid to meet Alexa's. Smiling brightly, he said, "Good morning, Miss Owl. How are you today?"

Slater snatched the report from Joe's hand. "She's fine." He opened the file to begin reading. "Okay, so, Bobby didn't ingest the cyanide at all. It was absorbed through his skin."

Alexa pushed up from the chair. "How?"

"Doc found a bunch of fingerprints on the shirt, probably Pooky's, Bert's, Bobby's, but who knows? Maybe someone else too. He said he had to test the shirt three times, but he found trace amounts of the poison along the collar of the shirt and the cuffs," Joe supplied.

"Trace amounts *now*, but a year ago, the cyanide would have been fresh and probably easier to detect. I've read several historical novels that used this method of poisoning. It's quite old and was very common in the early eighteenth and all the nineteenth century. Alchemists used clothing to poison people quite often. In fact, a political figure would hire them to kill a traitor, a woman to kill an unfaithful husband, or a man to kill a lover if she turned up pregnant. Whatever the situation called for, the alchemists would take care of it for the right price," Alexa explained. "Think about it. Bobby was under hot lights, and I'm sure he was nervous. He was probably sweating, and the skin absorbed the poison quickly, especially at the neck and wrist areas. Smart. We've got a very smart killer on our hands."

"Now we have to find out who wanted Bert Mateer dead, why they wanted to kill him, and who had access to the shirt," Slater said.

"Bert's wife, Pooky, is the most obvious suspect," Joe put in.

"Absolutely. She had plenty of opportunity. Although, you said no cyanide was found at the music hall, and Wheeler claimed they found no poison at the Mateer's apartment. It *appears* Pooky had no means, and what would have been her motive? You told me yesterday Pooky and Bert were a happily married couple," Alexa reasoned.

"That's true. We still need to talk with Mrs. Mateer," Slater said.

"I agree. Let's go," Alexa said.

Slater headed for the door with Alexa close behind. Joe hurried to his desk, grabbing up his jacket. "Right behind ya," he announced. Slater stopped short to shoot a look at Alexa. She shrugged. Joe followed them out to the car and opened the car door for Alexa. "I'll sit in the back," Joe said. "You shouldn't have to sit behind the caging."

"Thanks, Joe," Alexa said as she slid into the car. Joe closed the door, and she glanced across the cab. Slater was rolling his eyes while turning the ignition. "Who else in the cast do we need to talk with?"

Slater steered the Rambler out of the station's lot. "No need to talk with that new singer, Jack Holland. He wasn't around last year. Nick Ferroni, one of the baritone leads, didn't seem to know Bobby very well, if at all. It's still bugging me that Mrs. Starr and Royce Hathaway talked Bobby into taking Bert's place, and then they're married less than a year later. Now, that said, if Mrs. Starr wanted to get rid of Bobby, she could've just divorced him. She certainly didn't need to kill him. Although, I can't say that I blame her."

Alexa shot him a look. "Seriously, Slater?"

He replied with that bad-boy grin that was so Bobby Starr, and yet, there it was on Slater's lips. Alexa opted to ignore the smirk and continue the debate. "I suppose that depends on how her family felt about divorce. In the sixties, divorce was still looked down upon, right?" She caught Slater taking a quick glimpse at Joe. Oops, as far as Joe Randolph was concerned, it still was the sixties. She needed to choose her words more carefully. "I mean, are Katherine's parents, Mr. and Mrs. Fields Catholic? If so, are they strict Catholics? It's possible Katherine and Royce planned to kill Bobby in order for her to be free to remarry. That said, why would they poison Bert, and if they weren't involved in his poisoning, how would they have known Bert would be too sick to perform and Bobby would take his place that night?"

"She's right, Slater," Joe said from the back seat. He scooched forward to almost press his nose against the caging. "Seems a bit far-fetched. Although, it also seems too soon to remarry, especially after your husband hasn't just died, but has been *murdered*."

"It still bugs me," Slater said. He maneuvered the car through the Fort Pitt Tunnels. "And when something bugs me, it's usually valid."

"Noted," Alexa said.

After traveling up Greentree Hill and off the Greentree exit ramp, Slater pulled the Rambler into the parking lot of Greentree Manor, turned off the ignition, then twisted to face Joe. "You stay here. I don't think Mrs. Mateer would like all three of us barging in on her."

Joe's questioning gaze slid toward Alexa, then returned to Slater. He plunked back against the seat. "Whatever you say, Slater."

Alexa tossed Joe a withered smile as she slipped out of the cruiser and followed Slater up the sidewalk toward the building. "You probably should've left me behind. Joe is your partner."

"He's not my partner." Slater held the door to the apartment building open for Alexa, and they stepped inside.

She made her way to the elevator to press the button. "Still, he's far more official than a nun." Slater chuckled. Alexa added, "And I'm sure he's going to be questioning why I'm so involved."

"I'll cross that bridge when I come to it," Slater said as the elevator door skated open, and he stepped inside.

Alexa stood next to him and sighed. "Ah, the infamous bridge."

The elevator climbed, the light indicating the second floor lit, there was a *ding*, and the doors glided open revealing a tall, skinny, middle-aged woman wearing a blue overcoat, a blue, tulle bucket hat, big, round sunglasses, a blue leather purse slung over her right wrist, and a pair of white gloves waiting in the hallway. Alexa and Slater stepped off the elevator. The woman grinned at him with her too bright red lips as she entered the car. Slater nodded. "Good morning, ma'am."

As the doors closed, she said, "Good morning, Detective."

Alexa and Slater exchanged wide-eyed, panicked glances. Alexa said, "Surely, that wasn't…"

Slater made haste for the stairs, "Pooky Mateer, yes!"

Alexa rolled her eyes, then chased after him down the stairs. Now she understood why Pete had selected such a casual wardrobe for this case. When they reached the lobby, Pooky was just moving away from the elevator. Slater called out, "Mrs. Mateer…"

Pooky turned and smiled again. "I'm on my way to visit my sister, Detective. I don't want to miss the bus."

"Yes, ma'am, but we need to talk to you about your husband."

"Sally, that's my neighbor across the hall. She told me you stopped by yesterday. But I already spoke to that nice Detective Wheeler. He said he has everything under control, and that I don't need to talk to anyone else. He knows how hard this has been for me. I miss Bert so much, and what he went through before he died was just awful." Her lips quivered and her voice turned watery. Fumbling with her gloved fingers, she finally managed to unsnap her purse and fetch a handkerchief embroidered with delicate blue violets. Quickly, she dabbed her nose.

"Please, Mrs. Mateer, why don't you sit down for a moment? I'd really like to know what Mr. Mateer went through. I'm here to help," Slater said. He palmed her elbow and shepherded her to a bench near the front doors. Alexa was impressed. Pooky was almost as tall as Slater. For some reason, she had pictured her as a tiny woman.

"But I'll miss my bus and Hazel is expecting me by ten," Pooky sobbed.

"Don't worry about your bus. I'll get you where you need to be by ten. Where does Hazel live?"

Pooky eased onto the bench. "Brentwood. I don't drive, you know. I didn't need to. My Bert was such a wonderful husband. He drove me anywhere I wanted to go. Now, I have to take the bus everywhere."

"I'll take you to Brentwood. Tell you what, why don't we talk while I drive?" Slater gently suggested. Alexa considered him almost as smooth a charmer as Bobby.

Pooky blew her nose into the handkerchief. Wincing, Slater helped her up from the bench. She said, "I suppose that would be alright. But Detective Wheeler said…"

"Come with me, Mrs. Mateer. Now, tell me what Bert was having trouble with." He held the door open for her, then attempted to hold it for Alexa. She waved him on, then trailed behind them.

"That's just it. I don't really know what was wrong. Bert was so nervous and upset. He'd pore over our finances almost every evening."

When they reached the cruiser, Alexa opened the door to the backseat to slide in beside Joe. Slater opened the passenger door for Pooky, then jogged around the front to get into the driver's side and started the car. Joe's face bunched in concern. He mouthed to Alexa, "*What's going on?*" Alexa lifted a finger to her lips for him to be still and quiet. She didn't want Pooky to notice him for fear a third person in the car would upset her.

"Were you having financial difficulties?" Slater inquired. He pulled out onto Greentree Road.

125

"We never had before. Bert had a very good job. I don't know what was wrong. I didn't take care of the bills and never wrote a check until my Bert…" She blew her nose in the handkerchief again. Wiping her nose, she continued, "When we were at the music hall, I noticed he tried to talk to Royce Hathaway a lot, but Royce didn't want anything to do with Bert, and sometimes he wasn't very nice about it. Once, I saw him push Bert away. After that, Royce avoided Bert completely, except on stage, of course. Hazel lives on Willett Road."

"Got it. Did Royce handle your finances? Investments, retirement, that sort of thing?" Slater asked, pulling onto the Route 60-East ramp.

"I don't know," she moaned, still mopping her nose. "I saw Bert talking to Bobby Starr, real private like. I saw him with Bobby several times in a corner back-stage." Alexa exchanged a chary glance with Joe. "I'd hear him whispering on the phone, but I don't know who he was talking to. When I'd asked him what was going on, he'd say it wasn't for me to worry about. I tried not to. Like I said, Bert always took care of ev-erything. I suppose most women would assume he was having an affair. Not my Bert. Not the way he was fret-ting about money. We were losing money. I don't know how or why, but we were. My sister, Hazel, has been helping me with my accounts. She's never been mar-ried. A very independent woman. She showed me how to write a check and how to read my bank statements. I seem to be fine financially, but Hazel says I don't have as much as we once did."

"When did Bert start getting sick?"

"About two weeks before…before he died. He just didn't feel well. Vomiting, he couldn't hold anything down. Dizzy all the time. I thought it was stress. I was worried he was getting an ulcer. It just wouldn't go away."

"Besides you, who had access to the costume room?" Slater probed. He turned onto Saw Mill Run Boulevard.

Pooky lifted her shoulder. "Anyone, everyone. The costume room doesn't have a door. Why?"

"Did you ever see anyone come out of the costume room or find someone who didn't really belong in there?"

Clearly searching her mind while twisting the wet handkerchief in her fingers, Pooky stared out the windshield. "I don't remember. People are in and out of the costume room all the time. The coffee service is just outside. Sometimes they wander in to say hello, even if I'm not working on their costume. We're a family at the music hall. Some are closer family than others, but for the most part, everyone's friendly. I can't imagine anyone from the operetta company wanted to harm my Bert. Everyone loved him."

Squeezing the handles on her purse, Pooky turned her head to look out the passenger window. "Nick tends to stay to himself." She turned back toward Slater. "Don't get me wrong, he's very nice when spoken to. He's just…shy, I think. He's got a fabulous baritone voice. Bert wished he had Nick's voice." She lowered her tone to a whisper, as if Bert were sitting in the back seat and she didn't want him to hear. "Bless his heart,

Bert wasn't a very good singer." Pooky chuckled. "But he sure was a character. I think that's why Piers always found a part for him. Oh, there's Willett Road, just to the right. Fourth house on the left."

Slater turned onto Willett Road. "So, you can't think of *anyone,* in the operetta company or outside of it, who would want to harm or kill your husband?"

"No, Detective Slater, not a soul. Bert was loved by everyone: the landlord, all the tenants at Greentree Manor. He even told jokes to the cashiers at the grocery. Why, some of the girls from the Shop-N-Save showed up at the funeral home to pay their respects. Everyone. At least, I thought so. I wish he had told me what was wrong. I don't know if I could've helped, but maybe I could've comforted him." Slater pulled into the driveway of a small ranch house with red siding and white shutters. At the edge of the well-groomed yard was a for sale sign with a bright red banner draped across the front announcing, *sold.* An older woman wearing a yellow-plaid house dress, a white cardigan sweater, and a scarf around her head was walking a small dog in the yard. Pooky lifted the handkerchief to her nose, trying to stifle a cry. Her voice came out waterlogged. "I don't know why someone killed my Bert. That glass of cider was meant for him. I just know it. Poor Bobby Starr. He had a little one at home, you know. Maisie, such a beautiful child. I felt so bad for Katherine." Pooky's damp gaze met Slater's. "I was shocked she and Royce married so soon. I don't want to think badly of either of them, but...but it does seem...funny, you know?"

"Is your sister moving?" Slater nodded toward the for sale sign.

"Yes." She waved at the woman with the dog. "That's Hazel there. She can't stand the Pittsburgh winters anymore. She's looking at houses in Georgia. I *might* go with her." When Slater turned to get out of the car, Pooky touched his shoulder. "I just couldn't continue at the music hall, you understand. I suppose I just got too overwhelmed. I tried, and I made it for several weeks, but the memories were getting to me. I heard they found someone to take my place. I'm glad, but I hope they'll forgive me and call me back someday…if I don't move away."

Slater favored her with a compassionate smile. "I'm sure they will, Mrs. Mateer." With that, he got out of the car, jogged around the front to open the door for Pooky, and when he turned around, Hazel was standing right there.

"Pooky! What are you doing in this car? I was just about to walk down to the bus stop to meet you," Hazel's voice dripped with reprimand.

Slater helped Pooky from the car. "This is Detective Slater. He wanted to talk about Bert's death. So, he gave me a ride."

Hazel's scolding gaze shifted to Slater. "*Another* detective? Pooky told me she's been getting visits from the police." She fixed her hands on her hips. "It's about time. *Someone* needs to find out who was taking Bert's money and who is responsible for his death."

"Yes, ma'am," Slater said.

"Hazel, you need to calm down. They're doing all they can. Especially that nice Detective Wheeler," Pooky said.

"Calm down? *I* need to calm down? No, Pooky. *You* need to get riled up. *Detective Wheeler, indeed,*" Hazel chided, while rolling her eyes.

Pooky favored Slater with an apologetic smile. "Thank you, Detective Slater." With that, she looped her arm through Hazel's and urged her sister and the little dog toward the house.

Slater opened the backdoor for Alexa to get out, and slip into the front passenger seat, then he trotted around the front of the vehicle to jump into the driver's seat.

"Wow, Pooky's one tall woman," Alexa remarked.

"Yeah, she was much taller than Bert, but her sister isn't as tall," Slater noted.

"Mm. I don't know about you, but for me, it's looking more and more like Bert or Bobby's deaths had anything to with the operetta company. I think it has everything to do with Bert's financial problems. Perhaps we'll find more answers at Lifetime Investments," Alexa offered.

"We need to have another conversation with Royce Hathaway, for sure," Slater replied as he jammed the gear shift into reverse.

"You read my mind," Alexa put in.

"There's someone else I'd like to talk to first," he said.

"Who would that be?" Alexa asked.

"Winnie."

"Winnie Mulaney? *Why?*"

"Because she babysat Bobby's little girl, Maisie, all the time. I think she still does. I have to wonder what she's overheard or witnessed between Katherine and Royce this past year."

"I would hope they'd be discreet in front of the babysitter," Alexa said.

Slater chuckled from deep in his throat. "C'mon, who are we talkin' about here? If there's one thing the Mulaney girls have learned from their mother, it's the art of observation. Molly knows everything about everybody. She isn't one to gossip, but if you need to know something, talk to Molly. I'll bet my whole pension Winnie is her mother's best student."

Alexa giggled.

Chapter Ten

Small Spaces/Big Accusations

Twenty minutes later, Slater rolled the cruiser to a juddering stop in front of The Lazy Hound Pub. *Plunk, plunk.* Alexa grabbed the door handle to steady herself when Slater hit that gorge of a pothole in front of the pub. Slater groaned and askance, Alexa glimpsed Joe rubbing his head. He must've smacked it off the roof. The amazing thing about the pothole along the curb of the pub was it formed over and over again, year after year, and even in the twenty-first century. The nasty thing existed right outside the Owl's Nest Couturier Shoppe too. She couldn't be sure if some kind of wicked troll lived beneath the pavement or if the road crew just never bothered to correct the original problem—whatever that was. Improper drainage, most likely.

"I'm callin' Penn DOT the minute we get back to the station and tell them to fix that dang pothole," Slater groused while shouldering the door open.

Like grandfather, like grandson, Alexa thought. Cliff was always threatening the same. And yet, there the chasm remained year after year, decade after decade, and apparently, century after century. Slater opened the backseat door for Joe, and the three made their way into The Hound. Slater checked his watch. "It's only eleven. Too early for lunch," he said as he held the door open for Alexa.

A hearty Irish lilt greeted them. "It's a wee bit early for a pint, Detective, but come in and have a seat. We're always glad to see ya," Brian Mulaney stood behind the long, cherry bar wiping down glasses with one towel and had another slung over his shoulder. He smiled brightly at the trio approaching.

"Unfortunately, we're not here for a pint, Brian. I was hoping to talk with Winnie," Slater said.

Brian stopped mid-chore. A look of concern replaced his grin. "What could Winnie have done to bring ya lookin', then?"

"She's not in any trouble. I just want to ask her a few questions about her babysitting job for the Hathaways."

Brian hitched his chin toward the stairs. "The girls are upstairs. They usually don't come down for a while longer. They're probably fightin' over who's workin' the lunch crowd and who's stayin' upstairs with the wee ones and watchin' the soaps. Go ahead up, then, but at your own risk."

Slater nodded, then with Alexa and Joe on his heels, they climbed the staircase. This was it. This was the moment Alexa had been waiting for. She'd visited the past three times and had been in the upstairs of The

Lazy Hound Pub each time but had never been in the Mulaney's apartment. At the top of the stairs was a bathroom shared by the two tenants and the Mulaney family. In the twenty-first century, the once communal bathroom was now Alexa's guest bathroom. Just beyond the bathroom, affixed to the wall, was a payphone. Much to her surprise, the old payphone was gone. Whoa, by 1965 had the Mulaney's and the two occupants of the apartments gotten private lines? Good for them.

Behind the first door was the apartment Bobby and whatever wife he was married to at the time lived in. The second was occupied by an old Irish couple, the Murphy's. In Alexa's time, she combined the two apartments to create her bedroom, walk-in closet, and master bath. As they continued down the hallway, Alexa's anticipation grew. Tiny voices of children and feminine Irish banter from inside the Mulaney's apartment resonated through the door. Slater rapped on the door. The women's natter instantly silenced, and then Molly's distinct Irish tone said, "Well don't just sit there, Wynona Mulaney, see who's at the bloody door, then."

The apartment was suddenly quiet, except for the sound of the children moving around, little feet pattering over the wood, and toys dropping to the floor. Slater glanced back at Alexa and Joe. The knob twisted, the door creaked as it opened, and a young, lovely blond peeked out. Clearly recognizing Slater, Winnie craned her neck to see who was in his company. "Detective Slater…what brings ya by?"

"Hello, Winnie. I was hoping to have a word with you. May we come in?" Slater asked.

Winnie's pretty face pinched in concern. "Have I done somethin' wrong, Detective?"

"Of course not, Winnie. I just need to ask you a few questions. That's all. Would you rather we talk out here, in the hall?" Slater inquired.

Molly stepped up behind her daughter with a small, curly-haired redheaded girl on her hip. Alexa figured the child for twenty-four months. "Absolutely not, Detective. You'll be questionin' me daughter right in front of me eyes if you don't mind. Now, step aside Wynona and let the detective and his friends inside. Let's see what he's got to say for himself, then."

Ever since the first time Alexa had been upstairs at The Hound, she tried to imagine what the Mulaney's small accommodations could possibly look like. How could five people live in what was now Alexa's living room and kitchen area? Winnie opened the door wider and stepped aside to give them entry. When Alexa stepped over the threshold, she took in exactly how tight the Mulaney's living arrangements actually were. Not only was Alexa in a different time, but it was a time when families survived more simply, and they did without more often than not. While the Mulaney's owned a business in a thriving area of Pittsburgh, they lived quite humbly.

The sun beaming through the kitchen window drew Alexa's gaze to the beautifully etched window that still existed in her apartment. The black and white design depicted a man and woman standing near a trough, offering water to a workhorse. Alexa remembered Winnie's delight when she first met the now old Irish gal. Winnie gasped at the sight. "Me grandfather made this window back in Ireland," she said. Alexa was so happy the woman who'd refurbished the upstairs had taken great care to preserve the window. Directly beneath the window sat a wooden highchair. The kitchen cabinets were much like those in Bobby's apartment, and probably the Murphy's as well. Metal cabinets with ordinary silver handles, and a green Formica countertop. There were only three cabinets on the top and three below. Very little storage space. Ah, there he was in all his glory, the dumbwaiter, Charlie. Only he didn't have a door at all, just an open wooden car stationed to the left of the sink. Ol' Charlie didn't have a button to control his up and down journeys between the apartment and the pub. Oh, no, the old waiter had pull-cords to make him go. At the end of the cabinets was a stove with several dish towels stuffed over the handle.

Where Alexa's large, black granite countertop island stood was a well-used, oval, wood table with four chairs. The white refrigerator was rounded at the top, a long, silver handle, and a silver logo announcing *Frigidaire*. The small space between the cabinets and the fridge held a broom. A mop rested in a bucket in the space between the stove and the wall. Every inch in this scarce apartment had to be utilized.

Molly gestured toward the kitchen table. "Have a seat. Would you like some tea?"

"No thank you, Mrs. Mulaney. We won't be long," Slater said.

As they made their way to the table, Alexa's gaze swept over the floor. Her twenty-first century apartment boasted the original wood flooring, only the Mulaney's wood floors were scuffed. They were clean and shiny, merely worn. No large throw rugs. The little redheaded girl and a blonde boy, about eight months in age, had to play on the hard, drafty floor.

Strategically, Alexa grabbed the seat that faced the living room. Slater, Joe, and Winnie filled the other three chairs, while Molly remained standing, bouncing the little girl on her hip. Alexa couldn't help herself. She continued to scrutinize the Mulaney's living quarters in amazement. When she attended Ohio State University, her campus apartment was as small, but only she and one other girl lived there. She couldn't begin to imagine her parents, Natalyn, and herself living in such close proximity.

Instead of the elegant electric fireplace with the large, flatscreen TV stationed above on the wall between the long windows that looked out over Penn Avenue was a radiator. Several pairs of itty-bitty pants, tops, and cloth diapers were lying over the only heat source to dry.

"Now, what's this all about, Detective Slater? Must be serious. Seems you've brought the entire police department with ya," Molly stated. Her voice was on the shady side of edgy.

"I'm sorry, let me introduce my…fellow officers. Sergeant Joe Randolph and Alexa Owl." Each nodded as he introduced them. Although Joe seemed a bit baffled by Alexa being introduced as an officer, he didn't contradict the detective. Slater cleared his throat, then inquired, "Winnie, I understand you babysit Maisie Starr, Katherine's daughter from her marriage to Bobby Starr."

"That's right," Winnie replied. "I still do. It started out at the Starr's apartment right down the hall, then they moved to the new house, and I started goin' there. Now, sometimes I babysit at the Hathaways' house, sometimes in Katherine's dressin' room at the music hall, and sometimes here." A shrug. "Mostly at the house."

Four feet from the kitchen set, a rust-colored couch of chenille fabric and thick, rolled fringe corralling the bottom separated the kitchen from the living room. Stationed at the farthest reach of the couch was an end table with a ceramic floral lamp, covered with a green, ruffled shade. Alexa figured the lamp to be circa 1930s and appeared more suited for a bedroom than a living room. Against the wall where Alexa's bookcase now stood was a long, narrow table that held a radio, a small TV, and sure enough, a black rotary telephone. She supposed the two other apartments had phones too, hence the disappearance of the payphone in the hallway. Pressed against the farthest wall in the room was a double bed and a twin bed. Both neatly made with matching blue bedspreads and a curtain to provide limited privacy for Winnie and her parents.

How awful.

There was no bed for Maggie. Clearly, the children belonged to her, and she must've lived elsewhere with a husband. She appeared just as bedraggled and undone as the day before. She sat on the couch pulling clothes from a basket, folding them, then laid them in piles on the couch. The baby boy sat at her feet fumbling with blocks, while the little girl studied the strangers from the security of her grandmother's hip.

"Was Katherine Starr close with Mr. Hathaway before Bobby's death?" Slater asked.

"Very close," Winnie began. "A little too close, if ya don't mind me sayin'."

Molly looked as she always had, a woman of average height, thin, dark auburn hair tucked back on the sides with hair combs. She always wore a dress. This day, she was wearing a blue striped dress with a Peter Pan collar. Winnie appeared to be nineteen, maybe twenty. She was wearing hip-hugger jeans, a wide leather belt, and a floral, short-sleeved blouse. Her pure blond tresses spilled about her dainty shoulders. She was quite the Irish beauty.

"What makes you say that?" Slater fished.

"Royce came into Katherine's dressin' room all the time. Especially when Bobby wasn't helpin' out at the music hall. Sometimes he had to work late at the dealership."

"Field's Ford? Katherine's father's dealership?" Joe confirmed.

"That's the one. Personally, I think Katherine and Royce were havin' an affair all along. I liked Mr. Starr well enough, but at the time, I remember thinkin' it served him right after the way he'd carried on with other women when he was married to his other *four* wives." Sagging deeper into the chair, Winnie crossed her arms over her chest. "Now, I've heard the whispers from people sayin' they got married too quickly, but if you're askin' me, they were already involved. So, waitin' six months was probably an appropriate time for an inappropriate relationship, I suppose."

Alexa was instantly jerked from her scrutiny of the Mulaney household. "Just because Mr. Hathaway came to Katherine's dressing room doesn't mean they were having an affair, Winnie. Can you give us more to go on than that?"

Winnie's gaze flashed to meet Alexa's, and there seemed to be some slight recognition within her stare. Not that she recalled Alexa from the twenty-first century, rather from her previous visits. It was as if the brunette across the table was at the very rim of her memory, and she was trying to find the connection. "Sometimes when Bobby was workin' late, Mr. Hathaway would bring Katherine home. Let's just say they lingered in his car for a long time. I couldn't see what was goin' on in there. It was too dark, but one can figure it out easy enough, can't they, then?"

"Winnie's right," Maggie piped in. All eyes turned to meet hers. "I remember goin' to put the trash out one night when Katherine went up the stairs to fetch Maisie, and there he was, just as sweet as ya please, Royce Hathaway waitin' on her in his car, in the parkin' lot behind the pub. Believe me, I know what a *blaggard* looks like first hand."

"Is that all you'll be needin' then, Detective?" Molly asked. It was quite clear she was done with the questioning.

"Yes, for now. Thank you, ladies. We'll be on our way," Slater said, pushing up from the chair. Alexa and Joe eased up and followed Slater to the door.

Molly held the door open. "Do ya think Katherine had somethin' to do with poor Bobby Starr's death?"

"I hope not, Mrs. Mulaney," Slater said. "I sure hope not."

After Molly closed the door behind them and they had reached the staircase, Slater turned to Alexa and Joe. "Like I said, it's time for another conversation with Royce Hathaway."

West Mifflin Park—Twenty-first Century:

Bobby eased down onto a park bench. The sun was warm on his face. A light breeze tousled his hair, and the park was alive and bustling with children on the swings, the slide, and monkey bars. He watched them running and chasing and laughing, and he thought about Maisie. She would be in her early sixties by now, no longer the little one he held to his chest, kissed, and rocked. He glanced down at his attire: jeans, a Nike T-shirt, and a pair of old sneakers, and then he noticed the Bassett hound, Walter, stretched out on the bench next to him, snoring. "Yo, Walter…" No response. "Walter, you gonna help me out here?" Still, the dog slept. "Nice work, Walter." In the distance, he heard the subject of his visit to West Mifflin Park approaching, Louis Shipman, escorted by his parents, Olivia, and Josh. Bobby considered Olivia a good mom, except she was wound tight when it came to Louis, and her father, and her husband, and pretty much everything in her life. Olivia was a bit of a control freak. Man, she sure could use a guardian angel. Not his assignment.

The Shipmans were making their way from the parking area. Louis and his cocker spaniel, Allister, running ahead.

"Don't go too far, Louis," Olivia called after him.

Louis wasn't paying any attention to his mother's warning. He tossed a red ball and Allister ran off after it, and when he retrieved it, the dog returned for another go. The boy grabbed the ball from the dog's grip and threw it harder and farther. Allister galloped after it. Bobby was ready and took control of the ball, making it fly even further than the boy's ability. It bounced at Bobby's feet, and he caught it. Allister bounded toward the stranger on the bench, then stopped and sat down in front of him, panting, wagging his stumpy tail. "Good boy, Allister," Bobby murmured.

Out of breath, Louis rushed to the bench. He studied the stranger, holding his red ball out of Allister's reach, and the sleeping Basset Hound lying on the bench. Louis pointed to the hound. "Is that your dog?"

Bobby glanced down at Walter and shrugged. "Must be."

Louis's face bunched. "What's wrong with him?"

"Wish I knew."

"Looks like he's dead," Louis surmised.

"He always does."

"Hey, that's my dog's ball you've got. You should give it back," Louis said.

Bobby examined the ball, then pitched the boy a half-smile. "I should, shouldn't I? It would be wrong to keep it from ol' Allister, wouldn't it? I mean, it's always best to do the *right thing*. Don't *you* think?"

Louis studied the man, then lifted a shoulder. "I guess."

Bobby lobbed the ball. Louis spun around to watch it fly across the park. Gleefully, Allister took off after it. "Wow, you sure can throw hard," Louis declared, then he turned back. "Hey, how'd you know…"

The man and the Basset Hound were gone.

Chapter Eleven

Follow the Money

As they drove toward downtown, Alexa stared out the passenger side window, considering what they knew so far and the conversation they'd had with Pooky Mateer. Finally, she said, "Pooky claimed they were losing money. Evidently, lots of money. She'd witnessed her husband, Bert, exchanging terse words with Royce, an investment agent at Lifetime Investments. That made sense, but why would Bert Mateer feel the need to talk with Bobby?"

From her past relationships with the angel, he never struck her as a financial genius. Quite the opposite. Alexa surmised Bobby lived paycheck to paycheck, and those paydays were few and far between in the private eye business.

If her memory served her correctly, Bobby's second wife, Cora Lee's father didn't approve of their marriage because of Bobby's low-income status. Likewise, his fifth wife, Katherine with a K's father was insistent Bobby sell cars at his Ford dealership so Katherine would be more financially secure. Yeah, Detective Bobby Starr wasn't exactly Mr. Wall Street.

"Is this some kind of review?" Slater asked, his tone drenched with sarcasm.

Alexa twisted to face him. "Yep. Stick with me. Could it be Bert wasn't talking to Bobby about his financial problems, looking for fiscal advice? Maybe Bert needed Bobby's professional expertise."

"What professional expertise?" Slater scoffed.

"*Slater.*" Alexa shot him a look. "Pooky said when she saw Bert and Bobby talking, they were tucked away in a corner. It sounded like their meetings were covert. Had Bert hired Bobby to investigate his monetary losses at Lifetime Investments?"

"Not all investments pay off, especially if the investor is into high-risk ventures. I've taken some of those risks, and lost my shirt," Joe supplied from behind the caging.

Joe was right, of course. Alexa had never met Bert Mateer, and she didn't believe Slater or Joe had either; therefore, they didn't know if he was a risk-taker or a conservative investor.

In the early and mid-twentieth century, many women, mainly housewives, had little to do with household finances, that was a *man's job*. Women were expected, even taught by their own mothers, to take care of housework, laundry, children, cooking, and in fact, during that time period many women didn't drive. Most households had one vehicle, one telephone, and if they had a TV, they owned only one. Women started breaking those molds in the late '70s.

With that reasoning in mind, Alexa said, "From Pooky's account of her marriage, it sounded like she took care of the apartment, and Bert took care of everything else. It seems to me the investment debacle must've been very serious for Pooky to even be aware of the problem. I'll bet Bert was so upset he couldn't hide it. He must've suspected foul play."

"She also said Royce Hathaway wouldn't help him. So, maybe Bert hired a private eye to investigate the investment firm. You could be right, Alexa. Maybe that's how Bobby got involved," Slater said.

Unfortunately, both Bert and Bobby were dead. The answer appeared rather simple: ask Bobby. Alexa was certain that would be considered cheating and very much against Pete's protocol. No. Slater had to solve these murders without the help of a fellow angel, much less an angel who was one of the murder victims. She had no doubt Slater was well aware of the rules.

Slater was right. They needed to talk to Royce, but there was someone else she felt the need to talk to: Katherine. Did Bobby discuss his cases with Katherine? Did she have some or any idea of what he was working on? Did Bobby have an office or a file cabinet in the house where he kept his case files? Seriously, Alexa couldn't picture Bobby keeping files at all. He wasn't that organized, responsible, focused, or accountable. He was definitely a fly-by-the-seat-of-your-pants detective, at best.

Joe cut through Alexa's muse. "I think that little review was very helpful. You'd make a great detective, Alexa, unless your heart is set on becoming a nun. I mean, I'm not trying to sway you one way or the other. Giving your *whole life* to God is a big decision and…"

Slater's gaze cut to the rearview mirror. His voice was concise. "*Thank you*, Joe."

"One thing's for sure," Alexa began. "Bert and Bobby's murders had nothing to do with one opera singer getting over on the other. Nothing to do with jealousy among artists. I think it's time to follow the money."

"Guess this means you don't need to go back to the music hall and work on costumes," Slater said, as he rolled the car to the curb in front of Lifetime Investments.

"I told them I would help. I'm not one to go back on my word, but more importantly, we need, or rather, *you* need to talk to Katherine. You need to find out if she knows what Bobby was working on when he died, and if, by any chance at all, there's paperwork lying around in their home to help us out."

"You got any faith in that, Sister Mary Alexa?" Slater asked, his tone filled with snark.

"Not at all, but it's worth a try," Alexa replied.

"If you say so. I'll show up at the music hall tonight to talk with her. Let's go," Slater said.

"Not me. Not this time. Again, I don't want to be connected to you. I'll wait here. You and Joe have at it," Alexa said.

Nodding his agreement, Slater shouldered the door open, slid from the car, opened the backseat door for Joe, then they made their way into Lifetime Investments.

Blowing out a frustrated breath, Alexa laid her head back. "Honestly, I wish I could just text Katherine."

"Mr. Hathaway…" the receptionist's voice sounded anxious. Slater was sure she was shaken by the return of the police. "Detective Slater and Sergeant Randolph are here to see you…again."

Royce's head jerked up from his paperwork. Slater couldn't be sure, but it seemed he swallowed hard. Pulling his glasses off, Royce's reassuring smile for the receptionist's benefit was forced. "Thank you, Mrs. Blake." The receptionist's uneasy gaze cut to Slater, to Joe, and then she skated past to make her exit. Tossing his pen on the desk, Royce pushed to his feet. "What can I do for you, Detective Slater? I've told you everything I know about what happened last year."

"Are you sure, Mr. Hathaway? You were seen arguing with Bert Mateer at the music hall. Can you tell me what that was about?" Slater asked.

Royce's gaze dropped to the desk as if a prudent answer would jump up and come out of his mouth. Finally, he looked up. "I had no problems with Bert. We got along just fine."

"Did Mr. Mateer have investments with your company?"

"He did, yes."

"Was he losing money because of his investments?"

"That's what *he* said, but I couldn't be sure. He wasn't my client." Royce plopped down into his chair. "He wanted me to help him, but I couldn't. I didn't have access to his file. I didn't know what investments he was involved with, and like I said, he wasn't my client. There was nothing I could do for him. He wasn't buying it, but I couldn't. He got a little hot under the collar, pushy, but the fact remained, I just couldn't do anything for him."

"Whose client was he?" Joe asked.

Royce pressed his lips together. Clearly, he didn't want to divulge any more than he already had. "I'm the only agent, and then there's the owner. He's out of town right now. He's on vacation with his wife in California."

"Does the owner of Lifetime Investments have a name?" Slater inquired.

"Steve Wheeler."

"*Wheeler*?" Joe questioned.

"That's right. Is that all you need?" Royce asked.

"Just one more question," Slater started. "Were all of Mr. Wheeler's clients losing money?"

Royce slipped his glasses back on. "I hope not. I need my job, gentlemen."

Slater nodded. "I understand." With that, he and Joe made their way back to reception. Slater could feel Mrs. Blake's wary eyes watching them as they walked out the front door.

Once they were outside, Joe asked, "Steve Wheeler, any connection to our Detective Wheeler?"

"They're brothers," Slater replied.

Joe sighed. "Great. Just great."

Robinson Town Centre/Twenty-first century:

Louis and his dad, Josh, stepped through the glass door of Rosie's Gifts. Bobby knew Olivia's birthday was this coming weekend, and he was anticipating the boy and his father's visit to the shop. Of course, the manager on duty couldn't see the angel browsing the aisles, searching for something suitable for a birthday gift. Invisible, Bobby clad himself in a pair of jeans, a blue and white checkered shirt, and a bib apron like the manager and the employees were required to wear with the words Rosie's Gifts embroidered across the top. The manager smiled and nodded at the man and his son as they passed the cash desk, heading toward the greeting card section.

Josh perused the vast selection of birthday cards while Louis shuffled from one foot to the other impatiently. After spotting the perfect gift for Olivia, Bobby sent a glint of light from the glass shelf that held a collection of darling ceramic angels. The display was merely ten feet away from Josh. As Bobby intended, the angels drew Louis's attention, and he abandoned his father to check them out.

While Louis admired the angels, Bobby made himself visible to the boy. "They sure are pretty, aren't they?"

Clearly shocked to see the man, Louis said, "Hey, you're the guy I saw in the park."

"Yeah, I remember you. Looking for a gift?" Bobby asked.

"It's Mom's birthday this weekend." Louis glanced over at his shoulder at his dad, still poring over the birthday cards.

Bobby nodded toward the angels on the shelf. "Does your mom like angels?"

"Yeah…" He glanced at his father again, then lowered his voice to a whisper. "I broke one when I threw the ball for my dog the other day. We were in the house. I'm not supposed to throw the ball in the house. Mom was really upset cuz it was Great Nanna's angel. And then…" Louis's voice fell away. It wasn't hard to see the boy had something to confess yet couldn't muster the courage to do so.

Bobby hitched his chin toward Josh, now immersed in reading a card. "Maybe you should suggest buying one for your mom's birthday. It won't replace the *fallen* angel, but I'll bet she'll love it, anyway."

Louis managed a stiff smile. "That's what I was thinkin'. I haven't said anything to Mom about how the angel really got broken."

"Hm, maybe when you give her the new one, it would be a good time to tell her about that."

"She'll be upset."

"Your mom loves you, Louis. She'll forgive you. That said, I don't think she's the only one you need to talk to, am I right?"

"Yeah…" the boy dropped his gaze to the floor. He was contemplating, then lifted it to meet the man's. "I'm gonna go get my dad, so we can look at the angels," Louis said, turning away, then he swung back. "Hey, how do you know my…" Louis looked up and down the aisle. Once again, the man was gone.

Bobby made himself completely undetectable; however, he stuck around to witness the boy hurry back to his father and grab his hand. Louis pointed toward the angel display and where the man had been standing. He wore an apprehensive expression and his father appeared baffled when the stranger Louis now claimed to have spoken with twice was gone *again*.

Trying to calm his son, and most likely himself too, Josh squeezed Louis's shoulder, and reasoned, "Maybe he went to the storeroom to get something. C'mon, let's take a look at those angels" Hand in hand, Louis and his dad walked toward the display, both scanning the store for the mysterious man.

Chapter Twelve

Tensions at the Music Hall

While Joe stopped to talk with another officer, Slater held the door open for Alexa, and she stepped into the station. They made their way to his desk to find a neatly rolled brown paper bag sitting atop the desk planner. "What's that?" Alexa asked.

Slater took up the bag, opened it, pumped his eyebrows at Alexa, then pulled out a sandwich wrapped in waxed paper. He closed his eyes and took a big whiff. "*Mmmm*, Janey's been here. She left me a tuna-fish sandwich. God, how I loved these. She made the best tuna-fish sandwiches and tuna-fish casserole too." He laid the sandwich on the desk, peeled away the waxed paper, then picked up half of the neatly cut sandwich and took a big bite.

Alexa's jaw dropped. "What are you doing? That's not for you. That's for *1965 Slater*. You're eating *his* lunch."

Slater paused mid-chew. "Oh…I guess you're right." After swallowing, he examined the sandwich. "I sure do miss these." Shrugging, he sunk his teeth in again.

"*Slater!*"

"What? I left him half the sandwich." He reached into the brown bag and held up a blue and gold snack bag. "And a bag of Wise potato chips."

Scraping her fingers over her forehead, Alexa said, "I thought you were different than Bobby, but you're really not. *Gawd*, how did *either of you* get into heaven?"

Quickly, Slater stuffed the rest of the sandwich into his mouth. Around a mouthful he replied, "I take offense to that."

Alexa snatched the bag from him, rolled it up, and put it back onto the desk. "Evidently, your wife expected you to be here, which makes me worry you will be soon. I think we need to get out of here before your 1965 counterpart shows up."

He let out a sigh. "You might be right. C'mon, let's go out the side door."

They made it around the corner and almost to the door when Alexa noticed Wheeler walk into the room and sit down at his desk. A nanosecond later, 1965 Slater walked into the station from the other door. He'd no sooner passed Wheeler's desk than the detective jumped up from his seat.

"*Slater…*" he called out. His face and tone held a sharp edge.

Alexa stopped, pressed herself and Angel Slater against the wall to peer around the corner.

The 1965 Slater turned. "Yeah…"

Wheeler stepped around his desk to get into 1965 Slater's face. "Who do you think you are? I don't want you messin' with my cases. I don't want you talkin' to my witnesses. You're workin' the Starr case. I'm workin' the music hall. We're not mixin' them together. You understand?"

Slater tugged Alexa deeper into the corner. She stretched to see what was going on over his shoulder.

The 1965 Slater looked baffled, as he should've. "What the heck are you talkin' about, Wheeler?"

Wheeler jabbed Slater in the chest. "I don't want you poking your nose where it don't belong. I'd take the warning, or your pretty little sister-in-law might not make it to the convent."

"My *what*? You've had too much to drink, Wheeler. Maybe you should go home and sleep it off." 1965 Slater attempted to pass.

Wheeler stepped in front of him. "Maybe you should pay attention to my warning. I'm not kiddin', Slater."

Slater grabbed Wheeler by the front of his shirt and threw him against the wall. "I don't know what you're talkin' about. But if you touch *anyone* in my family, you won't have to worry about your cases. Do *you* understand?" He bounced Wheeler off the wall, let go, then stomped toward the door he'd just come through, shooting his fellow detective one more abrasive glance before making his exit.

Slater hurried Alexa out the side door. "That wasn't good."

"Oh, I dunno. That little mishap may very well work in our favor," Alexa said.

"How so?"

"I'm not quite sure…yet."

"At least he didn't find the half-eaten sandwich," Slater put in.

"*Yet*," Alexa noted.

Alexa glanced over her shoulder to make sure Slater had driven away before she entered the music hall. Satisfied when he rounded the bend, and with no one else in the parking lot, she pushed through the stage door with confidence. She hadn't traveled far along the dimly lit, narrow backstage corridor when a movement caught her eye. She came to a halt so her footsteps wouldn't draw attention. Deep into stage left, among the heavy curtains, a couple was enveloped in a passionate kiss. Narrowing her eyes, she stretched to see who might be so engaged. It was hard to be sure, but it looked like the young man she'd seen yesterday coming out of one of the dressing rooms.

Now, Alexa hadn't met nor laid eyes on all the members of the chorus, yet she couldn't recall anyone else with dark, shaggy hair like his. Most of the cast and even the stage crew had clean-cut hairstyles. She didn't recognize the girl he was kissing. The women in the cast had at the very least, shoulder length hair. This young woman had a severe short hairstyle. Her pixie cut reminded Alexa of the overtly thin supermodel of the '60s, Twiggy. The couple were so absorbed in the moment, the whole world seemingly had melted away. Ah, young love.

Amused, but choosing to dismiss the make-out session, Alexa continued down the passage. Just ahead, Tallis Chamberlain and Piers Linney were absorbed in what appeared to be a rigid tête-à-tête. Not wanting to be detected, Alexa sucked her body against the wall and stood still to listen in on the discussion.

"My Leland gives generously to this operetta company, and he is becoming *very impatient* that I haven't been awarded a leading role. And now, you're planning to produce The Gondoliers and you're giving the role of Casilda to Katherine? The lead role *again* to that *common* soprano?"

Piers Linney's British accent was noticeably stiff, and yet from Tallis's comment, Alexa understood it was in his best interest to remain patient with the singer. He took a tolerant breath before he spoke. "Right. I *am* grateful for every cent your husband donates to our company, but I must cast the operas appropriately. Katherine suits the character, Casilda, brilliantly, and she is a favorite among our subscribers."

"*Of course*, Katherine is a favorite. She's the only one they get to see in a leading role. Piers, I simply don't understand…"

"There's nothing for you to understand, Tallis. Katherine will sing the role of Casilda, and that's that," Piers insisted, and then wasted no time in sliding past Tallis to escape further debate.

Tallis stomped her foot like a child denied a cookie before dinner. Letting out a whine of frustration, she marched along the corridor behind Piers.

Alexa remained still, giving them time to leave the backstage area before continuing on her way to the costume room. As she stepped into the hallway, a woman called to her. "Miss…miss…"

Alexa turned to see one of the singers from the chorus walking toward her. "Can I help you?"

The young brunette inquired, "Are you the new seamstress?" Alexa nodded her reply. "I'm Jeanette. Katherine Hathaway was looking for you. Something ripped or broke on one of her costumes." Jeanette lifted her chin toward the hallway. "Her dressing room is toward the end of that hallway." Just then, the young man who had been necking, stage left, rushed past.

"Thank you," Alexa replied.

Jeanette hiked up on her tippy toes, waving her right hand. "Hi Adam!"

Without a pause in his stride, the young man glanced in her direction, pitched a feeble wave, and murmured, "Hi."

Jeanette dropped back onto her heels. Her face bunched. "Is everything okay?" Adam kept moving.

Alexa's heart stung for the girl. It was obvious Jeanette had a crush on Adam, yet unbeknownst to her, he was smitten with another. Poor kid. Alexa strode along the hall, hoping not to find Tallis in the costume room. She wasn't keen on dealing with the woman after her squabble with the director. The thought had no sooner crossed her mind than she came upon Dorian talking on the payphone at the top of the hallway. "I'm very upset and disappointed. I'll see you tomorrow, and don't be late!" He slammed the receiver down hard, then meeting

Alexa's gaze, he tramped away. His long, silky ponytail tied back with a red bow bouncing against his shoulders as he went.

Grateful not to be the target of Dorian's frustrations, Alexa continued down the corridor until she reached Katherine's dressing room. She paused, recognizing the sound of Slater's voice coming from inside.

"Thank you for taking the time to talk with me, Mrs. Hathaway. I know your rehearsal will be starting soon." Alexa heard Slater say.

Hm. He was supposed to wait ten to fifteen minutes before coming into the music hall. Yet, in his defense, he must've used the main entrance through the library. Alexa had not seen him in the backstage area. She really wanted to hear what Katherine had to say about Bobby for herself, and since she had the excuse that Katherine had been looking for her to repair a costume, Alexa tapped on the door. Their voices silenced.

A moment later, Katherine opened the door, and Alexa said, "Hi Katherine, someone told me you needed a costume mended."

Katherine glanced over her shoulder, outwardly uncomfortable about letting the seamstress in. Evidently, Slater gave her some kind of gesture and she turned back, wearing an uneasy smile. "Come in, Alexa. I've got a zipper that's separated. I need it fixed right away."

Alexa stepped into the room, instantly grabbing Slater's gaze. She feigned pleasant surprise. "Oh… Detective Slater. I didn't know you were here."

"Hello, Miss Owl. Nice to see you again."

"I hope I'm not intruding."

Slater pitched her a knowing grin. "Not at all."

Katherine explained, "We're having some groups coming in tomorrow afternoon to see the show. A high school choral group and a superfluity." By the obvious stymied expression on Slater and Alexa's face, Katherine giggled. "That's what a group of nuns are called, a *superfluity*."

"I would'a thought they were called a gaggle," Slater said quietly.

Alexa shot him a look.

"The nuns from St. Elizabeth's always come to see the show the afternoon before opening night. We let them in for free, of course, and it gives the cast, especially newcomers, a chance to get some nerves out of the way. Although, this is the first time we've had a high school group come in. Should be interesting. I hope they're well-behaved," Katherine said.

"The nuns or the kids?" Slater asked.

Katherine chuckled.

"A superfluity. I'll have to remember that. What time is the show tomorrow? I'll need to be here," Alexa asked.

"Curtain is at noon. You should probably be here no later than eleven," Katherine said.

"I will be." Alexa gestured toward the clothing rack. "Is the costume on the rack?"

"Yes. It's the yellow dress. Seems I'm just the opposite of Tallis, so she likes to tell me. I've put some weight on. For now, anyway. I popped the zipper. I'm sorry." A subtle blush stained Katherine's cheeks.

"No worries." Alexa waved a dismissive hand. "Don't let me hold you back. I'll take a quick look at it here."

She glanced at Slater, then back to Katherine. "I mean, if that's okay?"

Visibly looking for confirmation, Katherine's gaze cut to Slater. He shrugged his reply. She said, "That's fine." Taking her time, Alexa picked through the four costumes on the rack, pretending to examine each for any possible alterations they may need. Katherine continued, "What was it you wanted to talk to me about, Detective?"

"Do you happen to know if Mr. Starr was working on a case at the time of his death?" Slater asked.

"Bobby was *always* working on something or other. His cases didn't pay the bills, but he was a private investigator at heart. I really shouldn't have complained about it. My singing doesn't pay the bills either. That's why Royce works at the investment firm, and I still work, on a part-time basis, at my father's dealership. Singing for the operetta company is a passion, not a career, I'm afraid." Wringing her hands, she dragged in a pensive breath. "Look…I've heard the whispers, and I know you have, too. Royce and I may have jumped the gun a little by getting married so soon after Bobby's death, but I assure you we were *not* having an affair. I loved Bobby, and after his death, Royce filled a void I didn't think would ever be filled again. I needed him, and that need turned into love. I have no regrets."

"I'm not here to judge you, Mrs. Hathaway. I'm here to solve a case. So, would you happen to know what Mr. Starr was investigating?"

"Not really. We didn't discuss his cases. To be honest, I didn't care to know. Especially if the case involved an unfaithful husband in the area. I mean, if I knew the woman personally, how could I have looked her in the eye if I bumped into her at the grocery? I'm pretty sure most of his cases involved infidelity." She held up a halting hand. "No thank you."

"Fair enough. Did Mr. Starr keep a log of his cases, or did he have an office in your home?" Slater fished.

Just then, the little canary in the gilded cage started to chirp and flutter. Alexa hadn't noticed the bird when she came in. Katherine crossed the room to open the cage. She quietly smooched at the canary, and it came to the gate. Holding out her finger while continuing to kiss, the bird hopped on her Katherine's pointer. "Shhh, Zippy…mind your manners," she cooed.

"Zippy…what a darling name," Alexa said.

Katherine chuckled, while reaching into a cup on the vanity and pinching some sunflower seeds between her pointer and thumb. She fed Zippy the seeds. "She got her name honestly. I hadn't had her for more than a day or so, and Bobby accidentally let her out of the cage. Well, it took us two hours to catch her. She was zipping all over the house. When we finally caught her, Bobby named her Zippy." She dropped her gaze to the floor. Alexa felt certain she was reliving the moment, and from the look on Katherine's face, it was a pleasant memory. "I've always had canaries. Ever since I was a young girl, and I started singing. They have such a lovely voice, and they are so pleasant to look at. I keep Zippy, and other birds I've owned before, with me at the music hall. They help to keep me calm. In a way, they're little luck charms." She chortled again. "Most people keep a cat or a dog for the same reason. I prefer canaries. To each his own, I suppose." She placed the bird back inside the cage, closed the gate, then shook her head as if to clear her thoughts. "I'm sorry, Detective Slater, you asked about Bobby's office. Yes, he kept an office, and yes, it's still there. I haven't found the courage to clean it out. Royce has suggested we use it for a playroom for Maisie, but we may need it for a…um…I'll look around to see if I can find anything to indicate what he may have been working on. But…why do you ask? Do you think one of his cases had something to do with his death? I always thought someone was trying to kill Bert, and Bobby was in the wrong place at the wrong time."

"We're not sure about that. Mr. Starr may have been the intended target after all," Slater began. "If you could take a look through Mr. Starr's office, that would be a great help. Especially, if you come up with a log book."

Alexa snatched the yellow dress from the rack. "I should get to work. I haven't been to the costume room yet. There may be a pile waiting for me."

"Thanks, Alexa," Katherine called after her as she made her way out of the room, closing the door behind her.

As Alexa crossed the hall toward the costume room, she heard another heated discourse. It certainly seemed the music hall was unsettled this evening. She paused to identify exactly where the deliberation was coming from. Yes, the costume room. Furtively, Alexa inched her way across the hall until she was standing outside and off to the side of the doorway. It wasn't hard to recognize Dorian Matias's voice.

"This is unacceptable. You need to stay out of the way, and yet you do nothing but get in the way," Dorian berated.

"I don't know what you expect, Dorian." It was Royce Hathaway's voice. "I can't be expected to know what to say or what not to say if I don't know what's going on."

"I've suffered as much as that *nitwit*, Bert Mateer, and I'm not carrying on the way *he* did," Dorian groused.

"Hello, are you the new seamstress?" A British inflection echoed through the corridor.

Alexa whirled around to see Piers Linney walking toward her with a smile on his lips. Within a nanosecond, Dorian filled the doorway. His tall lean figure garbed in a long, black tunic, and a pair of what appeared to be leggings. His silky ponytail tied up with a red ribbon fell over his right shoulder. Dorian looked Alexa up and down with wicked suspicion in his eyes. "Oh, good," he began. "It's our illustrious seamstress. I've been peeking at your handiwork, my dear. What a glorious job you've done on Tallis's gown. She'll be absolutely giddy." His impious gaze moved to Piers. "We've heard what your next project will be, Piers. The Gondoliers, one of my favorites." Gazing at his ponytail while petting it with the pads of his fingers, he quietly criticized, "Not that I'm particularly delighted with your casting choices. Perhaps you should *reconsider* before making any official announcement." His gaze jumped up to meet Piers. "Just a suggestion."

Clearly disgusted, Royce squeezed past Dorian, then made his way down the hallway. It appeared he was off the hook, for the moment anyway. Piers countered, "I'm standing by my casting, Dorian. Rehearsal for *this* show begins in five. Please inform Tallis." With that, the director spun on his heels and marched down the corridor behind Royce.

Rolling his eyes, then dragging his gaze to meet Alexa's, Dorian tossed her a toxic grin. "I've made you a cup of tea to chase the chill of this *dreadful* music hall. It's sitting on the cutting table. Enjoy." With that, he strutted into the hallway, pausing long enough to let himself into Tallis's dressing room. As Alexa watched him slip through the door, she had to wonder, what did he mean by he'd suffered as much as Bert Mateer? Did he have money invested with Lifetime Investments? Had Dorian lost money too?

Alexa stepped into the costume room. Indeed, a Styrofoam cup with a tea bag dangling over the side and steam swirling above sat on the cutting table. *Hm.* There was no doubt. Tensions were running high at the music hall, more individuals than Bert Mateer lost money. It was imperative they talk with the owner of Lifetime Investments, Steve Wheeler, and more importantly, she had *no intention* of drinking that tea.

It was karaoke night at Louie's Little Mardi Gras Bar, and the place was hopping. Every table was filled, the music was pumping, and the beer was flowing freely. Dressed in a pair of jeans and a black polo shirt, Bobby blended in while sitting at the far end of the bar, drinking a beer and keeping a close eye on Louie Santorini. Not nearly as garrulous with his customers as Bobby remembered, Louie haphazardly wiped down the bar, reset the beer glasses, and poured from the taps without much conversation or enthusiasm. Even the barmaid appeared concerned with Louie's lack of interest. The young woman glanced up at the clock.

"Hey, Lou," she called over the din. "It's eight o'clock. Time to get the karaoke started."

Louie looked down at his watch. "So, it is. You go ahead and make the announcement. I want to get the dishwasher emptied."

The girl was taken aback. "But Lou, you *always* get things going. They expect you to do it."

Louie opened the dishwasher. "Not tonight, Meg, you go ahead. I'm just not feelin' it."

"Are you okay?"

He managed a svelte smile for the barmaid's benefit. "Yeah, I'm okay. I just don't feel much like karaoke tonight. Go on now, or we'll run late."

Hesitation filling her every step, Meg made her way toward the stage.

"You're right, Louie," Bobby mumbled to himself. "We are running late."

Chapter Thirteen

Taking Notes

The sun was shining brightly as Alexa and Slater approached a cruiser parked in the back lot behind the police station. "Why are we using this old car?" Alexa inquired.

"It's my old cruiser before I got the Rambler. It still runs good. They use it as an extra, but it's going to the auction next month. The 1965 version of me has the Rambler today. So, we're improvising."

St. Pete never improvised when fitting Alexa. Today, she was sporting a casual and comfy royal blue boyfriend shirt with her black crop pants. The darts along the ribcage gave the shirt a fitted look, and the curved shirttail hem provided a casual yet put-together appearance. No hair scarf today. Nice. "I wonder when Steve Wheeler will be back from vacation," Alexa said.

"I dunno, but he's got some explaining to do. Let's get some breakfast," Slater said.

When they arrived at Deluca's Diner on Penn Avenue, Slater said, "I want to see Steve Wheeler's client list, and I want his investments audited. Something's going on, and I'm sure it's illegal."

Slater held the door open for Alexa. "If he doesn't come back soon, like today, you won't get a chance to do an audit. We're running out of time, Detective."

Slater shook his head in frustration. "That's right. I forgot. You've got to be at the music hall by eleven today, right?" Alexa nodded. "Let's hope Katherine found something we can use in Bobby's office."

"Are you coming to the show?" Alexa asked over her shoulder as she headed for a booth.

"I'll be at the music hall for sure. I think I should have a conversation with Dorian Matias, don't you? You overheard him threatening Royce last night, and you had the impression he lost money, too." They slid into the booth, one on each side of the table.

The waitress approached, pulling a pad from her apron. "Coffee?"

"Yes, please. Alexa?" Slater asked. She nodded. The waitress marked it on her pad, then moved away. Slater grabbed menus from a holder, handed Alexa one, then opened his.

"I don't know what you'll get out of Dorian, but he's definitely worth bumping into." Carelessly looking over the menu, Alexa lifted her shoulder. "I dunno, don't you find it strange that two people from the operetta lost money with Lifetime Investments, and yet Royce claims not to know anything about it? I realize investment agents keep their client's information confidential, at least in the twenty-first century they do, but if clients are losing money and are unhappy, panicked even, you'd think he'd know why. And what's with Steve Wheeler keeping the problem from his *only* agent? You'd think he'd want Royce to be able to calm their fears while he gets the situation under control. Unless, as you said, he's doing something very underhanded."

"After breakfast, we'll go straight to the music hall, and I'll press Dorian for information," Slater said.

The waitress approached and set two cups of coffee on the table. "What'll ya have?"

It was almost eleven o'clock when Slater turned onto Beechwood Avenue toward the music hall. "Look," Alexa said around a chuckle. "I never actually thought I'd have an opportunity to use this word, but there's a superfluity." She pointed to a throng of nuns walking in groups of two along the sidewalk. Alexa counted eleven in the superfluity headed in the direction of the music hall.

The noble group of women moved with their chins up and their hands tucked inside the pockets of their long, wide-sleeved black tunics. The morning's whisper of a breeze puffed their veils to reveal the white coif that encased their head and neck. Each wore a chain with a large gold cross, except for the eleventh nun who tagged along several steps behind the orderly procession.

The tagalong nun wore a blue tunic, and she did not wear a cross. Like the others, she'd burrowed her hands inside her robe, yet her demeanor didn't radiate the confidence the others emanated in their stride. While the nuns dressed in black held their heads high, eyes focused on their route, she appeared distracted, looking about at the cars passing by, the houses beyond the sidewalk, even the ashen clouds above. The nun dressed in blue appeared less resolute than the others. Alexa had to wonder if she was a nun-in-training, one who hadn't yet taken her vows.

"They're early for the performance," Slater noted, steering around the bend toward the Carnegie.

"Nuns are known for punctuality, aren't they?"

"They're known for more than that," Slater mumbled sardonically.

"Is there a hint of stereotyping in that remark?"

Through that Dean Martin, bad-boy smirk he'd suddenly developed, Slater chuckled. "Not at all."

Alexa raised an eyebrow. "I didn't think so."

Rolling into the parking lot, they saw a school bus parked at the farthest reach of the lot. Teenagers were filing off the bus and making their way to the main entrance. Alexa was amazed. The boys were sporting suits and the girls wore dresses. Yep, it was the 60s. Everyone, including teens, went to special performances in dress clothes, not jeans and T-shirts. Attending an opera, a play, a musical, or even an operetta performed by a small company was a special occasion and worth getting dressed up. In the distance, the parade of nuns gathered at the corner and waited to cross the avenue.

Slater pulled the car to the sidewalk outside the stage entrance. "After I talk to Dorian, I'll find a seat in the auditorium, then I'll meet you outside after the show."

"That works," Alexa said, then got out of the vehicle and made her way to the stage door and stepped inside. This was the first time she'd walked into such a bustling atmosphere. Members of the stage crew were moving scenery around the stage. An older woman, Alexa had never seen before, was busy putting wine glasses and trays and other small props on a table, stage left. The sound of the orchestra warming up in the pit filled the entire hall. She hugged the wall as she walked along the dimly lit, narrow corridor behind the backdrops as more members of the stage and light crew rushed past her.

Stage right was just as hectic. Alexa hurried through, relieved to arrive at the top of the hallway that led to the costume room. It was an hour before showtime, and she was hoping no one was in the costume room with last minute alterations. All the dressing room doors were closed. As she passed each, she could hear anxious voices and the fumbling of movement on the other side.

Alexa was almost to the costume room when Katherine's door whipped open, and she stepped into the hallway. Her hair was swept into a braided Gibson Girl updo. She was wearing the yellow dress Alexa had mended last evening, and she was holding a red note-book in her hand. "Alexa, there you are." Alexa met her in the middle of the hall. "I did as Detective Slater asked. I went through Bobby's desk, and yes, he did keep notes. At least, he was keeping notes on the last case he was working on. I don't have time to find Detective Slater. I've got to get ready, but can you give him this?"

"Certainly. I saw him come into the music hall earlier. I'll make a point to find him," Alexa replied.

Just then, a dressing room door opened and Tallis peeked out. Her hair was done up much like Katherine's and her stage makeup had been applied. She was wearing a pink satin robe. Her timbre was on the shady side of panic. "Have either of you seen Dorian?" Katherine and Alexa both shook their head no. "Where could he be? I've called his apartment several times. He's not answering. It's not like him to be late," Tallis moaned as she closed the door, hard.

Quickly, Katherine opened the notebook. Alexa's heart sunk at the sight of Bobby's handwriting. "I marked this page. Because he has notes about Bert and how much money he lost and who was handling his investments at Royce's company. I didn't show any of this to Royce. He was so...*uptight* last night. I could barely talk to him. He's never like that. Something's wrong. Something's *very* wrong. You need to give this to the detective right away." She shoved the notebook into Alexa's hand, then rushed back into her dressing room, closing the door.

Pressing the notebook to her chest, Alexa headed for the costume room. She would take the notebook to Slater as soon as the show started. She was about to step into the room when she looked up to see Detective Wheeler standing at the apex of the hallway, scrutinizing her. What was he doing here? It didn't much matter. Wheeler didn't know why Katherine gave her the notebook, nor did he know Bobby's connection to the case, if there was a solid connection.

Alexa decided she would wait for *The Merry Widow* to get rolling, then she would slip into the auditorium and hand off the notebook to Slater. Meanwhile, why not peruse the information Bobby had collected and see if any of it was pertinent to Bert Mateer's death or unknowingly his own. Glancing around the room to make sure no one had entered, Alexa dragged the wooden chair into the far corner, sat down, propped her feet up on the corner of the sewing machine cabinet, and opened the notebook. *C'mon, Bobby, tell us what we need to know.*

After searching the backstage area and asking around for Dorian Matias's whereabouts, Slater considered trying Tallis's dressing room. He was almost at the top of the corridor when he thought better of it. After all, the entire cast, especially the leads, were probably getting ready. Their stress levels were probably hitting crescendo. Deciding he could talk with Dorian after the show, or purposely bump into him during intermission, he asked a member of the stage crew for directions, then made his way through several passageways to the auditorium.

The nuns had taken seats on the right side of the aisle, second row. The high school chorus class filled four rows on the left side of the auditorium. The teens were giggling and talking, while the teacher walked up and down the aisle, making sure they remained seated and behaved accordingly. Slater smiled and nodded at the teacher as he walked past and found a seat in the back row on the right side of the aisle. He laid his fedora on the seat next to him. Maybe he would visit Katherine's dressing room during the intermission to see if she'd found anything pertinent in Bobby's office. He sure hoped so.

Alexa was proud of Bobby. Although his handwriting was sketchy, he kept good notes on his final investigation, and with good reason, the probe was complicated, involving many people, including one, Detective Vince Wheeler, in the most exploitative, shameless manner. The fact was, Bobby was very close to breaking it all wide open. She had to wonder if the players knew it. Alexa also wondered if someone called Pooky Mateer from her post in the costume room, then sent someone in to soak the collar and cuffs of the shirt Bert Mateer was supposed to wear for the party scene with cyanide. Alexa imagined news traveled at the speed of light through the cast, and the news that Bobby was to take Bert's place on stage spread like a California wild fire. After all, Royce Hathaway told her and Slater that Bert used to get dressed in the costume room. From Royce's statement, it was common knowledge among the cast and chorus. Who knew? The shirt may have been prepped with poison the night before.

Letting out a sigh, Alexa glanced up at the clock. Goodness, she'd been reading the notebook for over forty-five minutes. The closing scene before intermission, the party scene, would be on stage any minute. No one had shown up in a panic with a costume mishap, so she decided to grab a cup of coffee at the table and find her way to the auditorium to hand the notebook off to Slater. She had to wonder how his interview with Dorian Matias went.

Felonious Finale

Alexa kicked her legs off the cabinet, pushed up from the chair, and with the notebook tucked under her elbow, she started for the door, then drew up short. Something was missing on the cutting table. She'd rolled up the measuring tape and laid it on the table next to the pin cushion shaped like a tomato, and the shears, but the shears weren't where she *thought* she'd left them. A search of the room was in order before day's end. Alexa made her way to the coffee service, laid the notebook on the table, grabbed a cup from the pile, poured from the carafe, and was spooning in some sugar when she heard approaching footsteps echoing from behind.

"You sure don't look like a nun," Wheeler said. Alexa spun around. Grinning at her like some kind of deviant, he jabbed a thumb over his shoulder. "There's a whole passel of 'em in the auditorium."

"A superfluity…a gathering of nuns is called a super-fluity," Alexa supplied concisely.

"I suppose you outta know."

She grabbed the notebook from the coffee table and hugged it to her chest. "If you'll excuse me, I have work to do."

She attempted to step by him. He blocked her path. "I was wonderin' what Mrs. Hathaway gave you." Now, Wheeler resembled a hovering deviant. He smelled like someone had rolled him in cigarette ashes. Wheeler nodded at the notebook. "Can I have a look?"

Alexa pressed the binder tighter to her chest. "It's just a notebook. My sewing notes."

"Now, why would Katherine Hathaway want to see your sewing notes?"

C.S. McDonald

"She didn't. I left them in her dressing room, and she was returning them to me."

"Then you won't mind if I have a look see." He stepped closer.

He was way too close for Alexa's comfort. She could feel his hot, cigarette breath on her face. This would be a very good time for Slater to come around the corner. Her gaze flicked over Wheeler's shoulder. No Slater. "The notebook is my personal property. So, unless you have a search warrant, step aside, Detective Wheeler."

"Kinda bold for a nun, aren't ya? I'd like to search more than that notebook, *Sister* Mary Alexa of the *Holy Virginity…*"

That was the limit. Alexa hurled the cup of coffee in his face. Wheeler cried out, clutching his face. Alexa didn't hesitate. She skated past him and ran up the corridor toward the backstage area. She really didn't want to cause a ruckus with the show well underway. The auditorium, Slater said he would be sitting in the auditorium, and that's where she needed to go. The problem was she wasn't exactly sure how to get there from here. Checking over her shoulder, Alexa dropped to a fast-paced walk, trying to feign a calm demeanor, no doubt failing miserably.

Singers, dancers, and most of the leads were gathered backstage, all garbed in their formal costumes for the big party scene, the very scene in which Bobby had collapsed and died. Alexa wanted to inquire how to get to the auditorium, but there was already a quiet commotion going on.

The young singer, Jeanette, was fussed up, shouldering through the cast, searching. "I can't find Adam anywhere. Has anyone seen Adam?"

Everyone was looking about. One singer said, "We're about to go on. He should be here by now."

Another said, "I didn't see him in the dressing room when we were getting ready for this scene."

"He's my partner in the dance scene," Jeanette said, her voice thin. "What am I going to do without a partner? *He's got to be here*...somewhere."

Katherine made her way through the pack to place a calming hand on the girl's shoulder. "I'm sure he'll show up at the last minute. He's just delayed for some reason. If he shows up late, just find a good spot in the dance scene and make an entrance. It'll be okay. Remember, this is just a *practice* performance. It's better this happens today than tomorrow night."

Alexa shot a glance over her shoulder. Wheeler was charging up the hallway. No time for directions. She would have to find the auditorium on her own. Ducking down, Alexa wormed her way through the crowd toward the narrow corridor she assumed led away from the backstage and to the auditorium and Detective Slater. She sure hoped so.

Chapter Fourteen

Sister Act

Alexa darted down the dimly lit corridor until she came to a split. She paused. Continue straight or turn right? Looking back, she caught a glimpse of Wheeler rounding the bend into the passageway. His face was red, burned. He probably figured Alexa was headed for the auditorium, so she turned right. The hallway was short and at the farthest reach was a door with a sign announcing *Emergency Exit* above. The push bar had a red line indicating if it were pressed an alarm would sound. Not a good idea with the operetta on stage. She could hear the orchestra playing and singing in the distance. Unfortunately, if Wheeler came down this hallway, she would be trapped and forced to use the exit, and then Alexa remembered a ladies' and a men's restroom located in this hallway. She risked a look back. No Wheeler. At least, not yet. Just as Alexa pressed into the ladies' room, Pooky Mateer was coming out.

"Excuse me!" Pooky cried in surprise.

"I'm so sorry," Alexa said, once again glancing over her shoulder.

"I am too," Pooky said, digging in her blue purse with a gloved hand while holding the handle with the other bare hand. She was still sporting the blue outfit from the day before. Her blue tulle bucket hat was slightly crooked and her long, brunette hair lay on her right shoulder in a gathered spiral. Pitching a diffident smile, Pooky hurried down the hallway.

Alexa slipped through the door. Out of breath and terrified, she leaned against it, closed her eyes, trying to assemble some calm.

"Oh!"

A woman's shocked voice broke through Alexa's anxiety. Her eyes popped open to find the nun dressed in blue standing at the marble sinks. She clenched the white headdress in her shaking hands. Static electricity had her short shocks of brunette hair standing at attention atop her head, and her eyes held a desperation that, at this moment, Alexa was having no trouble associating with. As she suspected, when she saw the seemingly distracted nun lagging behind the others along Beechwood Avenue, she was young, possibly no more than twenty. Still trying to let her pounding heart catch up, Alexa put a finger to her lips, then listened for any sound in the corridor.

"Is anyone coming?" the nun asked. Her timbre was just short of a breakdown. Her face grew more pallid by the moment. The headdress quivered in her hands. Yeah, something was going on here, and Alexa surmised that something might work in her favor.

"Are you all right, Sister?" Alexa quietly fished.

Tears dribble down her cheeks. "I'm going to hell." She drew the headdress to her face to hide her weeping.

Alexa pushed away from the door to make her way to the girl and tenderly touched her shoulder. "I don't think that's true. Why do you think such a thing? What's your name?" That's when she noticed a white glove on the floor between the trash can and the sink. Pooky must've dropped it when she was washing her hands.

"My real name is Teresa, but I've taken the name Viviana in honor of my aunt. She's the abbess of our order, Mother Viviana Reverent."

Alexa glanced back at the door, listening. Still no sounds. Lightly removing the headdress from Teresa's hands, she inquired, "She's the *abbess*?"

"Yes, she's the head of our order at St. Elizabeth's." Teresa looked into the mirror, then wiped the tears from her puffy eyes with the palms of her hands. "I'm a Novitiate. I'm in training to discern whether I am truly called to take the vows."

Alexa examined the headdress, then the young woman standing before her. "How's that working out?"

"Not very well, I'm afraid." Teresa's voice was watery. "My mother wanted me to become a nun. Our family has had nuns in every generation for forty years. But...I don't believe I've been called. I...I haven't been honest with my mother or my aunt, and certainly not with God." Reduced to tears, Teresa buried her face in her hands.

Gently patting her back, Alexa whispered, "It's okay. I'm sure God understands. Especially since you haven't taken those vows. Why don't you think you've been called?"

"I've fallen in love with a man, Adam Gless. He's in the operetta company. He's in a situation much like mine. His mother wants him to sing opera, but he wants to go to Nashville and become a country western star. He's in the operetta, not a lead, just in the chorus. My church, St. Elizabeth's isn't far from here. I've been sneaking away in the evenings to be with him during rehearsals. He's waiting for me outside. We're supposed to run away together, but…but I'm afraid." She snatched a paper towel from the stack on the marble vanity to wipe her nose.

Ah, yes. The lovebirds who were making out stage left last evening. Her heart sunk for Jeanette. She didn't get to be part of the party scene. Worse, the man she was, at the very least, infatuated with was leaving town with someone else. Regardless, Alexa needed to get moving. Her gaze flashed to the restroom door. No one was coming, so… "Ah, you poor kid. You said you love Adam, right?" Dabbing her soggy eyes, Teresa nodded. "Look…I'm in a bit of a spot myself. I'm a…police detective." Alexa saw Teresa's gaze snap up and widen in the mirror's reflection. She wasn't sure how St. Pete would feel about the tall tale she was weaving or what she planned to do, but… "There's a man who wants this notebook. It's got information in it that I must get back to my partner…" *Not a total lie.* "This is a life or death situation." *Still, almost the truth.* "I'll help you escape if you help me."

Teresa looked frightened and baffled at the same time. "What do you mean?"

"We look to be close in size. Give me your nun… uniform…and I'll give you my clothes. You go your way, and I'll escape, dressed as a nun, to get this information to my partner so we can lock this guy up. Seriously, he's involved in something bad, like *really* bad."

"I don't know…"

"It'll be okay, I promise. Adam's waiting…"

Teresa's gaze darted to the door, then back to Alexa. "I need to ask for forgiveness…"

"Of…of course."

Teresa knelt on the floor, clasped her hands, closed her eyes, and bowed her head in prayer. Alexa stepped back to give her room. It wasn't very long before the young woman crossed herself and pushed up to stand. Immediately, Alexa started to unbutton her blouse. Teresa said, "Wait. In the stalls. In case someone comes."

"Good idea."

There were only two stalls, so they each took one. Laying the notebook on the floor, Alexa quickly unbuttoned and flung the blouse onto the wall separating them, then kicking her slip-ons aside, she shimmied out of the crop pants and draped them over too. Trying not to be impatient, she stared at the wall, waiting. Suddenly, she noticed something blue and satiny dangling from the personal hygiene box affixed to the wall. She lifted the lid, then with the very tips of her fingers, she tugged a long, yellow satin ribbon out. How strange for a girl to dispose of a pretty ribbon in the feminine hygiene box.

Felonious Finale

Finally, Teresa carefully draped the blue tunic over the wall. Stuffing the ribbon back into the box, Alexa pulled the tunic over her head and pushed her arms into the wide sleeves. A moment later, she tenderly laid the headdress and veil over the wall. These pieces were a bit more puzzling.

"If you need help with coif, I'll assist you once I'm dressed. This is a nice blouse, and it fits me too," Teresa said. She sounded more enthusiastic about the plan. Good.

"Yeah, I think I'm going to need assistance." Alexa pushed into her shoes, picked up the notebook, then stepped out of the stall to make her way to the door. Leaning in close, she listened to the muffled sound of the orchestra and the entire cast singing. Alexa knew time was running short.

A moment later, Teresa emerged from her stall. Her expression reconciled with her hesitation, she looked Alexa up and down. "I'll warn you. This coif is very hot. I hope God forgives me for this." She pulled Alexa's hair back, then pulled the coif over her head and smoothed it over her shoulders. "Your hair is so beautiful. I had to cut mine off. You know, to become a nun."

"Don't worry, hair grows. Can't you do some Hail Marys or something? I mean, to make up for not becoming a nun?"

Teresa cloaked the veil over Alexa's head. "I'm not sure there's enough Hail Marys to cover what I'm about to do." She let out a forlorn sigh. "But I'm not the first to fall in love and walk away from the calling."

"I'm sure you're right. Don't worry, sooner or later, your mother *will* understand."

"To be honest, I'm more worried about my aunt than my mother. She'll feel so betrayed." Teresa cupped her hand over her mouth to suffocate a sob.

"So will Adam, if you don't get out there." Alexa rushed to the door while waving her newfound accomplice forward. Opening the door, a tiny crack, Alexa looked up the hallway and down. No one. She listened. A woman was singing. Katherine? Tallis? It didn't much matter. Surely, they were well through the party scene. Good. That meant the entire cast was still on stage. She'd have plenty of room to maneuver backstage and sneak out the stage door. Alexa turned to Teresa, took her hand, and squeezed it. "Good luck, Teresa. I wish you all the best."

"I'll pray for you, Detective," Teresa replied.

"Thank you." With that, Alexa slipped out of the bathroom. She rolled the notebook up and tucked it, and her hands, into the pocket of the tunic. Even if she passed Wheeler, he probably wouldn't recognize her. That's what she was counting on, anyway.

Teresa followed Alexa down the short corridor and when they reached the end, Teresa waved and turned right. Her stride was visibly uneasy as she walked away from the calling, from her aunt, and yet into the life the young woman's heart was urging her toward.

Alexa turned left, headed to the backstage area. She couldn't afford to go to the auditorium now. Surely, Teresa's aunt was questioning what was taking the young nun so long in the rest room, and would inspect the girl upon return, instantly recognizing Alexa was not Teresa or Sister Viviana as it were.

In an attempt to project a confident manner, Alexa lifted her chin as she sauntered through stage right. Her mom's sage advice, *if you look as if you belong, no one will question whether or not you do*, had better work, given there was no real reason for a nun to be in this area. She dared a glance to her right. Piers stood at the edge of the main curtain, immersed in the dance scene playing out on stage. An older woman stood at his shoulder, craning her neck to watch. Quickly, Alexa swept past. She was almost…and that's when the woman quietly called out to her.

"Sister…excuse me, Sister…" she said.

Alexa cringed. *Dang*! She'd almost made it to the narrow passage that led to stage left and the door to the parking lot. Turning, Alexa forced a pleasant smile and tone. "Yes…"

"Are you lost? Can I help you find your seat?" She was the older woman who had been directing the singers in warm-ups the first evening Alexa had arrived at the music hall. Luckily, Piers was so absorbed in the action on stage, he didn't bother to investigate who the woman was addressing.

While she'd only seen the woman that first evening, Alexa hoped not to be recognized. Her lips arched. *Think fast, Sister Mary Alexa. What is a nun doing backstage?* "Good afternoon. The show is wonderful. What a *talented* group of singers," she managed. *Think Alexa, think*!

The woman favored her with a kind smile. "Did you make the wrong turn looking for the restroom? It happens all the time. Let me walk you back…"

Alexa raised her hand. "No…I…um…I'm meeting someone stage left after this scene. They've asked me for a…a…um…special blessing before act two. I promise I'll be very careful as I walk along."

"Are you sure, Sister? I'm more than happy to escort you."

"No, no, it won't be necessary at all." Just then, Piers Linney walked past. He shot her a bemused glance, then dismissing her for more important matters, he continued forward. Intermission was within moments.

"You're sure?"

"Yes, quite." With that, she nodded at the woman and proceeded toward the passage. Askance, she saw Wheeler stepping away from the hallway that led to the dressing rooms and the costume room. He stopped to scrutinize the blue nun. Turning her face away, Alexa picked up her pace.

Teresa was right. The headdress was hot and with all the lighting and the closed-in structure of the backstage area, not to mention the stress she was under, it was heating up fast. From under the white coif, sweat dribbled onto her forehead, her temples, and trickled down her neck, front and back. Picking her way down the passage, and finally arriving stage left, Alexa ducked behind a wing curtain. Fumbling with the notebook tucked inside the tunic, her hand slipped into a wide pocket sewn into the tummy of the tunic, and much to her delight, the notebook fit right in. Now Alexa's hands were free. Pinching the curtain back, she peeked around to see Wheeler coming her way, searching through the darkness for the blue nun. His face wasn't quite as red, the burn had eased a bit, or maybe he went to a restroom to splash his face with cool water. Alexa didn't much care. He was getting closer, and she needed to get out.

Alexa's gaze flashed to the door that led outside and into the parking lot. If she opened the door to run outside, daylight would burst through the backstage, alerting her exit, especially while wearing the nun getup. Did Wheeler suspect her? Would he follow? Probably. Where to go? She scanned the cluttered, dimly lit space for a prop or a piece of equipment to hide behind or under, then her head snapped to the right. A metal ladder was mounted to the wall just inside the main curtain. She didn't know where it led, but it would get her out of this situation. Quickly, she checked the security of the notebook in the pocket. Satisfied, she gathered up as much of the tunic as she could, grabbed hold of the first rung, and started up the ladder.

"Sister, where are you going? You're not allowed up there. That's the catwalk. It's *dangerous*. Please come down," a man's loud whisper beckoned to her.

Seriously? Now? Alexa dared a peek to see a member of the stage crew. Where'd *he* come from? During the week, she'd seen him around, but she didn't know his name. No matter. She had no doubt he had unknowingly informed Wheeler of her location. Stepping past the curtain, Wheeler pushed the young man out of the way. Feigning concern, Wheeler called up to her, "Please,

Sister Mary Alexa, I know you're lost and frightened, but please, come down."

Nice try. Alexa clambered up, up, up the ladder, trying not to look down. Taking a glimpse downward could be her undoing. Above, she could see the opening to a catwalk. Okay, that made sense.

"*Shhhh*!" the young man rebuked at Wheeler. "The audience will hear you!"

"It's just a practice audience," Wheeler groused. "Looks like the sister is a little stubborn. Yeah, that's the way I remember them. Not as pretty as this one, but just as stubborn. I'm goin' up after her."

"Wait!"

"Back off, kid!"

Alexa chanced a peek to see Wheeler take hold of the ladder, and then feel the shake from the ladder from his turbulent crawl upward. The young man hurried away. About ten feet more until she reached the catwalk. Then what? Had she hit a dead end? No time to fret over the inevitable, so she kept climbing.

"Stop, Sister Mary Alexa, I'm not gonna hurt ya," Wheeler said, then Alexa heard him add, "Too much."

Her heart beat felt like tiny fists trying to break out of her chest, while her panicked breaths pounded in her ears. Finally, she reached the opening to the catwalk. Thank God, the walk had a railing on both sides. Alexa looked over. The stage was far below. A fall would mean death. To the left, the walk continued about twenty feet and then ended at the wall and a large, round light. To the right, the bridge traveled all the way to stage right. It appeared there was another ladder to go down to stage right, but a dark and bulky object lay on the overpass. Alexa glanced back. Wheeler had about ten feet until he reached the catwalk. Stage right it was! She turned to go when the wide sleeve of the tunic caught on the railing. Alexa tugged and yanked. Wheeler smiled up at her as he drew closer to the top. Desperate to continue on, she ripped the sleeve and jogged along the caged floor, making an awful *clanging* sound as she moved. In any other circumstance, Alexa would've made every attempt to tread quietly. This was not that circumstance.

Sweat dripped down her back. The tunic was getting heavier, hotter, and terribly uncomfortable. Alexa dared another glance back. Wheeler had just managed his first step across the catwalk. He grinned at her. *Whatta creep*! The runway was dimly lit, clotted with shadows, and ahead, among the silhouettes, it looked like that object was lying in a heap, something big. Part of a curtain? *Clang, clang, clang*. Wheeler's heavy footsteps marched along the bridge. He wasn't attempting to be quiet. Whatever it was up ahead, Alexa hoped she could get past it without too much trouble. Breathing heavily she crossed over the center stage point, and noticed a thick rope tied to the railing. Alexa eyed the knot as she approached. The tie appeared to be a quick release knot connected to a boom that held a light affixed to some kind of track.

At last, Alexa reached the object in the middle of the catwalk. Only, it wasn't an object. Grabbing the railing, Alexa drew up short. She gasped. Good God! It was a dead body! The man sat slumped with what looked a knife sticking out of his back! She wanted to scream.

She wanted to wretch. Glancing back, Wheeler was about twenty feet away. He was still wearing that sickening sneer. *Clang, clang, clang.* The body was blocking her way to the ladder. If she attempted to step over the body, she had no doubt the tunic would get caught up on the knife. Alexa gulped. Only one way out. Only one way down—the rope. Swallowing hard, then taking a braced breath, Alexa checked the notebook. Still good. She pulled on the knot, then climbed onto the railing.

"What are you doin'? Wait!" Wheeler called out.

Yep, the audience and the cast on stage heard his cry. Everyone looked up.

The light lugged forward. Gripping the rope for all she was worth, Alexa let the light glide down the track. Wheeler lunged forward, trying to grab her. There was a hard jerk, and she allowed herself to be pulled off the railing, away from Wheeler, and over the crowd below.

"Oh, my God! I really am a flying nun!" Alexa exclaimed as she swooped over the audience toward the stage. The audience gasped almost in unison and the singers and dancers on stage screamed, darting in all directions.

A woman in the audience shrieked, "*Viviana*! Dear Lord! That's my niece, Viviana!" Her cries were followed by screams.

Pure chaos was erupting throughout the auditorium and on the stage. The singers and dancers tripping over each other, trying to get out of the way. Good. Because Alexa was plunging directly toward the stage. She wasn't sure if she could control her landing, but she was going to give it a try! Now would be an excellent time for St. Pete to intervene.

Not happening.

"Watch out!" Alexa shouted. She lifted her legs, then as the light was reaching the stop on the track, the rope swung forward with a jolt toward the stage like a rope over a creek. Alexa eased foot one down then the other, hitting the floor at an uncontrollable run. She let go of the rope, almost face planting, but managed to fall to her knees, then clambered up to look back. The rope swung and joggled overhead.

Wheeler was just stepping away from the ladder, stage right. Pushing several singers out of his way, he pointed at the sweaty, flushed, disheveled nun. "Grab her! Don't let her go!"

The singers, dancers, stage crew, and Piers Linney stood flummoxed by the shocking spectacle before them. Alexa wasted no time. Taking advantage of the confusion, she darted toward stage left. Wheeler took off after her. Then, out of nowhere, a nun was on Wheeler's heels running across the stage. Her long, black cloak flapped behind her, while she smacked him with her purse, yelling, "You leave my niece alone! You wicked man! You leave her be! Deviant! Deviant! Help! *Someone*, please help her!"

Jogging forward while glancing over her shoulder, Alexa plowed into someone. She felt the body give, then straighten and hands grasping her. "What's goin' on?" Joe Randolph asked, pulling the nun protectively into his chest. Looking into her face, he exclaimed, "Alexa! What…"

Panting for air, Wheeler came to a sliding stop. The nun behind him stopped, too. She was about to whack him with her purse when her eyes grew wide with the revelation that the nun before her was not Viviana. Around choking for air, Wheeler sputtered, "She…stabbed…my brother. He's *dead*! Up there…on the catwalk."

The nun's jaw dropped, and she was breathless when she announced, "This isn't my niece. She's wearing Viviana's clothes…but…what have you done with my Viviana? Have you killed her too?"

Feeling the notebook pressing against her stomach, Alexa tried to push away from Joe, then luckily, Slater stepped up to his shoulder to demand, "What's goin' on, Wheeler?"

"*Slater*," Alexa gasped. Slater's eyes narrowed. At that moment, Alexa realized she was looking into the puzzled eyes of Detective Slater from 1965. This couldn't be good. Not good at all.

"Pat her down!" Wheeler shouted. "Pat her down, now!"

"Frisk a *nun*?" Slater asked, his tone was beyond shocked. Alexa noticed him studying Wheeler's undone appearance. The brown stain on the front of his white shirt and the red flush on his cheek.

Joe threw his hands up. "I'm not friskin' no nun."

Wheeler stepped forward. "I'll *gladly* frisk her."

Alexa stepped back against Joe.

"No! I…I'll…frisk her," Joe protectively insisted. Slowly, he turned toward Alexa. Lightly, he touched the top of her shoulders with his fingertips, then he moved them down her shoulders and upper arms. Alexa's stomach clenched. He was going to find the notebook. He slid his fingertips gently down to her elbows, and finally her forearms and wrists. "She's clean. No weapons."

"You barely touched her!" Wheeler bellowed.

"We'll check her out better at the station. Cuff her, Joe. Let's go," Slater instructed, crisply.

"What about my niece? I'm Mother Viviana Reverent from St. Elizabeth's…"

"We'll need you to come down to the station, ma'am," Slater said over his shoulder as they rushed Alexa toward the stage door.

"This isn't over, Slater!" Wheeler barked after him.

"I'm sure it isn't," Slater said.

Darkness swept through Louie's Little Mardi Gras Bar. The only lights remaining were those over the bar. The small stage where customers performed karaoke each week was dim, and the glow from the bar area glinted off the tiny mirrors affixed to the disco ball dangling above the stage. The hundreds of masks stationed from floor to ceiling on every wall were draped in devilish contours. All the chairs had been turned up-side-down on the tables while the barmaid and table server swept up.

"You girls go ahead home," Louie told them. "I'll finish up."

"It's no trouble, Lou, there's only a half-hour more of clean up," Meg, the barmaid countered.

"You've got little ones to get home to. I know, they're probably in bed by now." He glanced up at the clock.

"They'd better be. It's past two a.m. It's just the bar clean up and the restocking for tomorrow night that needs doing. Now, go on, go home. I've got it," Louie insisted, shooing them toward the door.

The girls grabbed up their purses and jackets. "The restrooms are clean too," the server informed on her way out the door.

"Thanks, girls. Be safe going home. See you tomorrow," Louie said. He stood at the door and watched them walk to their cars, get in, and safely pull onto Liberty Avenue, then he closed and locked the door. Making his way back to the bar, he scanned the tables, the stage, and the many masks he'd collected over the years. The bar had been good to him, and he'd been excited about the wine tasting room that was about to open. Now…not so much.

Winnie had helped in the planning of the new venue. All of her enthusiasm kept him going on the project, but his zeal had since vaporized. He hoped it would return when the customers started pouring in and laughter filled the downstairs space. Who was he kidding? He missed Wynona Mulaney.

Letting out a careworn sigh, Louie whipped the towel from his shoulder and started pulling glasses from the dishwasher, wiping them down, and placing them back on the shelves.

"Winnie will show up for opening night," he mumbled to himself.

"Eh, I'm not so sure about that," a man's voice said from behind.

Louie swung around to find the man sitting in the shadows at the far end of bar. He wore a fedora, and what looked like a suit. He hadn't seen anyone dressed like that since...well, it had been a long time. "How'd you get in here?" Louie demanded. "*We're closed.* C'mon, I'll let you out." Pitching the towel onto the bar in frustration, Louie started for the door.

"Gee, Louie, I thought ya might offer an old friend a drink. I've only come to enjoy a cold beer and maybe talk some sense into ya," the man said.

Louie spun around. He eyed the shadowy figure, then panic washing over him, he whacked the switch on the wall, filling the bar with light. His eyes widened and he gasped. "It can't be...it just can't be. You've been gone since..."

"Yeah, yeah, yeah, I've been dead since 1964." Bobby slipped the fedora from his head and tossed it onto the bar. "It even sounds like a long time to me. Now, how about that beer?"

Louie was shell-shocked. He couldn't move. "Are you—you're...Bobby Starr, aren't ya?"

Bobby opened his arms wide. "In the fl—okay, well, maybe not in the flesh, but yes, I am Bobby Starr."

"You're...you're a ghost..."

Bobby held up halting hands. "*No.* I'm an *angel.* There's a difference. Ghosts are terrifying. I don't consider myself terrifying. I'm a fairly good-looking angel. Don't ya think?"

Louie could barely catch a breath. What in God's name would Bobby Starr be doing at his bar? Keeping his distance, he side-stepped his way to the bar, and with shaking hands, he grabbed a glass from the shelf, shoved it under the tap, and poured a tall, frothy beer, then he gulped it down. When the glass was empty, he looked up. Sure enough, Bobby Starr was still sitting there.

"Wh…whatta ya want?"

"I wanted that beer," Bobby said.

"Oh…oh yeah." Louie grabbed another glass and poured beer from the tap, then slid the glass down the bar. Bobby caught it, lifted it to his lips, and drank half the beer down. Louie stammered, "Is it…is it my time? Is that why you're here?"

"Not hardly." He wiped away froth from his upper lip. "I told ya, I'm here to talk some sense into ya. I don't know how long you've got left, Louie, but I do know you've got an opportunity to spend your remaining time being *happy*."

"Whatta ya mean?"

"You've got to stand up for yourself. You've got to defend your happiness. Now, you've got two phone calls to make. Wait…they don't have to be phone calls. You can have at least one conversation in person, and maybe that would be best. Especially, with your daughter," Bobby explained, then he hitched his chin toward the door.

Just then, someone knocked on the door. Louie's head jerked toward the door to hear Olivia calling from the other side, "Daddy! Daddy, are you in there?"

Louie turned back toward Bobby. He smiled, took up his fedora, placed it on his head, and raised his glass. "Balls in your court, Louie." He drank down the rest of the beer and slammed the glass onto the bar. "What's it gonna be?" With that, Bobby Starr was gone.

Olivia rapped on the door harder. "Daddy! Please come to the door. I need to talk to you!"

Louie raked a harried hand through his thick, white hair trying to catch his breath. Did he really see what he thought he just saw? Had Bobby Starr really been sitting at the bar. His gaze flashed to the end of the bar, and there it was, the glass the self-proclaimed angel had drunk from.

"*Daddy*! Open the door!" Olivia cried.

"I'm…" he swallowed, hard. "I'm coming." Louie hurried to the door, twisted the deadbolt, and opened it.

"Daddy…" Olivia threw her arms around her father.

"Olivia, what in God's name are you doing here at two a.m.?" Still trying to reclaim his composure, Louie pulled his daughter inside, closed the door, and locked it. "And I think it's time I've had a talk with you, Olivia Ann Shipman." He led her to a barstool, and then made his way around the bar, grabbing the beer glass, to pour another one from the tap.

"It's a bit late for you to be *drinking*, don't you think, Daddy?" Olivia asked, her tone dripped with reprimand.

"I'll drink when I want to, I'll stay out as late as I want to, wear a toga if I want to, and I'll damned well date *who I want to*, Olivia." He paused, set the beer aside, then looked into his daughter's watery gaze. "Look…sweetheart, I loved your mom, you know I did. I would've done anything for that woman, but she's gone now. I've got to make my *own way* now. I can't and won't depend on you and your brothers to be my social directors." Olivia opened her mouth to speak. Louie laid a hand on hers. "I've made a terrible mistake and let your concern for my welfare rule my decisions. I can't let that be anymore."

"Dad…I haven't come all the way downtown at two in the morning to give you orders. I couldn't sleep after what happened at home. I had to talk to you." Louie shot her a questioning look. She let out a beleaguered sigh. "Louis has been seeing something strange. It's happened twice now."

"What?"

Another sigh. "A man. He's claimed to talk to this man twice: once at the park, and just this afternoon at the gift shop in Robinson."

Louie glanced down the bar at the empty beer glass. Was Bobby Starr visiting his grandson? Why?

Olivia continued, "Louis wasn't willing to tell us what the man said, until tonight before he went to bed. He said the man kept telling him he should do the right thing. I don't know if there really was a man, we never saw him, and Josh said he searched the gift shop for him and couldn't find him. Anyway, Louis came into my room around ten to give me my birthday present, early. It was a beautiful angel statue. That's when he confessed Winnie had nothing to do with Nana's angel getting broken. *He* threw the ball. Winnie didn't want him to get in trouble, especially on his birthday. So, she said she had thrown it."

"And that's why you're here? To tell me Winnie didn't break the statue?" Louie was just this side of angry.

"Yes and no. I came because I've been wrong, Dad." Olivia held up a justifying hand. "Not that I'm in love with Winnie Mulaney. I still think she's too wild for you, but as Josh told me, I have no right to stand in the way of what *seems* to make you happy. At least, for now. I'm sorry. And I hope you can patch things up with Winnie."

"You do?"

Olivia half-smiled, then reached into her purse bringing out the red ball. Holding it up, she said, "Balls in *your court*, Dad." She tossed the ball across the bar. Louie caught it.

Chapter Fifteen

Strange Happenings

Alexa couldn't believe it, yet there she was sitting in the back of the Rambler, handcuffed, wearing a nun's tunic, suspected of stabbing a man she'd never met, never had access to, nor had motive to kill, Steve Wheeler. At least she was being escorted to the police station by 1965 Slater and Joe Randolph, not Detective Wheeler. Wheeler had been raising a ruckus about taking charge of her, but neither Slater nor Joe were having it. For that, she was thankful. Nonetheless, Slater's rigid gaze shifted from the road to the rearview mirror. It was quite obvious he was trying to figure out where he was supposed to know her from.

"I don't understand why you don't remember her, Slater. You introduced her to us as your sister-in-law. She went with us to question some of the old witnesses from the Starr investigation. In fact, Alexa took the position of seamstress for the operetta company when Pooky Mateer quit." Slater blew out an irritated breath. It wasn't difficult to see he was searching his mind for the moments Joe was describing, coming up with nothing, and not understanding why. He must've felt he was being gaslighted, like he was trapped in Rod Serling's Twilight Zone. Joe added, "Some of the guys said she was staying with you and Janey until she left for the convent. I figured that's why she's in the nun's dress."

"Janey's sister isn't Catholic or a nun, and she doesn't look like...*that*. I don't know *anyone* named Alexa Owl. That older nun, Mother Viviana Reverent, said she's wearing her niece's dress." Slater adamantly insisted. His eyes flicked to the rearview. "Who are you, what are you trying to pull, and where's Sister Viviana?"

Knowing all the answers to all Slater's questions and knowing not one of them were the least bit feasible, Alexa felt it was in everyone's best interest to stay silent. She turned her head to look out the window, trying not to focus on the tight ball of knots coiling in her stomach, and how hot she was under the tunic. What would happen when they arrived at the station? Where was Slater? Her Slater. The angel. How were they going to get out of this?

Never had she come face-to-face with the Bobby Starr of the past when she was visiting yesteryear with the angel Bobby Starr. What was the protocol for *this* situation? Would St. Pete intercede, or were they on their own? More terrifying: was *she* on *her own*?

The moment Alexa dreaded had arrived. Slater rolled the Rambler into the police station lot. Now what? At least they hadn't discovered the notebook. Then again, would that be such a bad thing? The door opened and Slater reached his hand out. "Come with me, Miss Owl."

He took hold of Alexa's arm and guided her into the station. Joe followed behind. Poor man. No doubt he was struggling with Slater's memory slip and questioning how this woman had duped them in such a spectacular manner. Slater led her to the chair next to his desk, and she sat down.

Wheeler burst into the room, pointing at Alexa, and hollering, "She stabbed my brother!"

"*Calm down*, Wheeler," Slater demanded.

"That's *impossible*," Alexa began. "I didn't have anything to stab him with. Furthermore, no matter what he was stabbed with, you won't find my fingerprints on it, because I never touched the man. Why would I? I don't even know him. I have no reason to want him dead. What was he doing on the catwalk? Was your brother part of the cast, a member of the stage crew, in the orchestra? Why was he there, Detective Wheeler?"

By the looks on 1965 Slater and Joe's faces, her quick-fire questions took them aback.

Wheeler was not so impressed. He lunged at Alexa. Joe pushed him back. "Her questions are solid, Wheeler! Now *back off!* I think we *all* need to calm down," Joe said succinctly.

Slater pitched his fedora onto his desk. "Joe's right. Take her down to booking and by the time you get back, we'll all have a chance to catch our breath." His gaze skimmed Wheeler, then Joe, and back to Alexa. "Then you'll have a lot of questions to answer, Miss Owl."

Wheeler shot Slater an abrasive scowl, then marched to his desk and plunked down. "And so will he."

"Come with me, Miss Owl." Joe helped Alexa from the chair. They walked down a corridor until they came to a door on the right marked *Booking*. Joe opened the door and Alexa stepped through. "Hey, Bernie, got one for ya," Joe called out as he removed the handcuffs from Alexa's wrists.

A tiny, bald, older man wearing what Alexa would consider spectacles rather than glasses stepped up to a counter. Bernie was wearing a pristine white shirt with a green tie. Green suspenders held up his trousers. She had him pegged at about sixty-two, maybe older. He pulled out a thick book from under the counter, an ink pad, and then, grabbing a hunk of pages, he flipped the book open with a heavy *clunk*. Screwing up his face as if he struggled to see the page, Bernie picked up a pen and began, "Name…" When no one replied, he squinted up over his spectacles at the woman.

"Oh…um…Alexa Owl. That's spelled O-w-l."

"Birthdate…"

"Um…um…June first, 19…19.." Good Lord, she couldn't mention her actual birthdate. Impatience filling his gaze, the man peered up again. Alexa blurted, "1934."

"Height…"

"Five-six."

Bernie's gaze moved to Joe. "Charge…"

"Suspected of murder," Joe replied, then under his breath, he added, "*I think*."

Bernie didn't so much as raise an eyebrow at a nun standing before him, suspected of murder. Most likely,

nothing surprised him. At his age, Bernie had probably seen it all. "Okay, honey. Gimme your right hand."
Around a beleaguered sigh, Alexa surrendered her right
hand. He took hold of her thumb, rolled it over the ink,
then pressed it against a square marked "*right thumb*" in
the book under her name and birthdate. Except…noth-
ing showed up but a big, black blotch. No arched lines,
no circles, no squiggles, only an inky spot. Bernie's baffled
expression mirrored Alexa's shock. He cleared his throat.
Alexa assumed he was attempting to project a dismissive
demeanor when he suggested, "Let's try your index finger…" he stretched out her finger, rolled it over the ink
pad, then pressed it against the next square marked "*right
index*", except this time, he pressed harder. Alexa feared
he'd break her knuckle.

"Ouch!" she griped.

"Sorry, just trying to get a good print." Again, Bernie
was taken aback as was Alexa. His eyes slid to Joe's, then
returned to Alexa. Again, no fingerprint, merely a black
blot. He wiped his fingers down his lips. "Ah, Sergeant
Randolph…I don't believe this woman has any fingerprints. It's a *rare* thing, but it does occur. I read an article
recently about a woman in Switzerland who doesn't have
them. I suggest we move on to taking her photograph.
I'll make a couple phone calls to see how to handle this.
Step right over here, honey."

Alexa wished he'd stop calling her *honey*. Joe urged
her to follow the little guy into a dark corner of the room
where a camera was sitting on a tripod next to a tall stool
stationed in front of a white screen with thin, black, vertical lines indicating heights starting at four-foot-one inch.

Joe ushered her toward the screen, and Bernie positioned her in front of it as he wanted her to stand, then he made his way to the Polaroid camera. There was a flash and the photo slipped out the front. Bernie snatched the photo from the slot and tossed it on the stool. "Turn to the right, honey." Alexa grudgingly complied. Another flash, and he set that photo aside too. "Now, to the left, please." She repositioned, and there was one more flash. "We're all done here, Sergeant."

Reluctantly, Joe snapped the handcuffs back onto Alexa's wrists. "Time for those questions Slater warned you about. I sure hope you've got answers."

What response could she possibly have for that? Alexa simply let him lead her out of the room. They weren't halfway down the corridor when Bernie burst out of the room. "Hey! Sergeant Randolph! Wait!" They turned to see the little man's bald head stained with a red flush and his face flattened in dismay.

"What's wrong?" Joe asked.

"Come back here. We've got a problem," he stated. Joe's perplexed gaze met Alexa's. Bernie held the door open for them as they stepped back into the room. He closed the door and handed Joe the polaroid photos he'd just taken of Alexa. "Take a look at these." Joe examined the pictures. His eyebrows raised, then he raised his gaze to meet Bernie's. "Th…that's just not possible. I know dang well the film in that camera is good. I'd just photographed someone not ten minutes before you brought *this one* in." Joe opened his lips to speak, but Bernie held up a halting hand. "C'mon, Sergeant, I want you to stand in front of the screen. I'm gonna take a picture of you. I gotta see for myself."

"What's going on?" Alexa asked.

Bernie held up a shaking finger. "Y-you just stand against the wall and *don't move*. Go on, Sergeant, step in front of the screen."

Alexa couldn't imagine why the man was so rattled.

Shooting Alexa another curious glance, Joe shepherded her to the wall, then stepped in front of the screen. A flash. The camera spit out the photo. Bernie blew on it to hurry the processing along. Finally, his eyes flicked to Joe. He held up the photo for them to see. "I knew the film was good. Look…here's the polaroid of Sergeant Randolph…" he held up another photo. "And here's a photo of you, Miss Owl."

Alexa gasped. Sure enough, the photo in Bernie's right hand was a clear picture of Joe, but the only image on the photograph in his left was that of the screen with the height chart. No brunette dressed in a blue tunic. No shadowy figure or double exposure. Nothing but the white height chart. Flabbergasted, the man displayed the remaining two polaroids he'd taken of Alexa. Nothing, except the image of the chart on those photos, either.

Bernie's voice was thin. "I'm coming to the squad room with you. No fingerprints. No photograph. Who the heck is this woman?"

Alexa's chest tightened. What now? C'mon, St. Pete, or Slater, or…or Bobby. *Someone* had to come to her aid. This situation was beyond her skills.

Bernie didn't wait up. He marched out the door. When Alexa and Joe stepped into the hallway, the man was almost to the squad room. For such a little guy, he sure could move fast. His stride resembled someone trying to get out of a burning house, or maybe a *haunted* house. There was no doubt Bernie considered Alexa some kind of freak or ghost or worse. Every few steps, he'd glance over his shoulder as if he wanted to be as far away from the weirdo as possible. Okay, Alexa always claimed weird was her super power, but this was getting way outta hand.

"He seems to be in a panic," Alexa said.

"Eh, Bernie's easy to wind up. Maybe you're like the lady in Switzerland who doesn't have fingerprints. As for the mug shot…" a shrug. "I'm sure there's a *reasonable* explanation. The camera's probably acting up. I'll bet it's twenty years old. They started using Polaroid's around 1948. That camera was probably bought in 1949. *God forbid* the precinct buy a new one."

They were only a few steps away from the squad room when they heard Bernie's distraught speech. "I've never seen anything like it in all my days, Slater. She's got no fingerprints. She's got no image. What the heck is goin' on here? I've heard she's your sister-in-law. What kind of family have you got?"

Joe and Alexa walked into the room. Everyone's eyes flicked up to stare at her. Slater barked, "I told you I *don't know* who she is."

"C'mon, Slater. She's been in this very room at least twice," Wheeler countered.

"Well, I don't remember seeing her." He swung around to face Alexa. "Wait a minute. Did *you* eat my sandwich?"

Alexa shrugged. "What can I say? I was hungry. Look, gentlemen, I *did not* kill that man. Obviously, you won't find my fingerprints on the knife. That said, no one saw me on the catwalk with the man, except for Detective Wheeler, and he was chasing me. I hardly had a chance to kill his brother at that time. No witness, no motive, no opportunity, and I didn't have a weapon; therefore, I had no *means*. I don't think you have much to hold me."

"Why was Wheeler chasing you?" Slater asked.

"It's like you said, Slater, he's a *pervert*. I had to throw my coffee on him to get away from him," Alexa stated.

Slater turned to look Wheeler up and down at his red cheeks and the big, brown stain down the front of his shirt. "So, that's what happened to your shirt?"

"Oh, you are a *bold* little nun. I'm not a *pervert!*" Wheeler yelled.

"While I don't remember telling her that, yeah, ya are, Wheeler," Slater yelled back.

"That woman is not a nun!" a woman cried out. Everyone turned to find Mother Viviana Reverent marching through the door. Letting the door slam behind her, she stomped toward the group. "I told you at the music hall, she's wearing my niece's tunic." Her aggravated gaze connected with Wheeler. "I had to call a *cab* to get here, but I'm here now. No thanks to *you, Detective Wheeler!* I *demand* to know what has happened to my niece."

In her peripheral vision, Alexa saw Slater, in spirit form, leaning against a nearby wall. It was about time. Obviously, he was only visible to her, providing instant comfort, even though she wasn't sure what he could do about the current state of affairs. Just then, Bobby showed up, standing next to Slater, also in spirit form. She heard him say, "Wow. You've got this all messed up, Slater. We *never* bumped into me when Alexa came to *my* past."

"*Shut up, Starr,*" Slater growled over his shoulder.

How angelic they are. Alexa sighed.

"Well, how 'bout it, Miss Owl? We may not have any solid proof you killed Steve Wheeler, but you *are* wearing another nun's clothing," the 1965 Slater said.

Alexa didn't want to rat Teresa out, and yet there seemed no other way. She attempted a soothing tone, "Mother Viviana Reverent, I promise I *did not* harm Teresa in any way…" How could she comfort the abbess of her niece's well-being without betraying the runaway Novitiate? "She…"

"Excuse me," a man called out in a British accent. Once again, everyone's attention turned to the door. Piers Linney and a young woman walked into the squad room. "Detective Slater, this is Jeanette Tustin. She has something very important to tell you."

"Can't it wait?" Slater asked. His tone fell somewhere between forced courtesy and controlled provocation.

"No, I don't believe it can. Jeanette, tell them what you told me."

Jeanette's cheeks were tarnished a fiery red, and her eyes were teary. She was still wearing the lovely blue ball gown from the party scene she did not get to participate in, and it was clear she now realized why. "I'm a good friend with a singer named Adam Gless. I thought we were more than friends, but he told me this morning he planned to run away with a girl who was supposed

to become a nun. He told me her name was Teresa."
Drawing a hand to her throat, Mother Viviana gasped.
Jeanette's wary gaze slid to the nun, and then back to
Slater. "I thought he meant he was going to run away
with her when the opera closed in two weeks, but evidently, he and she decided to go *during* the practice show
this afternoon."

The 1965 Slater said, "Thank you, Miss Tustin. We
appreciate you coming down to tell us that." He turned
to the nun. "I think you have your answer, Mother
Viviana. And I assume *you* changed clothing with Teresa.
Is that right, Miss Owl?"

The color in Mother Viviana's face instantly drained.
Her wide-eyed gaze flicked to the woman wearing the
blue tunic. There was no hiding the truth now. Alexa
said, "Yes, I did. I'm so sorry, Mother Viviana. Your niece
didn't want to become a nun. She wanted to be with
Adam."

Without warning, Mother Vivian let out a whimper
and collapsed on the floor. Slater and Wheeler rushed to
the nun's side. Slater gathered her into his arms. "Mother
Viviana…" He patted her face. "Mother Viviana…some-
one get her some water!" Joe rushed to the water cooler.
Slater looked up at Jeanette. "Thank you, ma'am. I think
you can go now."

"I don't think so," Piers supplied. "She's got more to
tell."

Slater helped Mother Viviana sit up. Wheeler grudgingly aided by supporting her head. The woman was in
a daze but coming conscious. Joe handed Slater a small,
pointy paper cup filled with water. While assisting the

nun to take a sip of the water, Slater said, "Please tell us quickly, ma'am." Still dazed, Mother Viviana took a tiny sip.

It wasn't hard to see Jeanette was shaken by the nun's collapse and being at a police station was adding to her distress, no doubt. "I…I think Adam might know something about that man…the man they found dead on the catwalk…"

Mother Viviana gasped again. Her head rolled, and she passed out in Slater's arms. Noticeably concealing his frustration, Slater's jaw clenched. He tapped her face again. "Mother Viviana…"

Wheeler stood, allowing the nun's head to fall back. "Go on, miss. What about the man on the catwalk…"

Jeanette's startled gaze shifted from the nun sprawled in the detective's arms to the detective pressing her for information. Pier's whispered, "Go on, Jeanette. This is important."

"I…I saw Adam shortly after he got to the music hall…in…in the dressing room. He asked me If I'd seen that voice coach on the catwalk with some other man. He said they were arguing. If they were there when I passed, I didn't see or hear them."

Wheeler's face bunched in agitation. Slater inquired, "*Whose* voice coach?"

"She's talking about Dorian Matias. Tallis Chamberlain's voice coach. Many of the singers employ coaches, but Dorian is exclusive to Tallis, and he's the *only* coach who hangs around the music hall. Believe me, he's more of a hindrance than a help," Piers reported.

"How did this kid know for sure it was Dorian? It's dark up there. It could've been *anyone*," Wheeler more demanded than asked.

Jeanette's fearful gaze swiftly slid to Slater. Alexa sensed she didn't want to talk to Wheeler, and she couldn't blame her. "Adam said it was the weird, tall, skinny guy who wears a big bow in his ponytail. That pretty much describes Tallis's coach."

Mother Vivian's head bobbed upward; her eyes fluttered open.

"Look," Piers began. "I don't mean to be…heartless, but they've cleared the music hall, there's coppers everywhere, and when Jeanette and I left to come here, the coroner went up to the catwalk to examine the dead man."

Around a moan, Mother Viviana fainted again. Slater simply couldn't hide his exasperation any longer. Scanning the group surrounding him, Slater said, "Bernie, you take care of Mother Viviana." Shocked by the order, Bernie stepped backward. Slater waved him forward and diffidently Bernie inched his way toward Slater. "I'm going to the music hall to see what's going on and what Doc knows so far. Joe, you take charge of the suspect and anything else that comes up."

"I don't believe *I'm* a *suspect* any longer, *Detective*," Alexa insisted.

"*Randolph? I'll* take charge!" Wheeler barked.

"*I don't think so*, Wheeler. You'll *recuse* yourself from the entire case," Slater said. "This is about family for you. And Miss Owl, *I'll say* when you're not a suspect any longer. Joe, put her in a cell until I get back." He wiggled his index finger at Bernie, and the little man hesitantly helped Slater lift the half-conscious nun from the floor and into the chair Alexa had just abandoned. Slater grabbed his fedora and hurried toward the door, while Joe led Alexa toward the same hallway where the booking room was located.

"I'll call a cab to take her wherever she needs to go," Bernie called after Slater.

Piers stepped forward to implore, "Please, Detective Slater, I don't want to close the show again like last year. I know it sounds callous, but the operetta company *needs* this show."

Slater paused at the door. "I understand, Mr. Linney. Miss Tustin, do you know where Adam Gless and Teresa may have gone?"

"Adam doesn't have a car. He takes the bus everywhere. I think they planned on heading to Nashville. My guess would be the train station, or maybe the Greyhound station," Jeanette replied.

"Thanks. Mr. Linney, I'll see you at the music hall shortly," Slater called over his shoulder as he made his exit.

As Joe led her away, Alexa glanced back. Angel Slater and Bobby were gone. What were those two angels up to?

Chapter Sixteen

Unlikely Team

Joe gently directed Alexa into a holding cell, removed the handcuffs, then quietly closed the gate. Even using a light push, the gate *clanged* when it struck the hitch and locked. Peering through the bars, Joe murmured, "Sorry."

Alexa waved a flippant hand. "No worries. I understand. Just find the person who killed Steve Wheeler so I can get out of here. The sooner the better."

Pitching her a withered smile, Joe nodded his reply, then exited the small, four cell block, closing a heavy door behind him. Alexa was alone. Funny, Bernie stated he'd booked another prisoner ten minutes prior to booking her. Where had that prisoner been taken? Canceling that silly, unimportant worry, she made her way to the bench attached to the block wall and plopped down. She scanned the other three cells. Not so much as a hooker lounging on a bench in any of the cells. Hm. Maybe they'd already paid their debt to society or to Detective Wheeler. Another thought she pushed aside for the sake of her own sanity. Leaning her weary head against the wall, Alexa closed her eyes.

"So, you ready to blow this joint?" Bobby asked.

Jerking forward, Alexa's eyes popped open. "Bobby! What's going on? Where's Slater?"

"I knew you'd be happy to see me…for once." She shot him a look. Grinning, he slipped the fedora from his head and sat down next to her. "Slater followed Slater to the music hall to see what's goin' on. I'm supposed to bust you outta here…" he pumped his eyebrows. "Guardian angel style."

"Let me get this straight…you and Slater are working together? I find that…unlikely."

Bobby shrugged. "Hey, an angel's gotta do what an angel's gotta do. Especially when our favorite MIT is involved. Right?"

Alexa snorted, "Mortal in Trouble. I think I fit into that category the moment I met you, Starr."

"That's what ya get for bein' an earthly guardian sponsor."

"*What*? How did I become a…a…*sponsor*?" Alexa rolled her eyes in self-reprimand. "Was it one of those links that I shouldn't have clicked on a social media site? They were probably advertising a gorgeous dress I thought I *had* to have, and I fell for it. *Ugh*!"

"Um…I don't know what you're talkin' about. The way it was explained to me, your name came up on the list, and that's why I showed up at your place three years ago."

Alexa expelled a suffering sigh. "Do you know how I got on the earthly sponsor list and, more importantly, how do I get off?

Bobby tossed the fedora onto the bench next to him. "I dunno."

"That's not helpful, Bobby."

"Sorry. Anyway, Slater says you've got my old notebook and I'm gonna ask a really *stupid* question: did ya look through it?"

"Of course I did." Alexa leaned forward to check the door, then tugged the notebook from inside the tunic. "Thankfully, Joe did a light pat down at the music hall, then never got around to a more detailed frisk when we arrived at the station. Things got a bit too chaotic. I think they forgot all about it."

"Why didn't you hand it over to Slater? It would've got you off the hook immediately. My notes indicate everyone who was, or should I say, *is involved* in the real estate fraud. They'll know Steve Wheeler was collecting money from clients to buy up properties in Washington county that didn't exist, then using the money to invest in high-*high*-risk commodities, skimming the profits too heavily, and using them to buy cars and jewelry, but not paying the clients their fair share. Then everything came crashing down when those commodities started collapsing all around him, and his clients, like Bert Mateer, took the financial fall."

"Yes, and according to your notes, he took good care of his brother, Detective Wheeler. The list of clients who lost tons of money was extensive, Bobby, great work. So, why did Steve take such good care of Dorian

Matias? Your notes indicate he lost very little money. Only a few hundred. Meanwhile, the others were losing thousands."

Bobby scrubbed a hand across his chin. "Something was definitely going on between Steve Wheeler and Dorian Matias. I didn't have a chance to get to the bottom of that before…well, you know, I died, or rather, I was murdered. Maybe somehow Dorian got a hold of the financials and was blackmailing Steve Wheeler." He shook his head. "Although, I didn't think so, because if that were true, Steve would've told his big brother, the detective, and I think *he* would've taken Dorian Matias right out of the equation."

"I think you're right. Detective Wheeler is quite unscrupulous. So…you had another theory?" Alexa delved.

"I did…I still do, but I'm not ready to talk about it, not yet" Bobby said. "We've got to get the notebook to 1965 Slater. He'll put it all together."

"I've got to ask…was Royce Hathaway involved?"

"Thankfully, no. I was *relieved* to find he was innocent. He's good to my Maisie, and now Katherine's pregnant," Bobby said. Alexa sensed a touch of regret in his words. He missed his little girl, and she felt he was sad that the new baby wasn't his.

"I'm relieved too," Alexa softly said. "But here's the catch: Slater, who's running out of time quickly, was instructed to find *your* killer, not Bert Mateer's, not Steve Wheeler's, and certainly not to shut down or even expose real estate fraud. I get it. All these things are connected, but will it all lead to the original objective? Finding *your* killer?"

"For Slater's sake, I sure hope so," Bobby said. "Look, I think they knew I was closing in on the truth. Problem was, I didn't know they were closing in on me. One of them did it. I just don't know who, and obviously, I don't know how, since I didn't even realize I was murdered."

"Slater and I know the how. We've got to get the who, and we've got to get there fast. With all that in mind, how are we getting the notebook to 1965 Slater?"

Dean Martin would've loved Bobby Starr. His naughty grin was reminiscent of the famous crooner, and presently, Bobby was flaunting it. "Like this…" He snapped his fingers.

Gasping, Alexa leapt to her feet in pure awe. "Oh, my God! I'm…I'm *invisible*!" Arms open wide, she turned in a small circle looking for any trace of herself, then she looked up at the still grinning Bobby Starr. "I don't know if this is breaking protocol, but it is so cool! Can I stay this way through the rest of the case?"

"Now, *that* would be breaking protocol. I'm only do-ing this to get you outta here and get the notebook into Slater's desk." He held up his hand. "That doesn't mean the notebook is invisible, as you can plainly see." He was right. Alexa held up the book, and sure enough, it was floating in midair, as if no one was in the cell. Bobby warned, "So, there's still a good bit of sneaking around to be done, Mrs. Owl."

"I understand. Still, it should be easier to sneak a notebook into the squad room than a whole person."

"Don't bet on it. Let's go," Bobby said. He grabbed his fedora, stuck it on his head, and then opened the cell gate.

"Wait…I don't understand. Why can't they see our clothing?"

"Because I'm an angel and I don't want them to." They stepped out of the cell. "Unfortunately, the notebook is an outside object. If someone sees you, the notebook will be floating on air. Like I said, not as easy as you think."

Just then, the door to the small cell block opened and Detective Wheeler furtively stepped inside, closing the door behind him. "Okay, Sister Alexa, it's time for you and me…"

Alexa hurried into the cell across from the one she'd just occupied, knelt down, and shoved the notebook under the bench, holding it against the bottom. Obviously stunned to find the cells empty and the gates open, Wheeler slowly made his way along the cells. "Sister Alexa…" As he passed, Bobby slipped the keys to the cells from Wheeler's pocket and dropped them to the floor. Wheeler stepped toward the cell Alexa was squatting inside. Bobby shot her a look, snapped his fingers, and suddenly, she was visible! What was he doing?

Wheeler's lips curled into a disgusting smirk. "Whatcha doin', Sister? Prayin'? I think your prayer has been answered. I've come to keep you company." Flabbergasted, Alexa jumped up with the notebook in her hand. Wheeler's eyes widened. "Hey, you've still got that notebook…" He moved toward her. Alexa's gaze whipped to Bobby. Grinning, he nodded. She let Wheeler come close and when he tried to grab her, Alexa ducked under his arms and elbowed him hard in the ribs. Wheeler toppled forward, falling onto the bench with a grunt. Alexa made haste for the cell gate. As she jumped through, Bobby slammed it shut, and with another snap of Bobby's fingers, she was invisible again.

Frantic, Wheeler scrambled to his feet and across the cell to grab the bars. He shook them violently. "Hey! Where'd ya go?" He yelled, and then his jaw dropped open, and his eyes bulged in distress when the notebook floated past the cell and toward the door.

"You move pretty good for a nun," Bobby remarked as they stepped out of the cell block, closing the door behind them.

Once in the hallway, Alexa could not contain her giggles. Bobby raised a finger to his lips to whisper, "They can't see you, but they can hear you, darlin'. C'mon."

The hallway was empty. They had a clear path to the squad room, and as far as Alexa was concerned, with Wheeler detained, they had one less cop to worry about when they got there. Wheeler cried out, "Hey! Hey! Somebody! Get me outta here!"

Even though the notebook was in Alexa's very own hand, it was astonishing to see it gliding down the hallway, four feet from the floor. She had no sooner passed the booking room than the door whipped open. Alexa whirled around to see Bernie step into the corridor, looking up and down. There was no question he'd heard Wheeler's calls for help. Then his eyes found the flying notebook. His spine stiffened. His mouth formed a long, slender 'O'. Making the most unusual sounds, Bernie grabbed the door jamb as if he would fall backward while his gaze clung to the notebook drifting in the hallway.

Alexa kept moving, slowly walking backward. Bernie couldn't see her, but he had no problem seeing the notebook. *Now what?* Instantaneously, Bernie answered her question. The horrified man backed into the booking room and closed the door. There was no uncertainty. Bernie had had his fill of strange happenings for one day. Wheeler was on his own.

Alexa turned to see Bobby leaning against the wall, stifling a good laugh. Yeah, they didn't have to worry about ol' Bernie. He wasn't going to admit to anyone what he just saw, or what he *thought* he saw. In the short distance, behind the door that led into the cell block, they could hear Wheeler's muffled calls for assistance growing more intense and the gate on the cell rattling and banging. Encouraging her to ignore the uproar, Bobby waved her on to the biggest challenge: the squad room.

When they reached the threshold to the squad room, Bobby stepped forward to peek in, then turned to Alexa. "There's no one in there except for that sergeant. The other detectives must be out on cases. He's busy writing something. Probably a report. You stay here. I'm gonna cause a commotion, and when he reacts, you'll have a few seconds to get to Slater's desk and put the notebook in the middle drawer."

"What kind of commotion?"

"The sergeant's back is to us. Go to the water cooler…" Bobby hitched his chin toward the cooler along the same wall where the archway was. "Stand next to it with the notebook hidden behind, then get ready to put it in Slater's desk. I'll be back shortly, unless I'm having too much fun."

"Now I'm terrified," Alexa stated.

Bobby winked. "It's all about trust, darlin'."

Trust or not, there was not another minute to waste. Alexa stepped through the arch and scurried to the water cooler, slipped the notebook behind it, and waited for the disturbance to begin. Within a nanosecond, Wheeler's cries for help and the *banging* of the cell gate were amplified as if he and the gate were in the squad room. "Where is everybody? I need help in here! Hey! Prisoner escape! Prisoner escape!" Joe's head jolted up. Baffled, he spun his chair around, looking for Wheeler. Wheeler hollered again, "*Help! I need help!*" Joe sprung from his seat to dart down the hallway.

Alexa couldn't resist. Keeping the notebook behind the wall, she returned to the arch to peer down the hallway. Bernie had just come out of the Booking room and was headed her way with a briefcase in hand. Joe came to a sliding stop. "Bernie! What's goin' on with Wheeler?"

"Don't know. Don't wanna know," Bernie replied, then without so much as a peep at the closed door that led to the cell block, he picked up his pace toward the squad room.

Joe rushed to the door and tried to turn the knob, but it wouldn't move. "Hey!" Wheeled shouted. "Somebody come get me!" Joe pushed and shoved at the door, to no avail, while Bobby leaned against the wall enjoying the struggle.

Bernie was almost to the squad room. Alexa knew it was time to get the notebook to the desk drawer before he came in. Swiftly, she went to Slater's desk, opened the middle drawer, stuffed the notebook inside, then slammed the drawer closed. Alexa watched Bernie make haste out the door. Wheeler's cries weren't as loud as before, yet he was still shouting, and the sound of pounding had Alexa heading toward Bobby's "commotion."

She had just arrived at the top of the hall when Joe was attempting another heave-ho. Bobby winked at Alexa, then allowed the door to fling open, sending Joe floundering into the cell block. Alexa jogged toward the brouhaha to follow Bobby into the cell block.

"It's about time, Randolph! Where've you been? That little witch escaped and we gotta find her before Slater gets back! Now, get me outta here!"

Picking himself from the floor and yanking a pair of keys from his hip pocket, Joe groused, "Hold on a minute, Wheeler. How'd you let a *nun* get past you?" He hesitated. "What were you doin' in here?"

"You heard that old lady. She ain't no nun! C'mon, hurry up!"

Joe stuck the key into the lock on the gate, then attempted to slide it open. The gate rattled but didn't budge. He wiggled the key. Still the gate remained solid. He pulled it out and tried again. The gate remained closed. Letting out a vexed breath, Joe tried again. Wheeler yanked and shook the gate. "That's not helping!" Joe groused.

"Gimme that key," Wheeler snarled.

Joe shoved the key through the bars. Snatching the keys from Joe's hand, Wheeler reached around the bars and pushed the key into the slot. He twisted it right, then left. Still, the gate was locked tight.

Bobby took Alexa by the arm and led her into the hallway. "That outta keep them busy for a while. Let's head to the music hall and see what Slater's up to."

"Which one?"

Bobby chuckled. "Pick your poison."

Knowing his 1965 counterpart would be in the music hall somewhere, Slater remained invisible. By the time he had arrived, the backstage area had been cleared. The main curtain was open, revealing the auditorium. Members of the cast, stage crew, and orchestra were seated in the auditorium, waiting to be interviewed. Slater noticed the school students and the nuns had been released. As Slater rounded the side curtains, stage right, two medics were carefully lowering a basket, cradling a black body bag from the catwalk. Two police officers standing on the stage were looking upward, ready to lift the body bag from the basket and place it on a gurney stationed nearby to be transferred to the coroner's lab.

His hands clasped in front of his torso; the tall, lean coroner supervised the basket's descent. Doc stood beside the1965 Slater. Once the basket was in the officer's grasp and carefully steered toward the gurney, Doc reached down to his bag and passed a pair of bloody scissors by the tips of the blades to Slater. "These are dressmaker shears. My wife has a pair. They are *very* sharp and were used as the murder weapon. Mr. Wheeler hasn't been dead long, four hours perhaps. Rigor mortis has only formed in his facial tissue."

Examining the shears, 1965 Slater said, "I hope you can get prints from the handles."

"Unless the killer was wearing gloves, I'm sure we can," Doc supplied.

"Yeah…" Slater murmured thoughtfully. He handed the shears back to Doc. "I suppose you're the man to ask…it is possible for someone *not* to have fingerprints?"

"It's called Adermatoglyphia. Very rare. We believe Adermatoglyphia is genetic, and we're just starting to study the how and whys of the condition. Why do you ask?"

"We have a woman in custody, a suspect in this stabbing." The 1965 Slater held up the shears. "She's looking more suspicious than ever now that we have the murder weapon, and it's *not* a knife. She was the seamstress for the operetta company. We tried to fingerprint her and came up with nothing," Slater explained.

"Interesting. I haven't heard of a case in the United States, only Switzerland. I'd like to examine this woman. Could you bring her to my lab?"

"Sure will." The *click, click, click* of the gurney's wheels over the stage floor drew Doc's attention. Slater gave him back the shears. Doc carefully placed them in his bag, then scooped it up and followed the medics pushing the gurney across the stage toward the door.

An officer approached 1965 Slater. "We've got everyone in the auditorium and have released the kids and the nuns, and Mrs. Mateer, although she hasn't left yet. Everyone else is ready to be interviewed and they're gettin' antsy."

"Thanks." The 1965 Slater took a peek at the auditorium. "I see you've got them all toward the front. Good. I'll take a seat in the back row in a few minutes, and you can start sending them back. I need some officers to go to the train station and some to the Greyhound station. We need to find a young man named Adam Gless. You can find a picture of him in the operetta program."

Angel Slater scrutinized the witnesses seated in the auditorium. He noticed Pooky Mateer sitting with Katherine and Royce chatting. Then his gaze found Tallis Chamberlain. The lovely soprano appeared frazzled, desperately searching the theater. The angel knew what she was thinking. Where's Dorian Matias? Good question.

"That might be complicated," the officer warned. "We just got word there's anti-war demonstrations taking place at both places. Seems there's a large group of soldiers coming home on both transits today."

"I don't care if the president is arriving, we need to find Adam Gless," 1965 Slater stated. "Has an officer been dispatched to Dorian Matias's apartment?"

"About fifteen minutes ago," the officer replied.

"Good. Let me know if he's found. If not, put out an all-points bulletin for him." With a nod of understanding, the officer walked away. The 1965 Slater looked up at the catwalk and then made his way to the ladder and climbed.

Still invisible to mortals, Bobby and Alexa appeared as 1965 Slater was stepping onto the catwalk. "What's happening?" Alexa quietly asked angel Slater.

"Nothing good, I'm afraid. Steve Wheeler was killed with a pair of *dressmaker's shears*," Slater said.

"I have no doubt they came from the costume room," Alexa put in. "Before I left the costume room, and before my game of hide-and-seek with Wheeler, I noticed the shears were missing. Have you seen Dorian Matais?"

"No. We need to find him *and* Adam Gless, fast," Slater replied.

"Come to think of it, I heard Dorian on the pay-phone yesterday telling someone he needed to see them and not to be late. Whoever it was, they were supposed to meet him here today. At the time, I dismissed the conversation. Now, I have to wonder if it was Steve Wheeler," Alexa explained.

"When were you planning to tell me all this?" Slater asked.

"I've been a little preoccupied if you haven't noticed."

"I just sent…er…I mean, 1965 me sent men to the train station and the bus station to look for Adam Gless. I think we should head there too. If I was Dorian Matias, I'd be leaving town. We might just get lucky," Slater said.

"What about the airport? Dorian seems to have a lot of money. More money than Adam, that's for sure," Alexa put in.

"If I were Dorian, and I'd just killed someone, especially the brother of a police officer, I'd try to get out of the country," Slater said.

"It's got to be after three o'clock. The international flights have left Pittsburgh by now," Alexa reasoned.

"Remember, this is 1965. Pittsburgh didn't become an international airport until 1968. No, his best bet is to jump a train or the bus heading north toward Canada. I believe he can catch a transfer in New York that travels straight through." Slater glanced up toward the cat-walk to check on his counterpart's movements. The 1965 Slater was examining the small, dark space where Steve Wheeler had been lying.

"What makes you think Dorian has a lot of money?" Bobby inquired.

"He dresses well, and he drives a very expensive sports car—a Corvette," Alexa replied.

"Looks can be very deceiving. Katherine used to talk about Dorian all the time. Seems Tallis pays for everything; his clothes, the rent on his apartment, and according to Katherine, he drives one of Tallis's sports cars around. He probably doesn't own the Corvette, unless Tallis gave it as a gift. That said, Tallis Chamberlain may be a lot of things, but I don't think she'd finance an escape to Canada for a murderer," Bobby explained.

"That explains why he's so protective of Tallis. Are they, or should I say, *were* they lovers?" Alexa inquired.

Bobby made a face. "Oh, I don't think so."

"I see. Then what's the attraction?"

"Katherine says he's a very talented pianist and vocal coach. Unfortunately for Dorian, he didn't have enough talent to be a singer. He's also very pushy about getting Tallis what she wants, well, except as a primary lead in the shows," Bobby said.

"We'd better get going," Slater pressed.

"Okay, but before we go, I need a change of clothes. I can't stand this nun's tunic for five more minutes. It's like a furnace under here," Alexa said.

"Just take it off," Bobby said.

"I can't just *take it off*," Alexa groused.

Just then, 1965 Slater came down the ladder. Alexa, angel Slater, and Bobby stopped talking until he passed. Bobby said, "Trust me, Alexa. Just take it off. It'll be okay, I promise."

Alexa searched Bobby's face. He was being sincere. It was all about trust. She lifted her shoulder. "Okay…" With that, she pulled the tunic over her head. Her smile stretched up to her deep brown eyes. Under the tunic, she was sporting yet another casual outfit. A pair of hip-hugging, bell-bottom jeans, and a cream ribbed turtleneck. Maybe that's why she was so hot. Her gaze met Bobby's.

"Better?" Bobby asked.

"Much. Thank you."

"*Good.* Let's go," Slater said.

"I won't be going with you," Bobby announced. "Squad stuff to tend to, I'm afraid. I'll walk you to the stage door, but once you pass through, Alexa, you will be visible again."

Alexa nodded her understanding. Slater set off across the stage with Alexa on his heels, while Bobby brought up the rear. Slater pushed the stage door open and as he stepped through, his invisibility swept away as dust particles in the wind and bit-by-bit his human form materialized. Utterly awestruck, Alexa followed, looking down to watch her invisibility vaporize and her body reappear. With the blue tunic flung over her arm, she swung around to say goodbye to Bobby. He was gone.

Slater was making haste across the parking lot when an officer rushed toward him. "Detective Slater! We found Dorian Matias at his apartment. He's dead. He was stabbed, but they don't know with what. No murder weapon was found at the scene."

Chapter Seventeen

An Eye for an Eye

As the officer hurried back to his cruiser, Slater started toward the Rambler.

"What now?" Alexa asked with an exasperated sigh as she picked up her pace to keep up with Slater. Time was running out, and the case was getting more complicated by the hour. Dorian Matias was dead? Murdered? By whom? Certainly not Detective Wheeler—he was too busy chasing after a nun with a notebook.

Alexa was trying to wrap her head around all the events: Bert Mateer's murder, Bobby's murder, Steve Wheeler's murder, and a real estate fraud that striped so many of their savings. Sewing shears…the Novitiate nun in the bathroom, and Pooky Mateer coming out of said bathroom.

Grabbing Slater's arm, Alexa stopped short. "Wait!"

"What?"

Alexa shoved the blue tunic into Slater's chest. "Hold this!"

"*What? Why?*" Slater asked.

But Alexa was already running toward the stage door, up the three steps, grabbing the knob, and rushing inside the music hall. Tossing all fears of being spotted to the wind, she darted through the narrow, backstage passage, and through stage right. Thankfully, the entire backstage area was quiet and abandoned. Police officers, operetta members, and 1965 Slater were in the auditorium area. Alexa scurried down the hallway and rounded the bend into the hallway where the ladies' room was located. Before she pushed through the door, Slater had caught up and grabbed her arm.

"What are you doing?" he demanded.

"I've got to get something out of the bathroom. C'mon!"

Slater took a step backward. "I'm not goin' in *there*."

Alexa rolled her eyes. "Suit yourself." With that, she yanked the door open and stepped inside. Quickly, she traversed the empty room to the stall she'd used earlier to change into the nun's tunic and headdress. Flipping the lid open on the feminine hygiene box, Alexa gingerly pulled out the yellow satin ribbon. She hesitated to study the white glove still lying on the floor between the sink and the trashcan. Pooky had to have dropped it and was searching inside her purse for the glove when she passed her in the hallway.

The bathroom door creaked open. Alexa flinched and spun around. Slater whispered through the slight gap, "What're ya doin' in there?"

"Come in and *see*," Alexa suggested concisely.

"*No way*," Slater insisted, closing the door.

Alexa bent down to pick up the glove. As she straightened, she noticed the lid on the trashcan was slightly ajar. She stood back, crossing her arms over her chest, analyzing the can. Had the can been bumped, or had someone shoved something into it? She lifted the lid and let out a tiny gasp. Lying atop discarded brown paper towels was a crumpled heap of black clothing. Alexa reached in to pull out the bundle, then pulled it apart to find a black turtleneck tunic and a pair of black crop pants.

Again, the door wheezed open. "*Alexa…*"

"You will not believe what I've found. Get in here, Slater."

"I don't go through my wife's purse, and I don't go into ladies' rooms," Slater stated. "We've got to get going. We've got to find Adam Gless."

"We don't need Adam Gless. He *didn't* see Dorian Matias on the catwalk. Look…" she held up the clothing for Slater to study through the crack.

Slater pushed the door wide open, then wincing while taking a look, he asked, "Whose clothes are those?"

"I bumped into Pooky Mateer on my way into the ladies' room when I changed clothes with Teresa. I think Pooky was in here changing, too. Look…a white glove and a yellow ribbon. She was wearing one white glove and searching through her purse for the other when I bumped into her. I think she was wearing the ribbon in her hair to make it *look like* Steve Wheeler was meeting with Dorian, but it was actually Pooky. Lord knows she's as tall and thin as Dorian, and *she* stabbed him with the sewing shears. I'll bet Dorian Matias was already dead by the time Adam saw Pooky and Steve on the catwalk. It's *Pooky* we need to find, *not* Adam Gless."

"Pooky's in the auditorium. Let's go!" Slater declared. He let the door drop closed.

Alexa gathered the clothing under her arm and darted out the door after him. They ran down the hallway, turned right, and jogged a little farther until they came to a door marked *Auditorium*. Slater pushed the door open just a bit to peer through. "Pooky's walking up the aisle toward the exit. We'll catch her in the parking lot." Slater swung around to race down the corridor toward the backstage.

"How far can she get? She doesn't have a car," Alexa reasoned, as she chased after him.

"She doesn't, but Hazel does!"

When they reached stage right, Slater bolted across the stage. Alexa slid to a stop, trying to catch her breath, and trying to rally the guts to cross the stage as he had. Not happening. She took the longer but safer route along the narrow corridor behind the backdrop. By the time she arrived at stage left, the stage entrance door was closing. Slater was already outside.

Alexa pressed through the door to see Slater charging across the parking lot toward Pooky, who had her hand on the handle of a red and white Ford Fairlane. Slater called out, "Pooky! Pooky Mateer, *stop!*"

Pooky's head snapped toward Slater. Her face flattened in fear. Alexa had no reason to rush now. Slater had the situation in hand. Alexa slowed to make her way across the lot casually. She could hear a woman sitting in the Fairlane yelling, "Pooky! Get in the car! Get in the car, *now*!"

Closer to the vehicle, Slater said, "Patrice Mateer, please remain still."

As Alexa drew near, she could see the woman in the car was Pooky's sister, Hazel. Her little dog stood on her lap, paws on the steering wheel, barking at the strange man. Hazel cried out once more, "*Pooky*! Get in!"

Pooky's hand slipped away from the handle. She bowed her head against the car in defeat. Slater touched her shoulder. "Mrs. Mateer, I want to talk to you about the murders of Steve Wheeler and Dorian Matias."

Alexa was now standing at Slater's shoulder. At last, Pooky lifted her head and dragged her soggy gaze to meet Slater's. "They killed my Bert, Detective Slater. They took our money, and they poisoned him. That Dorian Matias would bring Bert tea every evening during rehearsals. I couldn't figure out why he was being so kind to Bert. He told Bert tea was good for the vocal cords and might help his voice. Bert wanted so badly to be a good singer. He gladly drank the tea. Little did we know the tea was laced with tiny drops of cyanide. Not quite enough to kill him, mind you, but enough to make him sick and suffer, until it did kill him." She unsnapped her purse and dug through until she came up with a handkerchief embroidered with pink roses.

"Please, Mrs. Mateer, come with me. We'll talk in my cruiser on the way to the station," Slater said. He offered her his arm. Pooky accepted it and Slater escorted her toward the Rambler.

How very angelic of him, Alexa thought, as she followed.

"I'm calling a lawyer, Pooky! As soon as I get home! I'm calling a lawyer," Hazel yelled from inside the Fairlane, and then she pulled out of the parking spot, whizzing toward Beechwood Avenue.

Alexa leaned in to whisper, "You're taking 1965 Slater's vehicle? How will he get back to the station?"

Out of the side of his mouth, Slater replied, "As I recall, he's a smart guy. He'll figure it out."

"Once again, you're *just like* Bobby," Alexa grumbled quietly. Though she doubted anyone could hear their hushed conversation over Pooky's not-so-hushed sniffles.

"Hey, an angel's got to do what an angel's got to do."

"Where have I heard *that one* before?"

Slater opened the passenger door for Pooky, she slid into the Rambler, then he opened the backdoor, tossed the blue tunic onto the seat, and waved Alexa inside behind the caging. Pulling a pair of keys from his suit jacket, he jogged around the car to get into the driver's seat. Pooky was blowing her nose.

Wincing while starting the car, Slater asked, "How do you know it was Dorian Matias who was poisoning your husband?"

"I told you; my sister is very independent. She's savvy too. Hazel spent weeks poring over my financial information, making phone calls, and she visited with Steve Wheeler on my behalf twice. On both occasions, Dorian was either sitting in Mr. Wheeler's office or he came in as she was leaving. Hazel claims they were com-mitting fraud. Real estate fraud. According to Bert's account, Lifetime Investments was purchasing property in Washington County. Only, there was no property. Evidently, he was using the investor's money for personal greed."

Apparently, the blue tulle bucket hat on Pooky's head had become too hot. Alexa identified with her discomfort after her afternoon wearing that heavy tunic. Pooky lifted the hat from her head to lay it on her lap, and the long, brunette mane she'd tucked underneath spilled around her shoulders. Alexa blinked back in instant recognition. Pooky was the tall brunette standing at the coffee station just outside the costume room two nights ago when Katherine came to introduce herself. It must've been Pooky who'd left the mysterious note that warned, *Careful what you drink.* Now, Alexa had a complete understanding of why she felt compelled to alert her—she knew Dorian had poisoned Bert's tea.

Alexa scooched close to the caging. Holding up the black turtleneck sweater in her right hand and the black crop pants with the other, she asked, "Pooky, are these your clothes?"

Reluctantly, Pooky glanced over her shoulder. Lips quivering, she replied, "Yes."

Alexa held up the yellow ribbon. "And this too?"

"Yes…well, no. Not really. When the operetta company decided to perform *The Merry Widow*, and I went back to the music hall to work in the costume room, Hazel insisted we push for information on Bert's death. I knew Bobby Starr had to be a victim, too. Hazel pushed and pushed. She was relentless. She'd say, *stop being such a coward, Pooky! They killed your husband, for crying out loud!* But I was afraid, don't you understand? I was afraid if I went to the police, they'd kill me like they did Bert and that poor Bobby Starr."

"How do you know they killed Mr. Starr?" Slater asked.

"Dorian told me. You see, Hazel…and I…believed Mr. Starr was investigating the fraud for Bert. They found out, and they killed him too. I almost told that nice Detective Wheeler what we found out. He comes to check on me every now and then. But I was beginning to worry he might be related to Steve Wheeler."

Alexa heard Slater grumble under his breath. "*Really?*" He continued, "Okay, so after a whole year, how did you end up killing Dorian Matias *and* Steve Wheeler in one day?"

"Well, finally we, Hazel, and me, made a plan. She drove me to Dorian's apartment. I wanted him to tell me the truth, but mostly, I wanted an apology for all the pain and sorrow he and his *friend* caused me."

"You wanted an *apology?*" Alexa questioned before she could stop herself.

"Hazel wanted more. She wanted a confession, and amazingly enough, that's what I got. Dorian wasn't sorry for what he did. He was rather proud of himself when told me how they'd swindled people out of thousands of dollars. He bragged about how he slowly poisoned Bert and how they killed Bobby Starr too. In fact, he told me he killed Bobby the same way he killed his *own mother*— he doused her pajamas in cyanide. His *own mother*. He said she was a worthless drunk. He called them all, Bert, Bobby, *and his mother*, awful names. I was so angry. After about fifteen minutes or so, Dorian got up out of his seat. He said he had to meet Steve at the music hall. He was unhappy with him because he'd promised to leave his wife and run away with Dorian. I had to wonder if he was gonna poison him, too. Not that he didn't deserve it."

"And that's when you stabbed him? Where'd you get the knife?" Slater asked.

"That's when I demanded an apology. Dorian laughed and pushed me away. Well, I was *so mad*. Madder than I've *ever* been. I didn't kill him with a knife. I had the sewing shears from the costume room with me. I'd stopped in the night before, after rehearsals, and picked them up. They were mine, after all. And I shoved them *right into his chest*."

Slater's expression reflected Alexa's shock. Nonetheless, he fished, "And Steve Wheeler?"

"He wasn't part of the original plan, mainly because we didn't know where he was, but now I knew where to find the dirty scoundrel. I took my sewing shears with me."

"You mean, you pulled the shears out of Mr. Matias, and then took them with you?" Slater confirmed, his tone was on the edgy side of flabbergasted.

"Yes. I wasn't going to waste a perfectly good pair of shears on that awful man. When I went into Dorian's bedroom, I found a black turtleneck and a pair of black pants on a chair. He had a collection of ribbons on his dresser. He always wore one in his ponytail, you know. I couldn't believe how many he had, all colors. Do you know he had a *chartreuse* ribbon? Chartreuse is such an uncommon color for a ribbon. I almost took it, but I took a yellow one instead, I think. He also had a lovely satchel next to the chair with sheet music inside. I took the music out and stuffed the clothes and the ribbon inside. Oh…" Pooky dug inside her purse, then pulled out a tiny, brown dropper bottle. Handing it to Slater, she added, "I found this. I bet that's what he kept the poison in. I think there might be some left inside." Trying to hide his shock, but failing, Slater held the three milliliter bottle up for Alexa to see.

"Anyway, then Hazel drove me to the music hall. I didn't expect anyone to be around. It was early, about ten o'clock, but that nice young singer, Adam Gless, was standing outside the stage door smoking a cigarette. I asked if he'd seen Steve Wheeler, but he said he didn't know who that was. So, I went inside and changed my clothes in the bathroom. I looked around for Steve Wheeler, but I couldn't find him. Then, I saw him climbing the ladder to the catwalk."

Stuffing the bottle into his jacket, Slater probed, "Then what happened?"

Pooky dragged in a deep breath. "Well, normally, I'm terrified of heights, but I was *just so mad*. I climbed *right up that ladder*. We argued. To be honest, I don't even remember the conversation. I just remember feeling so outraged by what the two of them had done to my Bert, Bobby Starr, and everyone else they'd cheated. I remember him telling me to leave him alone, to go home, then he turned away from me, and that's when I *stabbed him* with the shears. An eye for an eye, Detective Slater." In a gesture of justification, Pooky crossed her arms over her chest and gave her head a stiff nod.

"But you didn't take the shears with you that time. They were found still stuck in his back," Slater pointed out.

"No…I knew I had to get out of there." She waved a flippant hand. "I'll buy a new pair." With that, Pooky gazed out the window as if they were taking a Sunday ride through the country. Slater exchanged a stunned glance with Alexa in the rearview mirror.

Clearing her throat, Alexa asked, "Pooky, obviously, you changed back into your own clothes after you stabbed Steve Wheeler. Why did you stay at the music hall? Why didn't you leave?"

"I wanted to see the show," Pooky replied, as if the question appalled her.

"But your sister was waiting for you in the parking lot," Alexa pointed out.

Pooky shrugged. "Hazel hates opera."

Alexa's baffled gaze shot to the rearview. Slater shook his head.

Chapter Eighteen

Crackin' Up

Slater hadn't driven very far down the parkway before Alexa inquired, "Where are we going?"

"To the station. I want to book Pooky before *you-know-who* returns from the music hall," Slater said.

"I don't think it's a good idea for me to go to the station. Not after recent events," Alexa put in.

"Where do you want to go?"

"Turn around. Take me to St. Elizabeth's. I have some unfinished business," Alexa said.

Slater met her gaze in the rearview mirror. Favoring her with a svelte, but knowing smile, he steered onto the next ramp and made the circle to return to Carnegie.

When they arrived at St. Elizabeth's, Slater got out of the car to open the backdoor for Alexa. Gathering up the blue tunic, she got out of the Rambler. "All the evidence I collected in the ladies' room is in the backseat," she said. "They may need to exhume Dorian's mother. Although, I'm not sure if…"

"We'll see what Doc can do. How will you get back?"

"I'm pretty smart. I'll figure it out." Alexa kissed him on the cheek. "Now, go finish this assignment, and don't dilly-dally, Slater."

"See ya later, Miss Owl," he said, as he slipped back into the car, then pulled away from the curb to drive down Third Avenue.

Alexa took in the majestic Catholic Church before her. An ornate mosaic portrait of Christ adorned the arch above the thick wood doors. With the tunic in her arms, she made her way up the wide cement steps and opened the door to go inside. She passed through the red carpeted narthex to enter the grand sanctuary. A long aisle lay before her, flanked by rows and rows of pews. The sun glimmered through glorious, arched, stained glass windows. A huge pipe organ stood behind the pulpit and kneeling in prayer at the candlelit alter was the woman she came to see, Mother Viviana Reverent.

A flicker of nerves washed over her as she slowly made her way down the aisle. Mother Viviana had been so upset at the police station, accusing Alexa of harming Teresa, fainting at the very mention of the dead man on the catwalk, and of course, hearing the news that Teresa had abandoned the calling for the love of a man. Yet Alexa felt in her heart she had to return the tunic and talk with the abbess before St. Pete sent her back to the twenty-first century.

It seemed like a two-mile hike by the time Alexa reached the front of the sanctuary. Not wanting to intrude on the nun's private moment, she eased into a pew. Finally, Mother Viviana lifted from her knees and, as if she'd sensed Alexa's presence, she turned.

"Miss Owl…I'm glad you've come. I prayed I would have an opportunity to speak with you again, and it seems the Lord has found me worthy of this request. I owe you an apology," Mother Viviana said.

Alexa pushed up from her seat. "Not at all, Mother Viviana. I am so very sorry you're disappointed by the sudden turn of events. I know Teresa struggled with her decision. She was terrified she would go to hell for what she'd done, but she was more heartbroken that she had let you down, and how upset you would be with her. She feared she had betrayed you."

A soft, svelte smile tugged at Mother Vivian's lips as she tucked her chin into her chest and her hands into her cloak. Slowly, she lifted her gaze to meet Alexa's. "I fear it is I who has betrayed her, Miss Owl. It is I who has asked for forgiveness in this matter. Not all are truly called to become a nun, and deep in my heart, I knew this was not the right choice for Teresa. I allowed family's traditions to skew my judgment." Her gaze found a sunbeam gleaming through one of the stained glass windows. "And now, she's out there, somewhere, with a heavy heart, instead of the joy she should feel when falling in love."

"I'm sure it will all work out. Teresa will make her way home, and the family can talk things out." Alexa held out the blue tunic. "I wanted to return the tunic. I'm sorry, but the coif and the veil got misplaced in the chaos."

Mother Viviana took the tunic from Alexa and unfolded it. The white coif and veil fell from the bunch. "No, everything is here, Miss Owl."

Alexa sucked in a breath. The items had not been with the tunic, and she wasn't sure when the last time she saw them. "My mistake. I should be going. I'm sorry for all the grief I may have caused you, and I wish you all the best, Mother Viviana Reverent."

The nun nodded her reply. Alexa turned to make her way up the aisle when someone stepped into the sanctuary. With the sun gleaming in the windows, the individual was a dark silhouette. Alexa couldn't make out who it was, someone coming to pray or for confession? And then, she heard Teresa's voice, "Aunt Viviana…"

Alexa's heart swelled. She swung around to see Mother Viviana with her arms outstretched toward the young woman. Teresa ran down the aisle, and her aunt enveloped her in a tight, loving hug. Just then, the young man with shaggy dark hair stepped into the church. It was Adam Gless, and he had a guitar slung over his shoulder. He shot Alexa a timid grin as he passed on his way down the aisle.

Alexa couldn't suppress the smile lifting her lips when she stepped out of the church. She was almost to the sidewalk when the tug and pull of the portal, transporting her back to her own time began. It felt good to be going home.

Exhausted and frustrated, the 1965 Slater marched into the squad room. Joe asked, "Where'd you disappear to?"

Letting the door slam behind him, Slater came to a halt. "What're you talkin' about? I had all those people at the music hall to interview. Took forever."

Joe stared at him as if his pants had just dropped to the floor. "What're *you* talkin' about? We just finished bookin' that Pooky Mateer woman for killin' Dorian Matias and Steve Wheeler. You told Wheeler and me all about how you stopped her in the parking lot at the music hall, and how she confessed." He shot his arms out. "You were right there while we booked her, and then you were suddenly...gone. Are you crackin' up or somethin', Slater?"

Slater slipped his fedora from his head, raked his fingers through his hair, and down the back of his neck. He glanced back at the door, then to Joe's befuddled gaze. At this point, several of the other detectives were looking up from the day's paperwork with questioning expressions. Slater crossed the room to Joe's desk. Leaning in, he whispered, "How did my Rambler get back to the station? I had to catch a ride with Clarence."

"You've been under a lot of pressure lately, Slater. Look, we've got the Steve Wheeler, Dorian Matias, Bert Mateer, *and* Bobby Starr case under wraps. Why don't you go home and watch some TV with Janey I'll finish up here. I'm almost done, anyways. It'll take me about twenty minutes to type up my report, then I'm headin' out. I'm gonna get a beer at The Hound, you wanna come?"

"I'm gonna talk with Pooky Mateer," Slater said as he took several steps toward the hallway.

"You've already done that, man," Joe called after him.

Slater stopped, searching his mind for an interview with Pooky Mateer, for any conversation at all with the woman. When he couldn't produce the memory, he turned. "Maybe I *should* call it a night. I'll join you for that beer, then I'm goin' home to Janey, but I gotta get an aspirin first." Shrugging, Joe sat down. Slater made his way to his desk, yanked open the middle drawer, reached for the bottle of aspirins, then hesitated when his eyes fell upon a red notebook. "What's this?" Tentatively, he tossed the fedora onto his desk, then lifted the book from the drawer and sat down. He opened the notebook and after allowing the revelation of what he was looking at, and who the wordsmith was to melt away, Slater settled back to study the information Bobby Starr had collected.

"Slater…" Joe stood next to Slater's chair, eddying into his jacket. "You ready to go?"

Slater's head jerked up from his deep examination of the notebook. "Where's Wheeler?"

"He left. He had a little mishap with a cell, the gate got stuck with him inside, then we had problems with the door to the cell block." A shrug. "They seem to be workin' fine now. I called maintenance, they'll check it out in the morning. Why?"

"How long has he been gone?"

"Half-hour maybe forty-five minutes. Again, why?"

Slater held up the notebook. "Forget the beer. We're on our way to arrest Detective Wheeler. Put an all-points bulletin out for his car." Joe stared at him with wide eyes and a slacked jaw. "Don't just stand there, man. *Do it!*"

Joe dashed to his desk, grabbed the phone, punched a button, then announced. "All-points bulletin for a black, Chevy Impala belonging to Detective Vince Wheeler. Repeat, all-points bulletin for Detective Vince Wheeler." Dropping the receiver onto the cradle, he returned to Slater's desk. "What the heck is goin' on?"

Slater handed the notebook to Joe. "You read. I'll drive." Grabbing the fedora, Slater dropped it on his head as he headed for the door. "No wonder there's been a shortage of hookers in the holding cells."

Following close behind, Joe asked, "Did you take that aspirin?"

"I don't need an aspirin," Slater stated.

Nineteen

Back for the Best

A lexa heard the sound of kissing…smooching…
smooching with an Irish lilt. She opened her eyes
and through the blur, she could almost make out
her good friend, Winnie Mulaney, and something yellow
perched on the back of the sofa in the showroom of the
Owl's Nest Couturier Shoppe. "There now, that's a good
little birdie," Winnie cooed as she came into focus. Now,
Alexa could see the old Irish gal was feeding a canary
sunflower seeds.

"Is that Zippy?" Alexa asked, her voice was a bit
groggy.

"Ah, welcome back, lass. I don't know if this is Zippy,
or some other canary Katherine kept. She had so many
over the years, and they all looked the same, to me.
Katherine used to say they were her good luck charms,
and I have to agree. Lord knows, this little sweetie has
been good luck for me."

"Good luck for you? How?"

A wide smile lifted to Winnie's blue eyes. "I've received a text message from Louie about a half-hour ago. Seems he wants to see me. He asked me to come to the wine cellar. It's Friday, ya know. Louie said he wanted me to be the first to see it before he opened the doors to the public at seven." She glanced up at the clock stationed on the wall behind the bar and directly above the dumb waiter. "Now, I'd love to hear all about what went on with the new guardian angel trainee, but I'm supposed to be there at five-thirty. That's in an hour."

"That's right. Tonight's the night the wine cellar opens. How exciting for Louie. Do you think he's looking for a reconciliation?"

Winnie offered the canary another seed. "It's possible. Louie wrote the most peculiar thing in his message. He said, the ball will be in your court now, Wynona Mulaney. I'm not exactly sure what ball he's talkin' about, but I'm interested in findin' out."

Alexa chuckled. "Winnie, I've got to ask, since I've known you and Bobby Starr, you've never mentioned that Katherine with a K remarried a fellow opera singer shortly after Bobby's death. Why?"

"I don't really know. I remember thinkin' Katherine and Royce were havin' an affair. *Everyone* thought so. Especially when they married so quickly. Thinkin' back now, I believe we misjudged them. They fell in love during a troubling time in Katherine's life, and they were married for a long time. Produced two children together. Royce passed on three years ago. Katherine's still alive and sings for the operetta company now and again." A chortle. "Maggie used to say Royce was a blaggard, but as the years flew by, I think she changed her mind too."

"Mm…when I was in 1965, Maggie made the comment she knew a blaggard when she saw one," Alexa offered.

"I'm sure she did. Maggie was married to one for several years. Too bad she didn't recognize the blaggard in Cullen Duffy *before* she married him. Ahhh, I suppose she had *stars* in her eyes."

"Speaking of which…what's it going to be, Wynona Mulaney? Are you going to accept an apology if that's what Louie presents?"

Standing, Winnie grinned. "Well, it depends on the apology, doesn't it, then?" With that, she gathered her tote from the ottoman and made her way to the door with an extra nip in her step.

Alexa had to giggle to herself. Oh, yeah, Louie Santorini would be forgiven in a New York minute.

After taking a long, hot shower, drying her hair, curling it, then applying makeup, Alexa sat in front of her vanity mirror, brushing her full, silky hair. She'd been home from the past for well over two hours and hadn't heard from Slater or Bobby. She had to assume Slater got everything squared away before his time ran out. Requirement number one done, and successfully out of the way. Then again, neither Slater nor the scroll informed them of how many conditions he had to meet to get into the squad. Bobby, on the other hand, knew he had three to solve before acceptance. Was each guardian angel handled differently? Who knew?

She laid down the brush, picked up a lipstick, and gazed into the mirror. Letting out a tiny squeal, she flinched. Slater laughed. He was standing behind her. "Gotcha," he announced merrily.

"You angels don't play fair," Alexa stated.

Slater tried to smother his chuckle, failing. "Sorry. I couldn't resist."

"So, all went well, I take it?" Alexa asked, tugging at her emerald green, satin robe to make sure it was closed tautly.

"The case is solved. Pooky served a life sentence. Rather sad, since Steve Wheeler and Dorian Matias were responsible for Bert's death, and she may have gotten a leaner sentence had she only killed one of them, but she killed *two* people. And we now know Dorian murdered Bobby by a very old method of poisoning through clothing. We know this because Pooky broke the case wide open by committing those murders. And yes, that dropper bottle she gave me had some cyanide left in it. Detective Wheeler was arrested and convicted for his part in his brother's scheme. Wheeler served five years in prison. Let me tell ya, it was hard to get anyone to testify against him. Marriages were ruined and so were a few businessmen's reputations."

"I imagine so. According to Bobby's notes, when some of those *reputable* businessmen started asking questions about their disappearing funds, Wheeler not only roughed them up, but produced photographs of them with prostitutes, and threatened to show said photo to their wives. I'm surprised Wheeler didn't kill Pooky Mateer or her sister Hazel."

"Wheeler was a lot of things, but I don't think he wanted to harm an innocent woman. Surprisingly, Pooky beat them to the punch. Good thing, because sooner or later, they'd had gotten around to killing her."

Alexa pivoted on the bench to face him. "Hold the phone. I'm not sure I understand. Pooky was not arrested by the 1965 version of you. Rather, by the *angel* version of you. Isn't that a breach of protocol? I mean, Bobby and Bert's murders would have gone unsolved had we not returned to the past. Katherine gave the notebook to me, a person who didn't exist. That notebook may not have been discovered for another year or so until they decided to clean out Bobby's office for a nursery. For that matter, it may have gone unnoticed even then. Tossed in the trash, unopened. So, by solving those murders, *we changed history*, didn't we?"

Slater leaned against the wall, crossing his arms over his chest thoughtfully. "Yes and no. Seems to me, in general, this time travel stuff is a *circular* thing, and the future will be affected no matter how you cut it. I also believe St. Pete's protocols may vary from angel to angel, and circumstance to circumstance. We did what we had to do to fulfill the objective: *who killed Bobby Starr*? That said, we solved other crimes along the way, and I think St. Pete wanted it to go in that direction. Bobby told me the two of you usually ended up solving other crimes connected with his old cases. When you get right to it, this case was much the same. Everything walked hand-in-hand."

"I suppose you're right. Let me guess, nothing happened to Hazel, right?"

"Remember, conspiracy to commit murder was not on the books until the '70s. So, no, Hazel was *not* held accountable for aiding her sister in the murders. To tell you the truth, I'm not so sure they planned to kill Dorian. I think he made Pooky so angry, she stabbed him out of pure rage. Although Steve Wheeler's murder was quite premeditated, Pooky stole clothing, and changed into those clothes in order to not to be recognized."

"What about Dorian's mother? Were they able to confirm Dorian's claim that he killed her in the same way he killed Bobby, dousing her clothes in poison?"

"I'm afraid not. Even by today's forensics, cyanide poisoning is not detectable in a dead body after two days. But, in a way, it doesn't really matter. Dorian Matias is dead, and he had to answer for what he did to a higher authority—if he even got that far."

Alexa leaned an elbow on the vanity, then chortled. "Bobby is such a trickster. I don't know if you're aware, but we locked Wheeler in a cell, then Bobby jammed the cell block door as a distraction, while I put the notebook in your desk." She shook her head. "I felt bad for Joe Randolph, trying and trying to get into the cell block to rescue Wheeler, and then not being able to open the cell gate, either."

"Bobby told me how the two of you caused a free-for-all in the holding cells." Slater shook his finger at Alexa. "Ya know, come to think of it, I remember Murph, from maintenance, coming in the day after we arrested Wheeler. Joe told him the doors wouldn't open. Murph examined those doors for *forty-five minutes* and couldn't find a thing wrong with either of them. Joe couldn't get the gate to the holding cell to stick, no matter how he tried. Murph left, and we never had another issue with the doors. Joe didn't know why Wheeler went back there in the first place, and Wheeler couldn't remember either. I think everyone chalked it up as a weird week at the station."

"I guess Bernie calmed down, too? Hopefully, he didn't remember the woman, dressed like a nun, who had no fingerprints and couldn't be photographed."

"I'm sure you kicked up quite a commotion, but no, I don't believe he remembered. Bernie never said another word about it, and *trust me*, he wasn't the type to let *anything* go. It's like Bobby explained, they don't remember the circumstances, because you were never there." Slater cocked his head to one side. "Are you going somewhere? Looks like you're getting ready for an evening out."

"Yes, Cliff is picking me up. We're going to the opening of Louie Santorini's new wine cellar. We made reservations for seven."

"Ah, that should be fun. Glad to hear Louie was able to get that accomplished." Just then, the little canary swept into the room and alighted on the vanity mirror. "Hey, there you are. Don't want to forget you."

"I suppose it's time for you to go," Alexa said with a heavy heart.

"I'm afraid so." The silenced stretched between, and then Slater softly said, "Alexa, I know you felt bad when I died, because you thought it was your fault that I remembered everything from your visit to 1963. I wanted you to know you had *nothing* to do with my death. It was my time. I was called and I was ready."

"Thank you for that," Alexa whispered, trying to hold back the tears threatening to fill her eyes.

"Well, that's that. Maybe I'll see ya around. But when Cliff asks you to marry him, you say yes, ya hear? Or I'll be forced to haunt ya."

Alexa giggled. "In case you haven't noticed, you already are."

The shop door buzzed, alerting her that it had opened. Cliff yelled up, "It's me."

Slater shot her that Bobby Starr bad-boy smirk, and then with a casual tip of his hat, he was gone. She spun around to check the mirror. The canary was gone too. Slater made no promise of return, like Bobby always had. She wondered, was Slater required to solve only one murder? The opening and closing of the apartment door broke through her muse. "Alexa…"

"In here," she called out.

Cliff walked into the bedroom. "Almost ready?"

"Almost." Alexa stood. "Just have to get dressed. She turned and he gently caught her arm to pull her close.

"Alexa…I've been really slow."

"Slow? What do you mean?"

He lifted a small black box and opened it. Alexa gasped. Inside was an emerald ring. Surrounded by diamonds, the emerald shimmered. "I didn't get you a diamond, although there are diamonds with the emerald. I thought you should have something as unique and gorgeous as you. Something to reflect that uniqueness and beauty. I hope you like it, and I hope you'll say yes when I ask…will you marry me?"

"I love you, Cliff Slater, and yes, I'll marry you," Alexa said.

Grinning, Cliff picked the ring from the box and slipped it onto Alexa's finger. Drawing her closer, he kissed her lips, then pulling back from the kiss, he pressed his forehead to hers, and whispered, "Do you really feel like going to the wine cellar tonight?"

Alexa's eyes opened slowly to meet his sensual gaze. Her lips lifted. "It'll be so *crowded*."

"Noisy too."

"We could go tomorrow night. I mean, I've got wine here."

"Yeah, I've seen it." He kissed her deeply.

"Think I'll cancel that reservation," she whispered.

"Good idea."

On a braced breath, Winnie gingerly fingered the pure white mound atop her head. Satisfied all was in place, she snaked through the tables at Louie's Little Mardi Gras Bar. The masks affixed to the wall seemingly followed her progress toward the corridor at the farthest reach of the bar. As she passed the ladies' room, the door opened, and Olivia stepped out. The two women stopped in their tracks, waiting for the other to…Winnie wasn't sure what they were waiting for. Who would throw the first punch? Winnie was way too old for that nonsense.

Finally, struggling through her ambiguity, Olivia said, "He's waiting for you downstairs." She dipped her chin toward the spot where a door with a sign that read, *No Entry*, used to stand, now replaced by a spiral staircase winding downward, and a new sign announcing, *Louie's Little Wine Cellar*.

"Thank you, lass," Winnie said, then continued toward the stairs.

"Winnie…" Olivia called after her. Winnie pivoted. "I know you didn't break the angel. Louis confessed he threw the ball, and it bounced up and broke it. Thank you for trying to keep him out of trouble on his birthday, and I'm sorry for being so…difficult. It's just so hard…" Welling up with tears, her words faded away.

"I understand, lass. Losing loved ones is a terrible business, and those left behind *need* companionship, especially if they are up in years. We *all* need companionship. I hope you and I can start over."

"I'll try," Olivia said. Winnie turned toward the stairs. "Wait…you won't break his heart?"

Winnie smiled and touched her arm. "Not on your life, luv." With that, she painstakingly made her way down through the spiral. She paused near the bottom to admire the transformation of the once dark, musty, and cluttered basement. Her heart smiled at the sight of the charming wine cellar Louie had fashioned and she remembered his words, "*I want to create a cheerful atmosphere. I'm not interested in that old world look everyone else seems to go for. I don't want my wine cellar to resemble an old torture chamber that's been renovated. This basement has been a dark and spider infested place for too long.*"

Staying true to his vision, even when the contractor tried to sway him, Louie had succeeded in crafting an elegant, joyful, and alluring space. The old, grubby stone walls had been pressure washed and repointed. Winnie remembered the delight when they discovered the stones were light in color and full of character. The squared tiles on the floor sparkled in soft, creamy shades of sage and tan. A rich, glossy oak ceiling with inset lighting and brass lanterns on the wall provided a smooth, romantic flavor. Large barrels filled with wine bottles were stacked three high, on thick oak cradles posted in every corner, except for the farthest alcove in the room. The contractor had removed a heavy metal door and carved out an arched entry from the stones that beckoned guests into a private tasting room, featuring the finest vintages from France, Italy, Portugal, Oregon, California, and more. Straight down the middle of the room, Louie had positioned four long, oak tables. Winnie drew a hand to her chest. The wine cellar was a dream realized.

Louie stepped through the archway of the private tasting room to peek around the corner. He grinned when he found Winnie standing on the staircase. He opened his arms wide. "Do you like it?"

"Ah, if I said I liked it, I would be lying. I think it's grand, Louis Santorini, simply grand. You should be proud," Winnie said, stepping away from the stairs.

Louie reached a hand out to her. "I couldn't have done this without my favorite Irish girl, you know."

Accepting his hand and giving it a good squeeze, she teased, "I'm your favorite, am I? How many others have ya got?"

Chuckling, he pulled her into a tight embrace, kissing her forehead. "Only you, Wynona Mulaney. I only have eyes for you. God, I *missed you* so much." He stepped back from the embrace. "How could I have been so *stupid*? I should have set Livy straight right away. Forgive me?"

"Ahhh, Louis Santorini, you know I'm a sucker for that smile of yours. How can I not forgive a man who was torn between his daughter and his lover, but he's a father, after all, and he chose family? You're a good man, Louie. I feel blessed to have ya back in me life. Now, I want to see the rest of the cellar."

Without hesitation, Louie kissed her lips then, keeping her hand in his, he led her into the tasting room. A glimmering oak bar with five stools stood against the far wall. And in the middle of the room was a round table set with two plates, wine glasses, a bottle of wine, and a huge charcuterie board overflowing with cheeses, crackers, toasted paninis, and a pile of cannoli.

"This is beautiful! And what's this, then?" Winnie asked, pointing to the table.

"You might not believe it, but Liv made the cannoli. She's very good at it. She learned from the master: Grandma Santorini." Louie said as he scooped up the bottle of wine and poured some into each glass, then handed one to Winnie. "What shall we toast to?"

Winnie lifted a suspicious brow. "That there's no strychnine in the cannoli?"

Louie laughed. "C'mon Winnie, Liv felt terrible about it all. I think she made the cannoli as an olive branch. Besides, I told her, get used to having Winnie around. I said goodbye once, and I don't intend to say it ever again."

"Well, as me mum used to always say: if you're brave enough to say goodbye, life will reward ya with a new hello."

Louie raised his glass. "A very wise woman, that Molly Mulaney was."

Epilogue

Bobby crept through the bedroom door. The moonlight sifted gently through the curtains, casting a soft glaze over two sleeping figures snuggled under the blankets. "Is he always here?" Bobby murmured to himself. Once again, not a good moment to awaken Alexa. While it didn't turn out well the last time, he needed to move her. After all, Slater wasn't here to chastise him. Besides, he'd be more cautious this time, and with the decision made, he snapped his fingers.

Alexa's eyes fluttered open. Raking back her bed tossed tresses, she stretched, then froze. What? Once again, she found herself in the mauve living room that belonged to Winnie. Ugh! Bobby Starr couldn't be far…she rolled her head to the right to find the ornery angel grinning at her.

"I heard congratulations were in order. So, I thought I'd drop by to say it in person…or in spirit, that is. Congratulations."

"How did you hear so quickly?"

"Eh, Slater and his wife, Janey, were all-a flutter about it. So, you and Cliff are finally tying the ol' knot, huh?"

Suddenly feeling a draft, Alexa's gaze flashed downward. She let out a sigh of relief. She was wearing her emerald green, satin nightgown. "Yes, but nothing definite has been planned. Bobby, while I truly appreciate you wanting to see me, I don't think we should impose on Winnie. I'm fairly sure she and Louie reconciled last night, and…"

"Well, what have we here?" Winnie's Irish lilt slashed through the darkness. She turned on the lamp.

"I'm sorry, Winnie. I woke up, and here I am…*again*. Are we…I mean, is Louie here?"

Winnie waved a dismissive hand. "Nah, our relationship, as Holden likes to call it, is back on track. It was late so Louie insisted on driving me home, but I sent him on his way. I'm not easy, ya know."

Alexa chuckled. "Good for you, Winnie Mulaney."

"Now, what's this I'm hearin'? Let me see that ring, lass." Smiling brightly, Alexa held out her hand. Winnie and Bobby admired the jewels. "This calls for a celebration. I brought home one of Louie's favorite port wines for the next time he visits, but I think I should open it now." Winnie tugged the sash on her lavender terrycloth robe a bit tighter, then crossed the room to the kitchen to take up a bottle of wine sitting on the counter.

Alexa turned back to Bobby. "I guess you know the case is closed. We found out who your murderer was, Dorian Matias, and…as far as I can tell, we may have stepped over some protocol guidelines along the way."

"Yeah, Slater told me."

"How does *that* make you feel? I'm not sure St. Pete has as rigid protocols in place for Slater as he did for you."

Bobby shrugged. "We all lived different lives, Alexa. Our journey toward guardianship will obviously reflect what needed or maybe what *needs* to be done. Evidently, Pete wanted my murder and the other three murders to be taken care of, even if it compromised some rules. I'm okay with it. Slater will make a great guardian angel."

"You're not too shabby yourself, Bobby Starr. *I know* you pulled some angel strings to make things right for Winnie and Louie. Thank you."

"Here we go," Winnie announced, handing full wine glasses to Alexa and Bobby, then lifting her glass in the air, Winnie said, "May you live as long as you want and never want as long as you live!" They clinked glasses and took a drink. "Now then, you've turned out to be quite the angel, Detective Bobby Starr. So, it's *your turn* to give us a bit of advice, in the form of a toast. Let's hear it then…"

Bobby stood and raised his glass high. *"Never ignore those gut feelings you experience. That's your guardian angel talking to ya."*

"Here! Here!" Alexa and Winnie sang out, then took another gulp of their wine.

Bobby set down his glass, winked, and then he was gone.

Alexa wrapped her arm around Winnie and tugged her close. "Do you think he's really gone this time, Winnie?"

"I don't think so, but I'll go one better…how are ya gettin' back to your apartment?"

Wide eyed, Alexa gasped.

THE END

About C.S. McDonald...

For twenty-six years C.S. McDonald's life whirled around a song and a dance. She was a professional dancer and choreographer. During that time, she choreographed many musicals and an opera for the Pittsburgh Savoyards. In 2011 she retired from her dance career to write. Under her real name, Cindy McDonald, writes murder-suspense and romantic suspense novels. In 2014 she added the pen name, C.S. McDonald, to write children's books for her grandchildren. In 2016 she started writing the Fiona Quinn Mysteries, and in 2020, The Owl's Nest Mysteries.

Cindy resides on her Thoroughbred farm known as Fly by Night Stables near Pittsburgh, Pennsylvania with her husband, Bill, their cocker spaniel, Allister, and their King Cavalier, Charlie.

You can learn more about C.S. McDonald and her books here: www.csmcdonaldbooks.com

Be sure to check out books one and two from

Be sure to check out other books from **The Owl's Nest Mysteries**:

Back to the Burgh and Beyond

Maxed Out

Double Dog Dare

More cozy mysteries by C.S. McDonald

The Fiona Quinn Mysteries

Murder on Pointe

Merry Murder

Waves of Murder

Tastes Like Murder

Good Luck to Murder

Mambo and Murder

Saddle Up for Murder

Bon Voyage to Murder

Taking Notes on Murder

Matrimony, Mayhem, and Murder

Deep Blue Murder

Short stories by C.S. McDonald:

Fiona Quinn QUICK Mysteries

Banking on a Murder

Crystal Clear Confusion

Harriet's Heist

The Christmas Cameo

Thank you to these wonderful services:

Cover design: DusktilDawn Designs
Editor: Sherri Good, Silver Lining Editing Services

Formatting: Acorn Book Services

You can learn more about C.S. McDonald and her books here: www.csmcdonaldbooks.com

Made in the USA
Middletown, DE
28 May 2023